Sally Bone

Sheila Fields

Sally Bone

Sheila Fields

Blenheim Press Limited
Codicote

Published in 2009
by
Blenheim Press Ltd
Codicote Innovation Centre
St Albans Road
Codicote
Herts SG4 8WH

Previously published in Dutch in The Netherlands in 2005
under the title *De Bestemming*

ISBN 978-1-906302-16-0

Illustrations by Susan Davies

Typeset by TW Typesetting, Plymouth, Devon

Printed and bound by CPI Antony Rowe, Eastbourne

There is a website at www.sheilafields.com where you can
find out about the author and her other books

To my darling Aunt Jessie and Uncle Fred, who taught me the rules of life and who paved the way for my success in life. I shall always be deeply grateful to them. I know one day we will meet again.

ACKNOWLEDGEMENTS

My gratitude to my school friends still living in Chrishall. Because of the help and kindness shown, I have the feeling I have never left the village.

CONTENTS

The Balcony   1

The Room   89

The Wall   147

THE BALCONY

The Balcony was furnished as at all times. The crowds were screaming with joy. The statesman of the century waved to the crowd. The King, the Queen and the two Princesses were of irrelevant importance; our statesman had saved the nation.

The war in Europe was over, 8 May 1945.

Emotions could flow, embarrassment didn't exist. The nation was in a garden of unknown joy and freedom.

Among the many thousands of wives and mothers who were mourning the loss of their sons and daughters sat one still, very young damsel, beautifully dressed and groomed, on her bed crying her heart out. For her this was the day she had dreaded.

To her the balcony scene meant a new unwanted journey, a fear of the unknown. A journey back to her true parents: a mother she had seen five times in five years and a father no more than ten. Trains and all forms of transportation had been a disaster and an excuse not to see the children.

WAR

'Nursie, why can't you come with me tomorrow? You never leave me alone. There must be someone to tuck me in, see that my porridge is not too warm, brush my hair and read me a story before I go to sleep.'

Little Sally felt sad; she knew something was going to happen to her life, but she hadn't worked it out in complete detail.

'Sally, dear, I have told you so many times there is a war on. People go away, people become soldiers, ladies become nurses.'

'Will you become a soldier, Nursie? Or will you become a soldier's nurse?'

'Please, Sally, listen to me. We, your parents and I, have to make sure that little girls like you are safe from all the ugly things that can take place during war.'

'I understand that,' said little Sally, 'but Nursie, I want you to come with me.'

'We will stop this subject, young lady. You will finish your dinner, you will go to bed, tomorrow morning you will get up on time and the two of us will find ourselves heading towards the station.'

Little Sally couldn't eat any more. Her love for food disappeared; she couldn't get used to the idea that she was going out alone into the wide, wide world.

Nursie wouldn't be there to hold her hand and, oh dear oh dear, who would take care of her little rabbit? Who would feed Bunny?

'Nursie, have you packed all my clothes for me? Do I have enough socks because my feet must be kept warm. Nursie, have you put all my knickers in my suitcase because I must wear clean knickers every day.'

She was, of course, trying her best to work on the feelings of her faithful nurse and the only true friend she had known in her childhood years. Perhaps she might say, 'All right, Sally, I won't be a nurse, I won't be a soldier, I'll stay with you for ever and ever.'

Sally realised that none of this was going to happen, and the best thing to do was to go to bed and listen for the very last time to the story of the seven dwarfs, and say her prayers to Mr Jesus, asking him to take care of Bunny and Nursie, and thanking him for her daily bread.

Prayers had always been an evening ritual. It fascinated her to talk to someone that no one knew and if her wishes came true she was always promising him presents and inviting him to tea.

The last evening didn't end the way Sally wanted it to. Nursie wasn't herself. She kept dribbling on about the way Sally should behave with the kind people who were going to keep her safe, that the war wouldn't last long, and before they could say 'Jack Robinson' they would all be together again.

Somehow, Sally didn't believe all these promises. Nursie wasn't talking the way she usually did, and what's more, she didn't look at her while she was talking, which meant it was not really true. Her hot chocolate ended the day and after a very big hug and two kisses from Nursie she pulled the sheets over her head and started to cry.

'If I can remember the way Nursie looks she will always be with me,' whispered Sally to herself. 'I can always talk to Mr Jesus,' and with these comforting ideas, for the last time in the home of her nurse, her bear Soppy in her arms, Sally passed on into the world of dreamland.

* * *

Liverpool Street Station is one of the most crowded and busiest stations in London. Wherever you want to go, departure usually seems to be from Liverpool Street.

Black from the horrible smoke from the old fashioned trains, cheerful luggage porters rushed around hoping for a generous tip. Whistles were blowing a tone of announcement that everyone should get aboard. Two whistles meant the train was about to leave and that folks who were saying goodbye should leave the platform and return to the exit.

The cab would need approximately thirty minutes to reach the station from Sally's house. Her porridge had been consumed and there was absolute silence between the two people. The suitcase, gasmask and a new school satchel were lying in the front hall, ready to be carried by the driver to the cab.

By this time Sally was all dressed to go. She looked an absolute picture in a little fur coat, knitted hat and gloves to match, warm woollen socks and black patent shoes. Attached to her coat was a somewhat large badge with her name printed on it plus the number of the travel group. Sally Bone, Group 8, number two, age four.

The doorbell went. The cab driver had arrived on the dot. Sally rushed to the door to greet him.

'All ready, missy, got your luggage for me? Come on, now, we can't be late, can we?' Without further thought Sally followed the cab driver to the cab, took her place on the back seat, and watched him close the speaker's window; and by that time Nursie was sitting next to her.

Neither one said a word. Sally held Nursie's hand so tight it was as if she never wanted to let go. For the very last time Sally's nurse put her arms around the child, held her close and whispered, 'You will always be my little girl, Sally, and whatever happens, I will always love you.'

By this time the cab had arrived at the station. The luggage was unloaded and taken to a jolly porter who patiently awaited his instructions from the little girl's nurse.

Hundreds of children were standing on the platforms. Some had already said goodbye to their parents and were patiently waiting in their groups. Others were still sobbing and crying as goodbyes were in a question of minutes. The groups represented school classes, and in most cases the boys were with the boys, and the girls were with the girls. The jolly porter was politely asked if he would take both ladies and luggage to Group 8 and deposit Sally's case in the relevant luggage bin.

By this time Sally Bone was beginning to enjoy things. She had never before seen so many people together, except for when Nursie had taken her to see the King and Queen pass by in their lovely gold coach last summer. However, it didn't take Sally very long to discover that most of the children did look oh so shabby, and why were so many crying? Cry babies; even she knew that if you must cry, do it indoors and never outside, and certainly not in front of everyone.

She looked up at Nursie and gave her one of her mischievous smiles. It made the darling nurse feel better. She knew Sally so well: one of those smiles meant she was in command of any situation and you would have to be a smart little lad or grandfather not to fall for her natural charms.

Group 8 was right at the end of the platform but to Sally's delight right opposite the carriages attached to the steam engine. What absolute fun; she had never been so close to an engine before. Perhaps things wouldn't be so bad after all. Nursie shook hands with the infant teacher in charge of Group 8, asked her to keep a special eye on Sally, and said hello to the other little darlings who were all two or three years older than her Sally. Nursie bent down to give a final kiss to her little girl.

'Have you still got your hankie, dear? Don't forget to use it, there's a good girl. I'll see you soon . . . God bless.'

Nursie turned around, and walked past the crowds until she had found the exit. She didn't dare to look back. She hoped that Sally wasn't waving. Her heart and knowledge of life told her that she would never see her darling Sally again.

She sat in the back of the cab, tears pouring down her cheeks, and she prayed that her little girl would come through the war as beautiful and innocent as she was when it all started. The cab driver looked in his mirror and saw to his horror a kind hearted nurse completely at war with herself, trying to fight her emotions and not being very successful at it. What should he do? What could he do? What would the rules of etiquette allow him to do? After some twenty minutes he pulled the cab over to the side of the road, where he knew there was a small café on the corner, opened the passenger door and in a very timid voice announced his honourable intention.

'Please, Miss, may I offer you a cup of tea? There's a war on and we folks have to stick together.'

Sally, who was already getting bored, wished that she had brought her rabbit with her. She waved once or twice to the engine driver who had waved back, but she couldn't continue to get his attention although it would be great fun to help him drive the train. She racked her brains trying to decide whether or not she could drive the train and decided finally that she would leave that all to the great big men who liked getting their hands dirty and by the look of things didn't use their hankies.

She wanted everything to start. She was getting hungry and she wanted to go to the toilet. She tried to speak to the girls and boys, but no one would speak to her. Most of them were too shy to speak, still too upset from saying goodbye to their mums and dads, and most of them couldn't associate Sally with the kids in the street – she spoke real proper; she didn't forget her t's and h's. She took one final look at what she decided were a bunch of absolute shabby little horrors. She must find a way to get rid of them; what was Nursie thinking of, Nursie who was always so particular?

The schoolmistress in charge was wearing heavy shoes like men's, and an army-like khaki raincoat. Sally thought she looked like a man and to make matters worse she could see three long black hairs coming out of her chin. She was sure she could hear her teeth chattering when she spoke, an instrumental noise that made poor Sally want to sing a song very loudly, in order to avoid the poor lady being laughed at.

Nursie would have said: 'We must get ourselves organised, child, we can't go on like this forever.'

In the coming six years these words of genuine wisdom were used frequently by Sally Bone to get herself out of a plight, and frequently into one. As small as she was, little Madame had to be in complete control of her situation. Operation 'Station day' had to be reorganised. She couldn't possibly stay in this creepy crawly group; her rabbit had had more to say than this party.

Her eyes moved slowly to the group on the right. They were all boys, all had school uniforms on and all looked extremely smart. The gentleman in charge was twice the size of her Daddy and he had a lovely moustache. Her imagination went in all directions. Would all these nice young men take her with them in their group? Would there be room for her? She did have a problem: she had no chocs to give them, she couldn't ask them back for tea because she didn't know where she was going to. One thing she did know, however: she definitely wanted to go with them and not with the cry babies around her. Nursie had taught her how to walk and sing; perhaps she could sing to them. They might like to hear a Christmas carol about Mr Jesus and how very handsome he was when he was a baby.

She decided, however, that her tactics had to be more ladylike. She must first wave: one slow wave; two quick waves; it didn't matter, but wave she must. Male specimens always had an unbelievable attraction for Sally, and vice versa, and within one second the whole male group was waving at her. She wasn't sure if Nursie would have agreed to this, but fun it was and she had already decided with all her childish vanity which hand she would be holding before the train left.

Whistles were blowing; the station was ablaze with dirty black smoke from the engines. Station porters were shouting, 'All aboard, please, all aboard,' and in the midst of a tumult which can only be described as children in a war at home, little Sally tiptoed between all the long and short legs from one group into the other.

'What on earth are you doing here?' shouted down the lovely man twice the size of her Daddy and with the lovely moustache. He knew he couldn't possibly send her away. By now all the groups were rushing off to their carriages. If he was not careful she would fall under the train; such a small young mite should never have been sent from home in the first place; what was this world coming to?

World or no world, Miss Sally looked up at him with her velvet green eyes and shouted at the top of her voice, 'Please, Mister, my name is Sally, may I hold your hand, may I come in the train with you? Please, please?' The poor man had no time to think; the trains were almost moving, the porters already closing the doors. 'Young lady,' he replied, 'we'll talk about this later.' He picked her up, threw her under his arm and strode into his reserved carriage where pupils had already taken their place. There was only one place for Sally, either on his lap or on that of a pupil's, and as it was obvious that Sally was not going to leave go of him, it was his lap and definitely no one else's.

For three hours this stranger's lap was a divine paradise of excitement for her. What an absolute joy this war was going to be. Everyone was so friendly! She chatted and asked non-stop questions to the boys, shared their sandwiches and homemade cakes, and used the steam on the carriage windows for drawing dolls and rabbits. No Nursie to tell her what to do, no visits to home at weekends. She felt completely safe in the arms of this perfect stranger.

Her short little arm moved around his neck and she whispered in his ear, 'Mister, may I call you Uncle? I don't have any uncles.'

He turned his gaze and looked into the child's face. He felt an overwhelming desire to save her; to protect her; he mustn't let her out of his sight. How could he say no to such a request? No one had ever before asked him to be their uncle.

'Sally, you may call me Uncle.'

'Uncle what?' said Sally, 'you must have a name.'

'Uncle is sufficient for the time being. Now let's have a little peace and quiet; in an hour's time we will all arrive at our destination.'

Sally had no idea what destination meant, but one thing she was absolutely sure about, she had found a new uncle. He would find her luggage and write to Nursie and Bunny and tell them both that she was well and extremely happy. She was tired and the shaking of the train didn't help matters. Slowly Sally cuddled up to her new uncle; she held his hand very tightly and said, 'Goodnight, Mr Uncle.'

Her new friend laughed; he longed to give her a kiss on the cheek, but war or no war he knew he could only reply with a 'Goodnight, Sally. I'll wake you up when we get there.'

THE STATION

Audley End station I am sure has not changed in all these years. It may have received a few gallons of paint, a lavatory chain and a new door to keep the draught out of the waiting room. Maybe their ticket office has been modernised, but in those days it was what young and old called a dump. Audley End was the station used by the folks in the lovely villages when going to the city of London and the University city called Cambridge. Every day you would see the same porters, every year you would see them getting older and fatter, but everyone knew each other.

The rich were in the first class carriages, the poor in the third; the rich dressed in their pin-stripes and bowler hats; the farmers in their plus-fours and check caps. The poor and the happy wore in those days grey caps and spit and polish shoes.

On this Friday in September 1939 four buses were waiting at the railway station to take the children to their various destinations. Some of the foster parents had come by car to greet and pick up their London evacuees. No one knew anyone else; the meeting was in most cases extremely timid. The head or chief of the arrival committee, whatever we like to call him, was a certain Mr Fred Cranwell.

Fred was a builder and landowner living in one of the nearby villages. He was all over the place, shaking hands with the teachers, trying to be friendly to the children and making sure that all the luggage was placed onto the right bus. And yet somehow he knew that a problem was going to arise; it was all going too well for his liking. He knew he had everything on paper but mistakes were only human. The weather had let him down, it was raining; the buses began to steam up. He gave the okay for some of the cars to leave. Buses one and two were allowed to follow. The children were each clutching a bag of toffees in one hand and a comic of their choice in the other. He waved them out, knowing that all of them would be well received at their final destination.

He checked his list and came to the conclusion that the party now leaving the station must be the last one to leave the train, but why did he have a feeling that an unpredictable problem was slowly coming his way? There was, however, no mistake as marching towards him as if she was royalty itself, hand in hand with the headmaster, was a very excited little girl with a trail of schoolboys behind her.

He quickly checked his final list: teacher in charge a certain Arthur Tatwell. There was no indication of a young daughter coming with him and what's more Arthur Tatwell was staying with him. Jess his wife had given Arthur the posh guestroom. Fred decided that the best thing to do was to act as if everything was under control.

'Mr Tatwell, sir, welcome to our county. Perhaps we should let the boys seat themselves down in the bus first. There's food and drinks waiting for them. Jack and Marge over there, sir, have come to pick up two boys in your group, John Simpson and Brian Jones; perhaps you might like to say hello to them?'

Arthur thought the time had come to release Sally's hand and leave her for one minute in the care of Fred, who to him at that moment, appeared to be the best organiser in the world. Sally gave Fred one of her inquisitive looks. Poor Fred didn't know what to say. He truly thought he had everything spot on, but who was this child? He could, thanks to her name badge, see that her name was Sally Bone and he certainly hoped that Arthur Tatwell could tell him more.

The last bus pulled out. Arthur called, 'See you all tomorrow, chaps, at school, be good.'

The boys as a welcome present had received ballpoint pens, in those days an absolute American dream, so if there was any depression in the bus the ballpoint pens certainly revived the atmosphere.

Can you imagine a more bizarre situation? Two men: Fred was short, with a bald head, braces showing from under his suit jacket, tie knot more to the right than the left, but certainly not in the middle. He loved his grub, he was three stone overweight and had the most cheerful and honest face one could ever imagine. Arthur however represented the typical Oxford graduate, in those times with grey flannels and a woven jacket with leather covering the elbows. He spoke as if he was rehearsing the King's Christmas speech. However, there was something genuinely nice about him. He was without any doubt an attraction for women, and little Miss Sally was over the moon with him.

'Mr Tatwell, sir, who may I ask is this young lady?' Sally by now was playing hopscotch as if the day would never end. 'Is she family, is she registered as an evacuee? She is certainly not on my list.'

Arthur, who was feeling tired and strained from all the emotions around him, explained in very few words what had happened and without a word of hesitation inquired if Fred could find a suitable place for a very, very young evacuee.

Sally stood by now hand in hand with her friend Arthur. She was tired. Her eyes went searching up to Fred and the expression on her young face was that of loneliness.

'Let her come back with us. Mum will find her a bed for the time being.' He hadn't the heart or desire to send little Sally to strangers. He too felt a sudden longing to look after the child. What the war doesn't do to you, he thought, before I know where I am I'll be sleeping in my own chicken run.

Arthur promised to phone London, explain what had happened, and arrange for her luggage which undoubtedly had gone to Cambridge to be returned, and to apologise a thousand times to Miss What's her name for the behaviour of Sally. After all, the poor woman must have had kittens when she discovered that one of her group was missing, or had she?

The three war victims took their seats in Fred's car. Sally was flat out at the back, blanket over her to keep her warm, Arthur's raincoat rolled up under her head. This really was magic, what absolute fun. She decided to remain quiet, not to talk to anyone, and just listen to the grown-ups. Nursie would have said, 'Don't speak until you're spoken to,' and for once she decided to follow her rules, and remain seen but not heard. Arthur was not in the mood to do much talking; he couldn't get his fiancée out of his mind. He was deeply in love with Barbara, the maths teacher, who owing to the illness of her father was obliged to remain in London. In order to rescue himself from self destruction, he took his pipe out of his pocket, filled it with what later turned out to be Highland's Gold tobacco, closed his eyes and spoke to the unknown: 'I hope to God this war will soon be over,' and decided thereafter to enjoy the beautiful scenery.

CHRISHALL

Fred Cranwell's house was of course extremely grand. He had a toilet inside, probably the only one in the entire village. Toilets were always outside, cold, damp, and too repulsive to talk about. He had a bathroom and an actual wash basin, two large halls, one up, one down, a lovely big kitchen with a built-in stove and oven, and fireplaces in the dining room and sitting room, not forgetting a telephone and a piano, all evidence that Fred was truly a successful master builder and a highly respected citizen of his village.

The name of the house was Banyards and he lived there with his wife Jessie, aged sixty, and his daughter Pearl, aged thirty-eight. Let us be perfectly clear on one issue: only a very special evacuee would find his or her way into Fred's house.

Many secret documents found their way into his office. As chief warden of the entire district, very little could happen without him being informed, and he certainly didn't want any peeping toms moving around in his domain. Security was number one for Fred Cranwell; he was fully equipped from his Red Cross case to his rifle. Although if the time should arrive for destruction of invaders Fred would have felt more at home with a saw and shovel than a rifle that was nearly the length of the man himself.

Sally felt that the car had stopped. She felt very cold but excited. She peeped out of the window and to her utter amazement she found herself looking at a lovely big house, much bigger than hers in London. She had never seen so many windows before and windows meant window sills, and window sills had so many interpretations for Sally.

Arthur helped her out of the car and before he could wink an eye she was gone. She saw the chickens; a yard dog who was later to become her honourable friend number one; cats, all sizes; and above all, far in the distance, a horse. It was as if the whole of Fred's animals had turned out to greet her. She knew she couldn't pat the chickens even though they

The Red Cow Inn, Chrishall

gave her eggs; cats were not her favourite but the lovely brown yard dog with his faithful brown eyes must certainly have a hug. She was approaching the old dog without any sign of fear, when suddenly she felt a hand on her head, and a voice behind her.

'Are you Sally? Are you the little girl we are going to look after?'

Sally looked quickly back to the car. Mister Uncle had disappeared and she couldn't see the driver; there was only her, the dog and this strange lady.

AUNT JESSIE

'Why don't you come indoors with me; I'll give you a nice warm bath and then we can have tea together.' Jessie felt sorry for the child. She couldn't introduce herself as Mrs Cranwell. Something had to be done to make this little girl forget why she was here, make her feel at home and not completely lost.

'I'm your new Aunt Jessie, how about that? Do you think we could be friends, Sally?'

So many things had happened that day Sally didn't know what to think or say and it was her longing for warmth and someone to talk to that persuaded her to follow her new guardian into the lovely big house. She couldn't believe her eyes. If only Nursie could be here, she would love the big fireplace and the piano, and the flowered settee.

11

Before Sally could have a quick peep into all the rooms she found herself laughing and playing in the most soapy bath ever. There were funny sponges with holes in them, bath bubbles, coloured hair shampoo; she couldn't remember having such a treat before.

Aunt Jessie, a name Sally very quickly adopted, rubbed her dry with a huge white lovely warm towel and this was the start of Sally's first theatrical game in the house which would protect her for the coming six years.

'Aunt Jessie, I think I look like the Queen with this long towel around me, so may I have a peep in all the rooms? If you could tie the towel please under my chin, the towel will look like the Queen's robe.' She thought of her silver cardboard crown back home, and asked her new aunt if she might have a paper crown suitable for her to wear. She couldn't wear the robe without the crown; it didn't have to be gold or silver but it did have to look like one. Playing the role of Queen was one of Sally's favourite roles and if it meant using a tea cloth, sheets or her favourite prop, the patchwork bed quilt, then so be it.

Crackers! thought Jessie. We must have some left over from last Christmas. They always contain paper hats, which look somewhat like crowns.

The bathroom scene resembled Christmas. Crackers were pulled by the two of them, paper flying everywhere. Jessie had never realised before what utter cheap rubbish was packed in such expensive crackers. Sally took her pick from three paper hats. She was sure even the Queen would have worn the one she chose; it was red and looked, in her fantasy, extremely royal. As a reward for being such a brave girl that day she was allowed to have a peep into all the rooms. She must not touch anything, and perhaps tomorrow they could play the piano together.

Little did Sally know that her new aunt had a rather painful problem: Sally had no clothes. Jessie had heard Fred say that if they were lucky her case might arrive at Audley End the next day, upon which he would go and fetch it, but at the moment she had nothing to rely on except her own hope and imagination. Although she was really too old to look after such a young child she couldn't help enjoying the sparkling enthusiasm which surrounded Sally in everything she said and did. Jessie knew only too well that her young lodger would captivate the hearts of everyone in the village let alone her house.

One of Fred's shirts was the answer to her clothes problem. Buttoned up from top to toe, sleeves rolled up, one of his ties around her little middle, and she would look absolutely grand.

'I didn't touch anything, Aunt Jessie, honestly not. I did have a little lie down on your bed. I've never seen such a big bed before. Do you sleep there alone?'

Jessie decided to stay silent and started to dress Sally in Fred's shirt. The same underwear, socks and shoes would have to do for the time being.

Sally expressed her wishes to wear her paper crown at the tea table and that, as far as Aunt Jessie was concerned, was the final solution of the day.

Sally knew she had to remain quiet; there was a lot of bustle going on in the house. Men's talk, thought Sally. They spoke quietly so it was obviously not for her ears. She was all curled up in the reading chair next to the radio, little did she know it had been Fred's chair for twenty years, and she decided to look in all the magazines which she found neatly piled next to the radio. She was sure tea wouldn't be much longer. She was hungry and eager to discover what her new family would present for tea.

Already she was rehearsing the questions she wanted to ask them. She must not forget the cows; what was the name of the house? could the dog come into the house? He must be very lonely outside and how many times a day did we feed the chickens? Aunt Jessie started to lay the table. The child couldn't believe her eyes. The tablecloth and the china was the same as at home, but all the goodies, 'Jiminy Cricket,' an expression used by many a child, is all of this for tea? She was looking at pâté sandwiches, treacle tarts, fruitcake, custard tarts, plain bread and butter, and lastly homemade jam. She knew it was homemade jam because there was a plate and a spoon to go with the pot, and Nursie would always get cross if she didn't put the spoon neatly back on to the plate once she had used it.

She couldn't imagine Aunt Jessie ever getting cross and she decided there and then that she would ask Mr Jesus to make sure that she could stay with this very kind lady for a long, long time.

Sally with her three grown-ups around her resembled the magic of theatre. Crown on her head, hands folded neatly in her lap, eyes moving from one adult to the other, she secretly remembered the table manners which Nursie had taught her. Ladies first, children last. Don't take before offered, always take the smallest cake, and finally, never speak with your mouth full.

The teacups were full, sandwiches were being enjoyed, and the men were talking about the war. Aunt Jessie was walking backwards and forwards with fresh bread and butter.

Why didn't someone say something to her, admire her crown, tell her she looked lovely? She must be able to attract their attention somehow. Against all rules and regulations she placed her elbows on the table and whispered loud enough for everyone to hear: 'Please may I have a bucket? I want to milk the cow. My Daddy said he was sure someone would let me milk the cow.'

This unique cry for attention followed her for many years. Fred never stopped telling anyone who would listen about his little girl from London asking him for a bucket so that she could milk the cow. Unfortunately builders didn't have cows; however, Sally had from day one established herself as a permanent resident of the Cranwell family.

It was as if she had always been there.

She took the cups and the plates to the kitchen, carried each cup as if it were made of gold, sat on the floor and tried desperately to be quiet while Aunt Jessie did the washing up. In those days this involved a primitive combination of rubber gloves, if you had the money to buy them, hot water from a boiler, and at least three teacloths.

'Aunt Jessie, can we feed the chickens tomorrow, please?' It was as if Sally thought she was only going to stay for a short time and everything must happen before she went back to London.

'Sally, dear, I promise you, you can feed the chickens and find the eggs but we mustn't let the chickens escape from the run.'

This was all too much. Sally couldn't believe it and she had no one to tell this wonderful news to.

'If we can find five big brown eggs we'll boil them for tea tomorrow and now, young lady, it's bedtime.'

Sally ran into the dining room where the two men were still talking about their past and present lifestyles. She gave both men a goodnight kiss and ran upstairs to the lovely room that she had long guessed would be her very own bedroom. Aunt Jessie helped her into bed.

'Are you warm enough, Sally?' she asked. 'Would you like me to stay with you for a little while?'

Sally could no longer be brave. She threw her arms around her new aunt and tears began to flow . . . 'I miss Nursie, Aunt Jessie, I miss Nursie so much.'

Jessie held the child, as a mother who would comfort her own child, and told her that tomorrow was going to be a wonderful day and she would stay with her until she went to sleep.

Satisfied that Sally was truly fast asleep, Jessie tiptoed out of the room, leaving the door ajar and the light remaining on the landing so that the child would not awake to darkness, and found her way quietly downstairs to the dining room.

Further words about Sally were not needed. Both Jessie and Fred knew this young mite would stay with them for a long time to come and that they would treat her as if she was one of their own.

'Mum, why don't you sit down for a minute, you must be tired; you've had a busy day.' Fred always called his wife Mum, something he had taken over from his own children.

'I must just wash Sally's clothes and put them in the airing cupboard, then she'll have everything clean for tomorrow,' said Jessie. 'It may take a week before her suitcase arrives.'

The two of them looked at each other and both started to laugh, but behind the cheerfulness both knew their lives, like thousands more, would never be the same again.

The village was so exceptional; everything was so neat and tidy. Everyone knew each other, and yet the folks were extremely select as to whom they should speak to. There was a beautiful Anglican church with a permanent Vicar and his wife Mary. The Methodist believers were blessed with a more down-to-earth building, built sixty years back by Fred's father. Every Sunday a church minister abiding in a nearby village would visit them and perform the services that the church members required. Christenings; funerals; festivals, the favourite of which was always the harvest festival; not forgetting the famous church choir singing – an extremely important issue in the lives of so many church goers.

The local school was the most eccentric building one could possibly imagine. Whenever an excuse could be made, the flag was always put out to air: St. Patrick's Day; the Royal Family birthdays, which meant in those days four times a year; Poppy Day, remembrance of the first world war. Warm weather or cold, the children had to group around the flag pole, say a prayer, and sing a national song. Miss Miller was the headmistress and Mrs Clark her extremely kind and compassionate assistant. Sally, because of her age, had to keep herself occupied for the first year; or rather, the people around her were obliged to readjust their programmes so that Sally could enjoy all the attractions and delights which the village and surroundings had to offer.

By this time Pearl, the unmarried daughter in the family, had become Sally's favourite friend. She called her 'dear Aunty Pearl', mainly because she knew that Aunty Pearl would never say no, and her knowledge of children's stories was inexhaustible. The two of them would always feed the animals together. She was allowed to help Pearl with the dusting and occasionally, but only occasionally, was she allowed to creep into Pearl's bed and rehearse Christmas carols. Sally sang carols throughout the entire year; it was the magic of the tree that never left her mind and one of the few family traditions which, war or no war, continued to exist.

So much happened during her first year of residence at Banyards. It was a year of curiosity, watching big folk's emotions, travelling in her world of worlds to all the towns one could possibly imagine and lastly the weekend trips to the big cities to buy ice cream and a new dress, shoes, or whatever Sally and her Aunt Jessie thought were necessary.

FRED'S CAR

The days were never boring. There was always something to do. Fred would always take her with him in his car to the nearby town in order to go to the bank and draw out the weekly money for his employees. Sally loved these weekly trips with Fred. It meant she had him all to herself; she could sit in the front and rehearse with him the names of all the villages they passed and she was always sure that her driver would give her at least two toffees going and three coming back. Only in later years did Sally realise that Fred needed some sort of confectionery in his mouth in order to keep his false teeth in and the time that she saw him take his upper dentures out was for her an unbelievable monstrosity. The two of them would each sit on a cushion, Fred because his feet couldn't reach the accelerator and Sally because she couldn't bear the thought of not seeing everything. The bank manager would receive them with immense hospitality. Tea and lemonade in his office, the traditional shortbread biscuits, which were not Sally's particular favourite, but as Nursie would have said, 'Be polite, child, take what is given to you and say thank you.'

Thursday was baking day and no one, truly no one, could have enticed Sally out of the house on this particular day. Sally could never wait till it was Thursday. She loved it! As soon as the breakfast table had been cleared of plates that had held eggs, bacon, sausages, tomatoes and a few fried potatoes, then out came all the tins, bowls, flour, eggs, butter and so on: everything that was required to produce the height of luxury in a time of war. Most ingredients were on ration, but somehow Jessie, undoubtedly owing to Fred's status, always managed to get, as she would quote, 'a little extra'. Sally's task was to clean out all the storage tins and wipe them clean, to line them with fresh paper and sprinkle the bottom with flour. How she loved to watch Aunt Jess soften the butter and add any flavouring essence that Sally had chosen. She was allowed to roll out the pastry and make special designs on the meat and plum pies.

Cooking started to become pleasant again for Jessie; it was years since she had had so much attention paid to her chores and Sally, as young as she was, didn't miss a single trick. Her enthusiasm and skill was always rewarded with the promise she could clean out the bowls, a delightful task which Sally completed with her finger and not the spoon.

As time went on Sally became more and more inquisitive. She noticed that Arthur kept going away and no one would tell her where he went to. And across the meadow she could see there was a lovely, lovely bungalow. She knew people lived there because smoke came frequently out of the chimney. But why didn't she know who they were? Perhaps she could creep across one day and have a peep through the window. Perhaps she could ask them back to tea one day. She was sure Aunt Jess wouldn't mind and then they could all get to know them.

For some unknown reason she didn't ask anyone, not even dear Aunty Pearl, about the bungalow and decided to wait until the right moment occurred, giving her the chance to explore the unknown.

HYMNS, HYMNS, OH LOVELY HYMNS

Sunday was chapel day. Sally would go hand in hand with Aunt Jessie, who played the organ, to the front seat in the chapel. She couldn't really understand what was going on, but she stood up and sat down at the same time as the grown up folk did, held her hymn book tightly in her hands and looked with utter adoration to how her Aunt Jessie was playing the organ. Her Sunday clothes were indeed only for Sunday. If Aunt Jessie wore a hat, then she too insisted on wearing a hat, and what fun it was to try on all the many, many hats that Pearl and Jessie had collected over the past years. In reality Sally was an absolute scream. If there were verses in the hymn that she thought she knew, she would sing one tone

Methodist Chapel, Chrishall

higher than the rest, and if she liked the hymn she would sing it for the second time.

Her favourite hymn was 'Onward Christian soldiers, marching on to war, With the cross of Jesus going on before.'

Only later would she discover that her darling Aunt Jess had arranged with the minister to choose that particular hymn, together with his sermon, practically once every six weeks so that her Sally could sing to her heart's content.

The bungalow began to take on a form of magic for Sally. She tried to imagine who lived there. She made drawings of a car, a dog, and a tall thin lady. She was sure by now that she had seen a man walk down the drive. In fact she was absolutely sure that she had seen Aunt Jess wave to him.

Perhaps if she waited until it was her birthday, then she could invite them to her party, or Christmas perhaps: take them some fresh baked mince pies, Aunt Jess couldn't say no to that idea, surely.

The mince pies it was, and no sooner said than done, when our Sally plunged into her *plan de campagne*. 'Aunt Jess, may I please visit the bungalow and take them some mince pies for Christmas and if they are nice people invite them back to tea?'

Luckily for Sally, Jessie decided, there and then, to forget what happened in the past; there was after all a war going on, and why shouldn't this child bring them all together again? The same afternoon Sally and her Aunt Jess wandered across to the bungalow, Sally carrying her mince pies for Christmas neatly on a white kitchen plate.

Jessie's offering was more appropriate; she thought four fresh eggs in a simple kitchen bowl would break the ice. A perfect stranger would have anticipated looking at a rehearsal of the nativity play.

'Will you knock at the door, Aunt Jess, or shall I?' Sally's voice caused the most peculiar barking from somewhere inside. 'Aunt Jess, I think I'm going to be frightened by something, let's run back home please.'

Jessie opened the door and called out, 'Anyone at home? Joyce, are you there? Can we come in?'

A terrified Sally stood with her knees knocking and mouth slightly open. She grasped her Aunt Jessie's hand. She was absolutely terrified, as standing before her was the tall thin lady whom she had seen in her imagination. Under her arm she carried a white ugly looking little dog who looked at Sally as if he was going to make minced meat out of her, any minute now.

'I've come to introduce Sally to you,' said Aunt Jess. 'Sally is an evacuee from London, has no one to play with until she goes to school, and I'm sure she would love to play with Robin when it's not raining.'

Sally had by now a vague idea that Robin was the name of the dog and she secretly wished that she had never started on this bungalow adventure. She didn't like the dog; water was coming out of his nostrils, and the little horror wouldn't leave Sally's shoe laces alone. Sally couldn't decide whether to spill her lemonade over him or just push him away. The problem was, where to? She knew the only solution was to attract Aunt Jessie's attention and ask if she might go back home; she felt sick and would like to go to bed. She said her polite goodbye to Mrs Joyce who by that time had opened the door for the two ladies. There was no waiting for Aunt Jess, no goodbyes to 'Wobin'; she literally ran as fast as her little legs could take her to the big house she now called her home. Sally was extremely quiet that evening, and no one could get her to talk. Fred tried to do his best to cheer her up, but nothing would help. She kissed them all goodnight and disappeared to her bedroom.

'What's wrong, Sally? Why are you so upset? Tell me, then I can help you.' Jessie knew the child was hiding something, she wasn't her usual self.

'I don't want to go to the bungalow again, please, Aunt Jessie, not again, it frightened me. The dog frightened me, the lady kept looking at me, and . . .' and poor Sally started to shiver. She wanted her Aunt Jessie to hug her and tell her that the bungalow no longer existed; it had gone up in the air and would never come down again.

'Sally, dear, you wanted so much to go visiting; now let's forget our little adventure and go to sleep.' Sally decided that night that her prayers to Mr Jesus would have an additional request.

He still had to take care of Nursie, her bunny, Uncle Fred, dear Aunty Pearl and an extra portion for Aunty Jessie; however, would he please help her and get rid of, preferably as soon as possible, the dog called Robin. And if possible he would do her an extra favour if the lady could go along too. Sally was always convinced that her unknown Mr Jesus was listening to every wish or demand that she made and she was positively sure that the bungalow and all its inhabitants would disappear from the planet before the coming morning.

Sally's birthday and Christmas were very close to each other, and war or no war, everyone did their best to make Sally feel that nothing had changed in her life.

Her first birthday cake was a great success. Jessie cooked the cake and Pearl did the icing. The upper layer was decorated with edible flowers and five candles were planted in the middle. A special cake stand was polished for the event and all the lights were turned off so that Sally could enjoy the magic glow of the candles.

Dear Aunty Pearl had knitted her a cardigan, Jessie gave her slippers, and good old Fred gave her her first savings box which quite by chance was in the form of a house, plus money to the value of two pounds and the key to open and shut it.

Sally was out of all her daily routines, what a day of excitement. She gave all the animals an extra portion to eat. The yard dog received two additional hugs, and in addition she promised him a thin slice of her wonderful, wonderful cake. Long after Sally had gone to bed Fred still sat reading the newspaper. Jessie knew he had something on his mind. It was long past ten o'clock and without fail, Fred always walked around his house in order to check if lights were showing through the curtains, or to check if the barns and garages were safely locked. But tonight he was delaying it all.

'Mum, dear, can you understand this? I'll be blowed if I can; there is not a simple card or parcel from London. You would have thought they would have sent her something. Poor little mite, you can't use the war as an excuse for everything.'

Aunt Jessie, who had the genuine habit of making an excuse for everyone, asked Fred not to be too harsh; after all, they didn't really know who Sally's parents were, and after all they might be quite nice people.

Fred had no time for his wife's chatter; he had his thoughts on the matter, and that was that. His nightly rounds completed, he decided to go up and join his wife in bed. Before saying goodnight to his Jessie he couldn't resist asking, 'Mum, did Sally really enjoy her birthday?' One second of silence followed.

'I think so, dear, she's lying in bed fast asleep with her new cardigan and slippers on. The little house is standing on the cupboard next to her. You're a good man, Fred Cranwell; now go to sleep, you've got a busy day tomorrow.'

> *Christmas is coming*
> *The goose is getting fat*
> *Please put a penny in the old man's hat*

Christmas was and always remained one of Sally's immense passions. To her Christmas never died, it never went out of her mind, it was a time to forgive, an excuse to spoil someone. For her it was the ultimate feeling of being alive.

Pearl was at all times in charge of the decorations. Coloured paper chains were extended from one corner of the ceiling to the other. There was fresh holly on the walls, and a special place was reserved for all the many Christmas cards that Fred received as a thank you for all the energy and attention that he was giving to his evacuees. It was oh, so English; no one would have thought there was a war on. The Christmas tree was established in the window, horrible coloured balls were tied to every single branch, and to complete the annual presentation, or rather Sally's world of wonders, the Christmas angel was released from her annual sleep.

Sally christened her Patsy, don't ask why; knowing Sally she undoubtedly wanted to attract inquisitive attention. If someone asked her a question it always meant that she too could ask one. However, my true guess is that she didn't want the people around her to determine her irritating difficulty in pronouncing her 'r's, and the name of Patsy was designed for Sally's romantic search for sensation.

'Aunt Jess, do you think that the angel Patsy is looking her best; she is sitting after all right at the top of the tree. She could fall down, you know, Aunt Jessie.'

'Sally dear, angels have never fallen from Christmas trees and your Patsy knows she has to sit still.' Aunt Jessie's tone of voice told her to be quiet. The postman had just been. He must have told Aunt Jess some morbid news, Sally told herself. Aunt Jess is always 'down' after he's been. I can't think why. She gives him coffee and bics; he doesn't cheer us up, he ruins the entire atmosphere, Sally whispered indignantly. Little did she know that poor old Joe had to listen to and tell the entire community the latest war news. Who had been called up; if not, why not! He saw tears, he heard fear, everyone wanted to read good news, but unfortunately Joe was too often the bearer of news no one could define or understand.

Sally kept counting the days to Christmas and her flow of questions was never ending. Which chimney would Santa choose; would they ask him to use the one in the kitchen? It was without doubt the largest. Would she find presents in her stocking or would Santa need a pillowcase? Who was coming to their Christmas dinner? Everything had to be organised in her mind. 'Please, Aunt Jess, don't be a spoilsport, tell me who's coming! Will I see Nursie and my Daddy?'

Jessie had dreaded this inevitable question, and decided there and then to be as short and acceptable as possible. 'I think your Daddy will come when the winter is over. I think he'll be here for Easter, but I'm sure that Santa has spoken to him, and I'll bet you, Sally dear, that he'll have some presents from your Daddy with him. Now let's remember, Harold and Marie are coming plus little Trevor, Eric and Joyce and perhaps Arthur and his fiancée.'

Sally began to brighten up; this really could be fun so long as Joyce didn't bring that horrible dog with her, 'Wobin', and as far as she was concerned they all could forget Trevor. Sally thought he was a nasty little boy; he came to the big house at various times to play with her, and when no one was in the room he would always pull down his trousers and insist that Sally looked at his what-what. Poor Sally couldn't become the least bit excited with the exposure of Trevor's what-what. It reminded her of the little sausages frying in the pan every morning for her Uncle Fred.

What a silly boy he was. How could any boy think his what-what was worth seeing?

The night of all nights arrived. Sally wanted so much to go to bed early. She inspected the chimney first in order to see if there were any blockages and insisted that the curtains remained slightly open. 'You never know, Aunt Jess,' Sally said, 'Santa might lose his way and I can always put the light on for him.'

Sally had no idea as to the amount of bother and hassle that was going on while she was in the planet of dreamland. The pillowcase was full to the brim and Fred, as quiet as a mouse, placed Santa's goodies at the bottom of Sally's bed.

Old folk always say Christmas is for the young ones and Sally was certainly an example of their statement. Dreamland captured Sally until six o'clock. It was dark outside. Sally asked herself, Has he been, shall we take a peep? Madame, in her romantic little nightie, glided out of bed and tiptoed in the dark around the room. She practically fell over the pillowcase ... 'Jiminy Cricket, this can't be true, he's been!' she screamed. The happiest young girl in the country forgot that the curtains were open, forgot there was a war going on and in her excitement she put the lights on. Sally Bone couldn't believe her eyes! There were parcels everywhere; her bedroom looked like a toy shop.

A doll's house had been made for her by the company's carpenter, and as if it wasn't enough a little shop had also been ordered and delivered by a special toy shop in Cambridge. Both items lacked nothing. Books, pencils, a little handbag and of course hankies, everything a child could dream of had been delivered by Santa.

There was wrapping paper and yummy goodies all over the place: on the floor, on the bed, and in all the tumult of Christmas we find Sally sitting on her bed singing at the top of her voice her favourite Christmas carol: 'Away in a manger, No crib for a bed; The little lord Jesus lay down his sweet head. The stars in the bright sky looked down where he lay, The little lord Jesus asleep in the hay.'

It was as if she and only she existed in what for her was a moment in her life she would never, never, forget. These wonderful, wonderful people would have bought the world for her if only to make her happy. Pearl got up and made tea for everyone. By this time Sally had established herself on Jessie and Fred's bed. She was completely over the moon, and couldn't for the life of her understand how Santa had got the doll's house down the chimney.

'Aunt Jess.'
   'Yes dear.'
   'May I whisper something in your ear'? It won't take long.'
   Sally whispered loud enough for dear old Fred to hear. 'I haven't seen

anything from Nursie and my Daddy. Do you think that Santa didn't get the parcels?'

Fred, although extremely early in the morning, thought it was his turn to intervene.

'Sally,' said Fred, 'maybe Santa has left something downstairs near the Christmas tree. Shall we both take a look?'

Sally, who needed no further asking, waited until Fred had dressed himself in his old brown dressing gown. The two of them side by side, and extremely slowly, descended to the living room.

'Open the door slowly, Sally,' said Fred, 'you never know what you might find.'

The total darkness in the room was somewhat scary but not for long.

The tree suddenly came to life, all the lights went on and for miles in the silence of the early morning, all the animals must have heard Sally scream with delight! Under the tree was a huge parcel yet to be opened and in front of, for Sally the most beautiful tree in the world, was standing a brand new bicycle. There was a little basket on the front and special pedal clogs designed for little ladies with short legs and small little feet.

'Uncle Fred, is this bicycle from my Daddy? Where is the bell, let me ring the bell, please, Uncle Fred!' Fred had long ago learned in life that if you can make someone content by telling a fib, then go ahead and produce one.

'Yes, Sally dear, your Daddy gave it to Santa a few weeks ago, are we happy now?'

The child couldn't restrain her emotions any longer. It was a bit too much and there was after all another present that needed her attention.

Fred suggested that both went into the kitchen to open the extremely big box that had been delivered by special mail a few days back and find out what was in it. And who had given it to Santa. The box contained an exquisite china doll with moving eyes and long eyelashes, dressed, in Sally's fantasy, like a beautiful princess. A Christmas card could be seen just under the doll. 'Uncle Fred, please read the card for me, I'm sure it's from Nursie.'

Fred, hoping to God that the child's wishes would come true, put his glasses on and began to read the handwritten Christmas message, in the quietness of the early morning.

'To my dearest Sally, who I hope is being a good girl and of whom I will be thinking on Christmas Day. Give Mr and Mrs Cranwell a big thank you kiss from me and I pray we will all meet each other soon. Lots of love and kisses, take care Sally dear, Nursie and Bunny.'

Fred was quiet. He had so much on his mind. He still had the job of telling Mum that Harold, their first born, had been called up and would undoubtedly go on active service in January. Evacuees were wanting to go back home. He knew only too well that this war was not going to experience a fast ending. But regardless of all his war and domestic duties he had done his utmost to make Sally's first Christmas in his home a truly memorable and happy one. He felt tired.

'Shall we go upstairs, young lady, and have a little sleep? We've got a busy day ahead, Christmas has only just begun.'

The skills of Santa were constantly on Sally's mind. Again someone unknown, who listened to her wishes and made them all come true.

Perhaps Mr Jesus and Santa were brothers. To Sally they definitely had something in common. The turkey, the Christmas pudding, cakes and guests were now of irrelevant importance to her. The bicycle was tested in the yard. The doll's house furniture was moved around and around and the shop finally looked as if it was open for trading. All the animals received their daily good morning and she wished each and every one a happy Christmas. The chickens received a double portion, the dog went for a walk in the orchard, and she decided that the cats' saucers should receive some of Aunt Jess's cream in their milk. She would take this up with her dear Aunty Pearl; then she was sure the whole family would enjoy their Christmas.

SCHOOL

Confrontation with Sally at school was, to put it quite mildly, not exactly a daily routine. She was admitted at an earlier age than the rest of the starters. She spoke a different language than the locals and the average evacuee. She was without any doubt the champion chatterbox of the class, her favourite chatter partners being the boys, who would give their last apple or sandwich to be in little Madame's favour.

Probably the youngest class monitor ever, it was Sally's task to collect the writing books and make sure that no pencils were stolen. Every day the pencils all had to be sharpened and counted. She was too young to realise such tasks had been granted in order to keep Sally occupied. The time she needed to exercise her lessons was no longer than one tenth of

Chrishall School

the time required by the rest of the pupils and although little Madame would dawdle off to do some painting or continue knitting her egg cosies, the books and pencils gave her a feeling of being needed; the school couldn't survive without her. It would just have to close down! She was always the first one there and the last to leave. The only person she left in utter peace was the cleaner. Brushes and water were never Sally's favourites.

Jess was well aware of Sally's ostentatious behaviour in the school class. She also knew that no one seemed to mind. She made them laugh. She could sing, tap dance, and play 'God save the King' on the piano. However, you did have to stand up when she played it, identical to the behaviour of Uncle Fred on Christmas Day. There was never a dull moment from the first day she entered to the day she left.

An invitation to Aunt Jess's tea was her favourite bribe; she knew Aunt Jess would never deny one girl or boy a place at the tea table, and dear old Jessie never let on that she was well aware of Sally's childish blackmailing schemes.

The announcement that Sally's father was making a visit to his daughter was indeed greeted with a sigh of relief. It meant he had to put his bike on the train, travel from Liverpool Street Station to Audley End and cycle in the rain, snow or sun to the village where his daughter was living, namely Chrishall. This cycling tour would take an average of two hours, total travel time – eight.

Her father's name was Frank William. He was a quiet, pleasant spoken man, five foot seven inches, well dressed and with a charisma that would set every woman's heart on fire. He, as a young lad, had been a valet to a general in the first world war, and he had served in France, but like most Britons, he never spoke about it. The subject was taboo.

'Do you think he will come alone, Aunt Jess? Can I walk down the road to meet him? The chapel will have to miss us, they'll have to find someone else to play the organ and pass around the bibles. My Daddy can't possibly go to the chapel; we must have him all to ourselves. You will love him, Aunt Jess, I'm sure you will.'

The thought of his coming occupied her entire being. Everyone at school knew of her Mr Special who was making his first visit to their village. The way she described the coming event, to anyone who would listen, one would have thought that Mr Churchill himself was arriving. But to Sally, it was her Daddy, whom she longed to tell her secrets to. He must know that she loved her village and all the nice people who lived in it, she must show him her school that she never wanted to leave, the playgrounds, the orchards, Uncle Fred's car; and her biggest secret of all was her love for Aunt Jessie and dear Aunty Pearl.

Perhaps he could come and live in the village. She knew he could sing, and they could certainly use an extra tenor in the chapel choir.

This arrival was, to be sure, the event of the year. The poor man was exhausted. Two and a half hours' cycling in wind and rain, up hill and down, is in the county of Essex an achievement. He had a book and some money for her savings box. Fred had already disclosed the history of Sally's bicycle and Frank played along with the charade.

'Eat your dinner, Sally,' said Jessie, 'it will get cold. When you have finished, you can take your Daddy for a walk and show him all the places you go to every day.'

Jessie didn't like the way things were going. This man from London seemed nice enough to her, but it was too obvious that Fred wasn't doing much talking and Sally was doing too much glaring. Frank described the anxiety and fear that surrounded families in London, especially the air raids. His mother's house had been totally blown apart, everything, the whole street gone. Hundreds of people were killed, friends they had known for years. Luckily, his mother had been visiting at the time. Just a few items in her house had been spared.

Frank, who was so proud of his little girl, thought she was so beautiful. He looked at her and inquired, 'Sally, would you like to show me the village? I can't stay long, the last train leaves Audley End at four o'clock, so I have just one hour to spend with you.'

27

Without a positive nod or reply Sally left the table, put her coat on, and started to walk down the drive. Frank felt that something was definitely wrong with his daughter. Was she not happy here? If not, he definitely had a problem.

Hand in hand they walked down the village lane. She showed him her chapel, her school, her favourite sweet shop, and the pond with its tadpoles and frogs. She pointed out the butcher and where Miss Rodgers the music teacher lived. She explained that next year Aunt Jess was going to treat her to music lessons and that Miss Rodgers, although very ugly, played the piano beautifully.

She knew the names of everyone, their occupations, and their illnesses. John played the violin, Marjorie played the piano, George rang the church bells, and Harry was not all there with his lemon drops. Aunty Maud and Uncle Len had sugar diabetes and Miss Watson had been buckled up with rheumatism for years. There was silence. Frank knew his daughter well enough to know that something was boiling. 'Okay, young lady, let's have it, tell your old Dad what's on your mind. Shall we sit down on the grass, or shall I take it standing up?'

What an explosion, out it all came; she almost choked over her own words.

'Brian Jones has gone home because he was homesick. The doctor says that silly Violet must go home because she wets the bed every night. Michael the hawk steals and steals, so he will be the next one on the departure list.'

Frank couldn't feel where this was all leading up to. He knew that some evacuees were returning to London but why all the sudden commotion from his daughter?

'Please, Daddy, please, let me stay in my village!'

In her childlike way she was so convinced that no one could function if she left them.

'I want to stay here for ever and ever. Aunt Jess will agree and I'll do my best at school, I promise.'

Frank didn't know what to say; he knew that all the commotion had nothing to do with the horrors of war. His daughter had found what every child longs for, a haven of love and security, for her a realm of magic and space to develop her exceptional talents.

'Give me a quick kiss goodbye, Sally, I promise I'm not going to take you away, at least not until the war is over.'

Everyone waved Frank goodbye as he cycled down the drive and off on his return to London. Everyone anticipated tears and perhaps a small tantrum, but not our Sally. She took one look at Pearl and said, 'I think it's time to collect the eggs,' and 'Please Aunt Jess, could we have tea a little earlier? I am feeling a little bit peckish.'

THE LETTER

Window sills are squatting shelves for cats, flower pots, the odd pipe, and in Banyards they were the look-out post for Sally's non stop urge to investigate what was going on in the outside world of Chrishall. Did the buses pass by on time and whose baby pram was Violet Hicks pushing? If the doctor's car passed by twice in one day then the entire household was kept informed; to her it meant someone was very sick in her village. However, Sally did have a secret, which she kept entirely to herself.

Something was definitely going on in the bungalow. The bungalow which belonged to Fred's son Eric, his wife Joyce and their horrible drippy little dog Robin. At regular times, ten a.m., one p.m. and seven p.m., she would see a man dressed in a sailor's uniform walk up their drive. Sally thought the man looked most uncomfortable in his uniform. He was much too fat for the tunic like top and the pork pie hat on his big round head looked absolutely hysterical. His strides were clumsy, almost childish; sometimes he would walk, other times he would bolt, it was as if he couldn't wait to say hello to someone, but who?

Eric was always out and about, that she was sure of. She had heard Fred complain so often about this hush-hush domestic problem, to Aunt Jessie. Thus there was only the dog and Mrs Joyce left over. Now she quickly worked out that the sailor man couldn't possibly be going to feed the dog, so Mrs Joyce must be feeding the sailor man! 'Jiminy Cricket', this was real grown up stuff.

She was certain no one knew about the sailor man's visits. She must tell her best friend Vera. Vera, by the way, was a right little cockney, two years older than Sally. But streetwise, we'll definitely raise the number to ten. The poor girl promoted poverty. It didn't matter what she wore, she always looked shabby.

Vera tried her best to tell Sally where the babies came from and how they arrived there. This was an impossible and quite unnecessary task as Sally was convinced that all babies came from cauliflowers and as for Vera's description of what-whats and their shocking behaviour, she, Sally Bone, decided there and then, she did not want to have anything to do with such behaviour and if Vera continued to be so sloppy, she would have to drop her and find a new sensible friend. Dicky, the boy in the back row with red hair and freckles, was quite nice; maybe he had seen a baby in a cauliflower.

The bungalow mystery kept her extremely occupied! She could of course take some fresh eggs over to the bungalow when she knew the sailor man was there. She was well aware that an excuse was not necessary if it involved doing a good turn, and eggs in those times were always associated with generosity and a good appetite, and they kept you healthy.

One of the few chores which were allotted to Sally was the posting of mail deriving from the big house, and of course the bungalow, every Monday and Friday. Letters were carried safely in her school satchel and handed, extremely elegantly, to Mrs Brown the post mistress. A dear old lady, extremely small, one could hardly find her behind and above the counter. Her hair was drawn back very tightly and her voice made one think of birds singing for their dinner. In true facts she looked slightly like a small little bird but a very nice colourful one. Sally liked her. She always remarked on Sally's clothes, gave her a toffee, and asked her how things were going on at school. Was Aunt Jess keeping well? Miss Brown also had an exceptionally good memory which meant that she could, without having to think twice, tell you how many letters per family had been posted, and on which particular day.

Sally knew she had to handle the letters with great care. She felt greatly honoured with this, for her, extremely important task, especially when she read HMS on the envelopes deriving from the bungalow. She hadn't a clue what HMS stood for, but she was sure it had something to do with the sailor man and his porky pie hat. Weeks passed by, summer arrived and Sally felt like a Queen in what was for her, her own little village. Letters can bring joy and they can also express sorrow but never will Sally forget the drama which exploded after she discovered an HMS letter which had been tucked away in her school satchel for seven full days.

An HMS letter which had not been posted! It had fallen into her reading book, which hadn't left the satchel for the last two weeks. What should she do? Everyone trusted her. She was equal to Mrs Joe. She couldn't make a decision, but she could of course discuss the mistake with Vera. Vera always knew what to do and after all Vera was her friend.

'What are you dribbling about, Sal? Blimey, it's only a daft letter, tear the thing up, I'll help you; no one will miss it. If they find out you ain't posted it they'll send you back home; remember what they did to poor little Michael the hawk, they certainly sent him packing.'

Vera thoroughly enjoyed the sensation, she liked her friend Sal, but she could be annoying at times, all that la-di-da and little teacher's favourite; now it was her turn to be the one in charge.

'Give me the letter, I'll tear it in half and we'll both tear each half into hundreds of pieces.' Sally was frightened out of her wits. The thought of being sent back to London away from her village was unbearable. She felt sick, she got up and did a wee-wee behind the tree. For the first time in her young life she experienced the feeling of fear.

'Come on, Sal, don't make a meal out of it, where is the bloomin' thing?' Vera was almost singing! 'At last somethin' is really happening in this ghastly village, can't think why Sally loves it so much. I'd leave it tomorrow if I had the chance,' Vera whispered to herself.

Paper was everywhere, big bits, small bits. Neither of the girls made any effort to read anything; they both had one thing on their minds, destruction of the wretched letter.

'Vera,' said Sally, 'we can't leave all the bits lying here, now can we, it's most untidy and the cows could do their pancakes on it.'

Vera couldn't associate the cow pancakes with the torn letter but if it would make Sal feel better she would help her to pick everything up. It was after all not her letter, and Vera felt a sudden urge to seal the whole incident off. She too didn't know what HMS meant, but it did smell a little spooky!

The letter snips were deposited in the apple bin at the bottom of Fred's orchard. The bin was used for rotten apples only and why shouldn't the paper snips rot along with them. HMS was gone and forgotten. Both ladies were confident their task had been accomplished and the subject was closed.

'Thank you for helping me, Vera, I feel much better now. Do you want to come back to tea?' Sally asked. 'We've got crumpets and greengage jam. Aunt Jess won't mind but you must ask to wash your hands first, and don't talk with your mouth full.'

Music lessons were a dream. Miss Rodgers, with her lovely long fingers, extremely clean nails, grey greasy hair, stained false teeth but the voice of a professional soprano was the weekly prize for Sally.

She lived in a truly beautiful ancient farmhouse, with animals everywhere, roses around the front door and a copper knocker that had be banged at least six times before anyone could hear it. Back doors were always prohibited. It meant you might step in the horse's dung and take the smell through to the sitting room, or in those days, the piano room.

'Miss Rodgers,' said Sally, 'I've practised every day, may I play my favourite piece for you?' Miss Rodgers knew that Sally's favourite piece was undoubtedly the only piece that she had truly practised, but she went along with the musical charade and listened for the innumerable time to Friedrich Handel's Water Music. Thank goodness Handel had never written a lyric to go with it, then everyone would have been in trouble. No one demanded that Sally should practise anything in particular; her Aunt Jess, who was a school friend of the music teacher, wanted her to learn and appreciate the joys of music. Little did both ladies know that it would take more than music to quieten the storm approaching the village. It needed more than music to temper the anger, fear, and gossip that was heading their way.

INQUIRY TIME

The children had said their early morning prayers, the history books had been distributed desk to desk, everyone was prepared to commence from page twenty-eight when in walked the headmistress, Miss Miller. She looked extremely stern. Sally asked herself why she was wearing her gentleman's tie on that particular morning, but before she could fantasise an answer she heard her name being called.

'Sally Bone, please come into my room and close the door.'

Sally, as Sally would, anticipated a pat on the shoulder for good or excellent work. Perhaps she had won a prize for needlework? Miss Miller was unpredictable; sometimes she was nice, and other times extremely strange. Her Uncle Fred would say, you never know which side of the bed that woman gets out of.

'Sally, how many times a week do you take letters to the post office?'

'Twice, Miss Miller,' Sally replied.

'And how many letters are there, Sally?'

'I don't count them, Miss Miller,' Sally said. 'I just hand them to Miss Brown who checks the stamps and that's that.' Sally had no idea where this was leading up to, why her, why not Miss Brown, why was the post office so important?

'That's all for now, Sally, go back to your desk and close the door on your way out.'

The same procedure occurred two weeks later. Identical questions, same stern look, the only annoying difference was . . . the questions were coming from the classmates. Has Sally been a naughty girl? Have you stolen something, Sal?

Sally didn't like what was happening and couldn't for the life of her sense what was going on. Joyce had stopped giving her letters to post; perhaps Mr sailor man was of no importance any more.

The county nurse Maud Day, a blonde lady with blue eyes and a nose far too long, visited the Chrishall school six times a year. She inspected the children in general, checking if they had lice in their hair, teeth problems and so on. Maud had been fighting the lice war for many years. Most of the village dwellers were on good terms with Maud. Maud knew all the village secrets.

It was common news to her that the stork didn't visit Mrs Joyce's bungalow, but that Joyce had asked her to question Sally on the HMS letter did appear, even to her, somewhat fishy. However, she regarded Joyce as her friend and thought it was her duty to assist when needed.

'Sally, be honest with me, did you lose a letter on your way to school?' Maud asked. 'If you did, just say yes and we will not talk about it any more.'

This time Sally had herself completely under control. She completely forgot the reason why she had destroyed the letter. Porky pie sailor man was the cause of all this trouble and all because he hadn't received his soppy letter from Mrs Joyce. Serve him right, thought Sally. He shouldn't be going to the bungalow anyway. What a way of going on, she was sure her Aunt Pearl wouldn't let fat sailor men with porky pie hats visit her, and if so Sally was certain that no HMS letters would leave the village.

'No, nurse,' Sally replied. 'I did not lose a letter but I could always look to see if I can find it, that is if you want me to?'

Maud knew she wasn't going to get anywhere with Sally. Deep down she liked the child and if Joyce got herself into such a mess then really it was her job to get herself out of it. If the letters were so important then she should mail them herself.

Sally's appetite returned, so did her chatter. Mentions of these goings on were never discussed at home, although it did seem strange that even Aunt Jess, who could smell a porky a mile away, was completely unaware of the HMS affair.

Sally continued to make her buttercup chains for anyone who would wear them. Her invitations to birthday parties increased; in fact, as far as she was concerned everything was back to normal.

Now, Sally never liked doctors. To her they were horn blowers, needle and thread makers, horrible pompous johns who made you say Aaaaah ... She couldn't bear the smell of them; their nails were never clean, and most of the time they had long hairs coming out of their ears. Her Daddy always said they were a stuck-up bunch and only the Jewish boys were any good.

The village doctor was indeed a pompous old so and so. Heart patients had to stay in bed for the rest of their lives, his word was law and Fred just couldn't stand him. Many a time Sally would hear him say: 'If you're not sick that bugger will make you sick.' His name was Wilson, George Wilson. He had seen Joyce grow up from a happy-go-lucky young woman to a childless unhappy middle-aged housewife. He knew the relationship with Eric's cousin was somewhat more than the average baked beans on toast and strong tea to go with it. He had warned her at various times of the consequences. He knew Fred only too well, the bungalow was his property. Eric, regardless of his dancing and prancing, was his son. There were times when he anticipated that Joyce would pack her bags and leave without saying goodbye to anyone. She begged George to put the child under pressure, to find out where the love letter was lying. She was desperate to get it back; there was enough gossip in the village and a war romance would certainly be a healthy juicy distraction from the daily newspaper and radio messages.

He promised Joyce that the next time he was near the school, he would try and put some sense into Sally's head and get the truth out of her.

Why is it that adults always underestimate the judgement and sensibility of children? Sally saw through Doctor George's tactics in one second. She knew he was about to blow his top. It was the way he was standing, almost bending over her, doing his utmost to look like the tower of Babylon, arms folded, eyes half closed – in reality the man didn't know what to say.

Sally was already hypnotising him with her eyes, and any second now she would have him in the palm of her hand. George cleared his throat and said the first thing that came into his mind. 'Sally, would you do me a very big favour? On your way home please call in at the bungalow, and tell Mrs Joyce what happened to her letter. Mrs Joyce is ill and I have the feeling that you, young lady, could make her much, much better.'

Sally detested the words ill, illness, disease, even pain; these words suggested to her that someone could die, abandon her, her ultimate being could be disrupted. If Mrs Joyce was a little bit ill then she should do something for her; after all was said and done, if Mrs Joyce would travel off to Mr Jesus, who would look after the dog? She didn't want to. It was as if the doctor had taken Sally into his confidence, totally disregarding the law of confidentiality.

'Can I rely on your help?' Doctor Wilson pleaded. 'Will you do me this one big favour?'

Concentration was truly not surrounding Sally during the last two hours at school. She was desperate, she wanted to talk to someone she trusted, someone who would help her. If Mrs Joyce was ill then she, Sally Bone, had to put her back on her toes again. She couldn't make her mind up as to whether she should act the role of the nurse or the doctor. That she was the culprit and the cause of all the commotion, had long left her busy little mind.

During the last minute of school she decided that Fred was her saviour. Uncle Fred would know the right way to do things, he knew everything. He didn't beat about the bush. Luckily his car was already standing in the drive. He sat in his office doing his paperwork, a sign that he was not to be disturbed. Sally forgot all the rules; she wanted to talk to Fred and talk she would.

Sally wasn't Sally this time. She spoke very slowly, gave him the whole picture, porky pie sailor man, the letters with HMS on them, the rotten apple bin, the interrogations from Miss Miller, Nurse, Maud Day and Doctor Wilson.

'Did they frighten you, Sally? Why didn't you tell me this before today?'

Fred's face was getting more like an over-ripe tomato every minute. He was boiling from inside. How dare these pompous buggers go behind his back and discuss affairs that involved his family.

'Sally, dear, we all do things we shouldn't. Do the ladies in the house know anything about these goings-on?'

He couldn't believe that Pearl would keep such news away from him.

'No, Uncle Fred,' Sally said, 'only the school children know that grown ups were asking me questions, no one else.'

Fred knew this meant the whole village was informed! Why couldn't that bloody doctor have come to him? The school nurse knew Pearl; surely she could have come to the house. They could have tackled Sally; they would have got the truth out of her. Only then did he realise where the root of all the trouble was. All three were protecting Joyce and his nephew and bollocks to his family.

'Sally dear, go tell Aunt Jess I'll be back at supper time and not before. I've got a few calls to make.'

No one ever knew what took place during those calls but knowing Fred, he, without doubt, practically crucified them, a task he had wanted to perform for many, many, years.

As far as the bungalow was concerned he knew he was wasting his time to interfere. Deep down he liked Joyce; he knew she was unhappy and that his son was to blame. When the war was over perhaps everything would change for the better.

The war took its toll in the village and surroundings. Harold, the elder son, was called up; he went into the army. In those days he was called an army mechanic. Eric went into an ammunitions factory. He lost one of his fingers, which meant he was put off for many months.

Mr Arthur had to leave teaching; he landed up in the RAF and was a pilot fighter. The whole family missed Arthur. Banyards was his home when he would come down from London to visit various schools to inspect the performance of the London evacuees. He would come in his two-seater MG which always meant a special trip for Sally. He was so handsome in his uniform. Sally insisted that his photo should remain next to her bed and nowhere else.

Every night after dark Fred would walk the grounds to see if all was well. He was always warned if there was a prisoner of war on the run; luckily he never found one or rather, the prisoner didn't find Fred. If so, Fred would have first given him a good fry-up: bacon and eggs; sausages, the flavour of his choice; fried bread and steaming tea or hot milk to wash it down. If the Italian had said, 'Papa, may I phone Mama?' Fred would have dialled the number. Anything to make the man feel at home before being taken off to the prisoner of war camp, fifty miles away from Chrishall.

Aunt Jess's war dialogue was extremely limited. It consisted of six words and these words were influenced by the time of day in which they were spoken: 'Fred, is that one of ours?' In the beginning everyone was completely silent, Aunt Jess wasn't going to accept any old answer, no way. Fred had to determine by the noise of the engines if it was a Jerry plane or one of ours.

If they didn't take her seriously then it meant a delay in meals, over or under cooked meat. In other words, Fred's food was grossly affected, and without his food our Fred could not perform. Thus the evaluation of the plane's noise determined the time and quality of the Banyards' cuisine!

The air raid shelter was an absolute work of art; it wasn't that there were flowers painted on the walls, but today it would have won a prize for international design. It was built exactly halfway between the big house and the bungalow, and it was open to both families; however, occupation was constrained mostly to the evening and night hours.

It was a combination of mud, cement and corrugated iron and there was a period when Aunt Jess had her tea flask, tins of sandwiches and comics all lying ready for the air raids. Shelter time was frequently from eight in the evening through to five in the morning. Sally loved every minute of it. To her it was sheer excitement. Madame had her own deck chair, Pearl always took the blanket to put over her, and Aunt Jess kept her quiet with cups of creamy hot chocolate and little egg sandwiches which had been released from all form of crusts.

The grown-ups had to speak quietly just in case Sally wanted to fall asleep, an assumption that was completely out of place. Sally wanted to discuss all the war stories at school. It was in the air raid shelter that Sally made friends with Mrs Joyce, who later would become a very dear and loyal friend. Sally was always the ring leader when it came to amusement in the shelter. I spy was the favourite game, and no one had the courage not to join in.

Sally was quick to notice that Mrs Joyce was never a winner; she would always lose. We can't let this continue, thought Sally, we must find a way to let her win. Let's take her red shoes. R.S. will surely make her think of the shoes she's wearing. Luckily for Sally it worked; the winning moment was exchanged with a nod of satisfaction and the following afternoon Sally gained sufficient courage to visit the bungalow after school for what she called a lady to lady chat.

'Mrs Joyce, may I come in, please. I have something very important to tell you. I know where your letter is, it's in the rotten apple bin, in Uncle Fred's orchard. It's all torn to pieces so no one can read it.' She was about to say 'I didn't read it' but stopped. Think of London, thought Sally, you've told her more than enough.

'I think you're very brave, Sally,' said a very sad and tired lady, 'very brave indeed. Would you like to stay and have tea with me? I'll show you all my miniature china shoes I collect from all over the world. We will phone Pearl and tell her you're staying.'

This was to be the beginning of a unique friendship. Joyce taught Sally how to swim. She took her to the films in the vacations. Sally could rely on a weekly surprise: a bicycle ride after school; picking bluebells in the forest; a picnic in her favourite park. Amongst all the joy and fun with the person she now called Aunt Joyce, she inevitably remembered that her new friend was ill. Doctors didn't tell fibs; that was only for the common folk. It would be rude to ask her, but she did notice that the bedroom curtains were often still drawn at the time she went off to school.

YANKS

The men were tall, beautifully dressed. They spoke most peculiarly, ran after the girls, handed out chocolate, cigarettes, nylon stockings, organised parties and late night dancing, made girls pregnant and all we could do was call them Yanks.

'Sally, you will not take a lift from any of these men, sweets you will not accept, or anything that looks like a present.'

Sally had never experienced that Aunt Jessie could be so strict. It wasn't like her to be offish about anyone. Sally had no desire to pay attention to these men in their Jeeps. She was secretly scared of them; their footsteps didn't somehow integrate into the beautiful English countryside. It was as if they were aliens rushed in from some planet, in order to save the world.

Sally's mind and thoughts were geared to one boy only, and what's more, he certainly was not a Yank. Sally had a crush on John. John was her first young boyfriend and John, in Sally's imagination, was definitely going to be a loving and devoted husband. During the last half of the war Sally's John would come and visit the family during the Easter and summer holidays. He had lost his mother, who had been a close friend of Pearl, at a very young age, a situation which Sally tried to identify with her own, and although grossly overrated, it strengthened her liking of John immensely. They were together every minute of the day, mostly in their wigwam on the front lawn. The wigwam was also the dressing room for their theatrical performances. When in residence the flag was established at the top of the wigwam, and no one was allowed in without hearing first, 'Come in, gentle people, we are awaiting you,' a phrase created by the gentleman of the wigwam.

Their stage trunk contained a collection of Aunt Jess's and Pearl's old clothes, hats and jewellery, most of which had been obtained from Christmas crackers. Pearl's shoes found their way into the trunk. Umbrellas, tea cups, sugar bowls which belonged to the dolls house, plus any type of prop that could supply a theatrical function, all found their way into the famous wigwam trunk.

Now, John didn't mind wearing dresses or necklaces. Come to that, he didn't mind wearing women's shoes or summer hats decorated with daisies. Sally even painted his finger nails; she thought it went with his ears. It made him look more cat-like, more like an actor, more 'beware of the dog' sort of thing. How they finally got the paint off the poor lad's fingers belongs exclusively to Sally's book of secrets.

When it rained they would stay in their wigwam and John would read Shakespeare's *Midsummer Night's Dream*. Sally loved the crazy hole in the wall and the silly donkey.

John was not the least bit good looking. His ears were far too big; they made her think of a donkey. Doesn't matter, thought Sally, I can always have them stitched back, but his voice and his nice blue eyes made Sally melt. In her eyes he couldn't do anything wrong. He wasn't a bully like most boys; he loved being at Banyards and it was so obvious his little girlfriend Sally, whom he called Sisi, was very precious to him.

Seaside visits were always arranged when John was at Banyards, a wartime luxury that very few children experienced. John wanted to be a teacher and Sally an actress, but one thing was certain, they had promised each other to be soulmates for many years to come.

More and more evacuees were going back home, some after three or four years. They wanted desperately to return to their parents and their local schools. Sally saw them go. Go if they must, she thought, as long as I can stay here. She was already enjoying her life in the chapel choir. Front row, hymns of her choice, what more could life offer her? She had introduced Ponds cream to the entire family, including Joyce. Bottles of Soir de Paris and Yardley's talc plus large size powder puffs were now additional bathroom items. Both ladies loved it and what Fred thought of the bathroom luxury was of no importance.

THE BABY

There's nothing like the coming of a child to make folks loosen up, to make them remember that death is always chained to life and that joy is inevitably more healing than sorrow.

During the beginning of the last autumn of the war, Joyce and Eric surprised the entire community of Chrishall. They adopted a baby boy from a nearby village. Maud Day had heard the news about a young girl who, during an affair with an American Captain, had become pregnant. The girl, name unknown, wanted to put the child up for adoption and Joyce was the first person who came into the nurse's mind. He was beautiful, chubby, blond, with blue eyes. Name: Geoffrey Cranwell.

The village folks had something new and positive to chat about. They all thought that Joyce was extremely brave, and that Eric would come to his senses and move into the role of a devoted house father.

No wedding had ever, or ever would, exceed the attendance in the Anglican church on the day of the christening. A cloud of almost indescribable magic went through every house in Sally's little village. Everyone felt they had a reason to celebrate. Six ladies appointed themselves to make all the flower arrangements. Miss Rodgers, Sally's music teacher, was asked to play the organ. Mary, the vicar's wife, put a catering committee together, and Fred was approached for advice on lawn preparations. They needed a marquee for the vicarage lawn.

Perhaps Fred Cranwell would be generous and help them complete their plans? Of course Fred agreed. . . . He thought it was a wonderful idea. Who wouldn't in a time like this; his family was still complete and although he had his doubts on what Joyce was doing, and rightly so, as long as she and the rest of his loved ones were happy, to Fred this was what it was all about. Fred promised to keep the delightful plans a secret from his family.

Nevertheless Sally knew something was going on. She could smell it. People avoided her; they obviously didn't want her Aunt Jess to discover what they were all digging up. Dramatic as it was for the vanity of Sally, her mind was completely occupied with the dress parade of the whole family including the baby's. She would wear her harvest festival hat, with yellow satin ribbons decorated with little yellow flowers. Aunt Jess should wear her new blue suit and her lovely light blue straw hat to go with it. Sally wanted no arguments; she was the 'fashion director' and everyone had to look their very best. Pearl asked Fred if he knew who the godparents were.

'No idea,' said Fred, 'no idea at all.'

The day of the christening arrived and although Aunt Jess would have preferred a christening in the chapel, she had made up her mind to enjoy anything that came her way. Breakfast took place an hour earlier than usual, and although the service would start at two o'clock, all four sat dressed and ready to go by twelve thirty.

'Aunt Jess, may I pop over to the bungalow and have a look at Geoffrey before he goes to church? Is there anything you want me to take them?'

'No dear, I'm sure they have everything, but before it's too late there is something I want to say to you. The vicar knows what he is doing so you do not have to interfere. He has christened so many babies, he won't drop anything out of his hands, and I'm sure he will not drop the baby. So please sit quietly and enjoy singing your hymns.'

One of the lads at the church door gave the sign that Fred's car and his son's were approaching the church. The church itself was packed. People who lived in surrounding villages and who had known Fred for years found their way to Chrishall's picturesque church building. Today they were all one huge family.

Miss Rodgers began to play the organ. What she played is long forgotten; however, knowing her love for Mendelssohn his chords must have been heard throughout the church.

Joyce, Eric, and baby Geoffrey entered the church first, followed by the godparents and Joyce's sister and brother. Following them were Fred and his family. Eric placed his arm over Joyce's shoulder; he had to steady her, This couldn't be happening, where were they? Were they dreaming? Was this reality, flowers, people, music?

Joyce and Eric walked like two robots to their reserved seats near the pulpit. The godparents, Fred and his three ladies followed. Everyone was simply dumbstruck, but oh so wildly happy. The service was carried out to perfection. The baby didn't cry, in fact Fred was the only one shedding a tear. He couldn't get over the attendance. What a war couldn't do to people, he thought. I wouldn't have missed this christening for the world. We English always like our traditional food, and the way all the guests were tucking in, one would have thought that food was going out of fashion and not on ration. The baby was admired, advice was whispered into Joyce's ear, and Aunt Jess thanked so many people whom she hadn't seen for years, for making her daughter-in-law's day so unforgettable. The clouds were a warning that it was time to depart, and everyone, intoxicated by all the emotions of the day, made their way home. No one did very much talking that evening, not even Sally.

'Sally dear, where were you after the service? I didn't spot you in the grand marquee,' asked Pearl.

'I stayed in the church, Aunty Pearl. I wanted to look at all the flowers; I wanted to smell them. I also read all the names of all the soldiers carved on the walls, did they die a long time ago?'

Fred thought, not tonight, and promised Sally that he would go back to the church with her and give her a special tour. They all went to bed early; they were what we would call 'whacked'. Sally didn't feel like staying in bed, she was still so excited with everyone's performance. The window sill was the place to sit and recapture the events of the day. Mr Jesus must not be forgotten. She thanked him for a wonderful day. Did he think that Geoffrey could become her brother? Would he please make sure that Geoffrey's mummy wasn't ill and finally would he give a little extra attention to all the village folks. The last hymn had made an immense impression on her.

It was a delightful verse which one can repeatedly hear in places of worship in England.

All things bright and beautiful
All creatures great and small
All things bright and beautiful
The dear lord made us all.

It was the last sentence that remained in Sally's memory and influenced from that day onwards her daily chitty-chat to her dearest friend Mr Jesus.

The after joy of the christening came to a sudden end. Arthur, who had been respected by all, had been shot down in his plane during a raid above Germany. Everyone, even Fred, was shedding tears.

He was a man one didn't just forget. Arthur Tatwell as a teacher had been such a inspiration to so many young people, even Sally felt the need to place his photo above the fireplace so everyone could see him. In her prayers to her Mr Jesus she asked that he, Arthur, be taken good care of and would he tell him that she was sure she would one day see him again. Would he please give him her love and not forget to tell him she would do her very best at school.

* * *

42

The baker's son, Bernard Jones: he too, never came back. He was killed in Burma. There was a memorial service held for him in the chapel. Even Fred attended in his black suit, black tie, and black band around his arm. In total five young boys in the surrounding villages never returned to their homes. Even Sally, in her daily world of joy and fantasy, could feel the sadness around her. She saw Fred attached to the radio listening to all the war news and heard him repeat so many times, 'It won't be long now, Mum, just a few more months and Harold will be home again.'

'Aunt Jess, I have a very special question to ask. Would you like to hear it now or shall we wait until bedtime?'

'There's nothing like the present, child, so let's hear it now.'

'Would you like me to stay for a little while once the war has ended? At least until it's time to go to another school?'

This question had taken Sally many weeks of preparation.

She dreaded the consequences: Aunt Jess could say no, but there again, do pigs have wings? Sally's fears were as usual unfounded. Aunt Jess had long discovered under Sally's pillow her 'book of secrets' and as founders are finders or vice versa, Jess thought it was her privilege to have a quick peek inside.

The following Sally secrets had been neatly written:

> *Stay with Aunt Jessie longer . . . I don't want the war to end.*
> *Go to school in Bishops Stortford.*
> *Aunt Pearl's birthday 7 June.*
> *Aunty Joyce is ill.*
> *Geoffrey has two teeth; Vera is leaving next month to go to her*
>   *grandmother.*

'Sally dear, we'll discuss this matter with your father and if Uncle Fred agrees, you may stay as long as the teachers here can guide you. The following year means another school, and then it's off into the world of the higher education; you must understand the village school can't meet such demands . . .'

Poor Jess wasn't allowed to continue.

'But that will mean I can always be here in the holidays, that's two to three months a year. There you are, Aunt Jess, it's not all that bad, is it now, you won't be alone all that long; I'll be back before you know I've gone.'

Right, thought Sally, that's got that settled. I'll see John three times a year and the family won't have to miss me too long.

LONDON

Gertrude Bone had made the occasional flying visit to Chrishall. Sally always managed to be ill at the time, or even worse they could, quite by coincidence, never find her. 'I'm sorry, Aunt Jess,' she would say. 'I don't love her, I only love you. She never kisses me. She really doesn't have to come at all.' To make matters worse, she was sharp enough to conclude that Fred's affection for the 'lady in question' had long reached zero. Thus any punishment for her improper behaviour towards the mother was out of the question. Sally was his little girl.

Sally did indeed stay in Chrishall for one whole year after the war ended. It suited the mother to have her daughter fostered. Her business after the war was a gold mine. People wanted houses, flats to live in, employment, new fashion shoes to wear, she couldn't go wrong; a child around the place was the last thing she wanted. If Frank wanted their daughter back home, then he would have to make sure he was there to look after her. Staff in the house was no problem, but they had to work and no diddle daddle with a child.

Sally hated both her new home and in actual fact what to her was her new mother. There was no contact between the two. Sally despised her manners; she thought them crude. She always took one shoe off under the table. Disgusting, thought Sally. She never had money in her purse, just a huge roll of banknotes rolled up with an elastic band.

She had blonde wavy hair which to Sally was dyed and unladylike, and when she drank her tea, Sally would look the other way. Sally's criticism reached its peak when her mother started to speak; even her voice made Sally shiver. Nowhere can we read, 'One must love one's mother,' and the word 'respect' had not yet entered Sally's vocabulary. I'll let you into a secret, however: it did later, but only when it was all too late.

The London schools and vacations in the village took place as anticipated. First came the fancy London prep school, attended by all the little posh horrors who knew their bread and butter had been taken care of. All you needed was to pass the necessary exams, have sufficient financial backing and go to the right schools, and the world wherever would open its doors to you. Sally had this system from day one at the school delicately drummed into her.

'Sally Bone, you've been sent here so that we can do our best to teach you to become a lady. You will work hard and your reward will be the best education this country has to offer. Our school will have produced again a pupil ready and capable of achieving her goal in life.'

As young as Sally was she knew that these wise words, regardless as to whether they conveyed class distinction or not, would influence her daily rules of conduct.

She always knew that her life in London, regardless of how many times her mother moved, the new house more ostentatious than the last, would be temporary. Her father did his utmost to make her life enjoyable, but he knew she missed her friends in the village and that Aunt Jess was never out of her mind. Whatever he said or tried, he could never replace the trust Sally had in Fred's wife.

The piano and theatre lyrics were Sally's and Frank's mutual interests, and even Sally's mother would join the party when she heard the two of them performing *Annie Get Your Gun* or 'Underneath the Arches'.

Uncle Fred or Eric could always be relied upon to come and fetch her on the last day of every term. Jessie would make sure they left on time, she didn't want her Sally thinking they had forgotten her, and as Jess would repeatedly say: 'I don't trust that woman, Fred . . .' She did, by the way, mean the mother. 'If we're not careful she'll put Sally in a holiday camp for the entire holiday. We know perfectly well she won't stop working to look after her.'

Little did Jessie know that their fears were completely uncalled for. The holiday agreement suited the mother to perfection. It didn't cost her any money, the daughter was in safe hands; let's be realistic, what more could a hard-boiled business woman like Gertrude Bone have wished for? Gertrude Bone was no fool; she knew that her daughter's talents, posh schools whatever, were definitive to her. Her favourite topic in her favourite environment, the work floor, was always geared to one single judgment: you don't have to be sorry for Sally, she can take care of herself. She's got her father's charm and my brains.

Holidays always meant school reports were discussed with Fred and clothes repaired by Pearl. Pocket money was given for their trips to Cambridge, and it was a tradition to buy two dresses, one for Chapel and one for Christmas, Easter, or Harvest Festival. John always came, and the music room replaced the wigwam. Baby Geoffrey, no longer a baby, was cuddled until he could hardly breathe. The village folks were visited; Sally was back in the world that she adored.

How, she often wondered, did I obtain all this? Is it because I work so hard at school? Could it be because I tell Aunt Jess that I love her so much? Sally always wanted to know why, she never accepted a situation for what it was, and no one ever gave her, with the exception of her school, a satisfactory answer.

What she always dreaded was leaving, having to go back to London. Poor Sally always cried. She knew her tears upset everyone, but she just couldn't help it.

Two years after the end of the war the first tragedy occurred in the family. Aunt Joyce passed away. She had cancer and there was nothing any hospital could do for her. Sally was in London when the news arrived; she was smitten with grief. Her village was trembling. Geoffrey, who in her imagination was her brother, had now lost two mothers, and who would look after him? She couldn't get the lost letter out of her mind. Had Aunt Joyce really forgiven her? Had she always said the things she wanted to say to her? It reminded her of a passage she had once read on a tile, 'Never say things you might regret, you may never have the chance to repair them.'

Why, oh why did Aunt Joyce have to die? She was so happy with Geoffrey. Where did this power come from that took us away from the people we love? Sally had much to think about, and no one near her to discuss it with. Maybe she could ask her scripture teacher next term, or the chapel minister; she was sure that someone must know why these things had to happen. She was certain her Aunt Joyce didn't want to die. It all felt so unfair; there must be an answer somewhere.

Her mind went back to Geoffrey's christening and the mass of flowers, Joyce so happy, and Miss Rodgers playing 'All things bright and beautiful' on the organ. What a wonderful day it had been. Sally was sure her village would never forget it. She would never forget Joyce, and she hoped that Joyce had taken nice thoughts about her to heaven, for in heaven she was, that was for Sally an unquestionable situation. Geoffrey went to live in the big house and Pearl took him totally into her care. Everyone made it quite clear that nothing would change for Sally; her home was still in Chrishall and her room would always be hers.

The months went by in London. Schools changed, pals changed, boyfriends changed. Sally was no longer faithful to her John.

She loved, during the holidays, having a good old giggle with Aunt Jess on the courting subject. Sally made Jess feel as if she were a teenager again.

'Aunt Jess be honest, didn't you have lots of boyfriends?' Sally asked. 'I only have to look at them and they run after me. I'm particular though, Aunt Jess, I only like the tall ones: brown eyes, no glasses, excellent teeth, and they mustn't be stupid.'

Sally used to love to listen to Aunt Jess formulating, in a slightly embarrassed manner, her courting days with Fred. 'Did he kiss you first, Aunt Jess, or did you give him a hint in the right direction?'

'Sally dear, really, a lady shouldn't talk this way.' But all the time Jess couldn't help laughing.

'Go on, Aunt Jess, tell me all the bits and pieces, I've got to hear it from someone, and you never know, I could fall for the wrong one.'

During that holiday there was more laughing and giggling going on in the kitchen than ever, and when Sally returned to London she felt she could handle the entire male establishment. She had promised her Aunt Jess that she would never do anything that Aunt Jess wouldn't do, a rule with an emotional flavour but certainly one that never lost its meaning.

Folks come, people go, but Sally's book of secrets and wishes always remained with her; her secrets and longings were hers only. She would predict what would happen the next day, the following week. The secret was often the result of her wishes. She was an absolute genius in predicting what was going to happen next.

'Plain common sense,' she would say to her fellow schoolmates. 'Take Davidson, for an example, she didn't have a twinkle in her eye last year, now, did she? She was a right grumpy so and so, dull shabby clothes. Look at her now, she's certainly found her way to some fancy store, lipstick, the whole lot! She's got a bloke and this is her last year here. Life is a formula, girls, you're either in formula A or if you are a nitwit you could end up in K or Z and what gets you there nobody knows, but truly, ladies, it's all worked out in advance.'

'Sally,' asked one of the crowd, 'do you know where you will go to? I think you're terribly clever to know so much.'

'I'm not clever, girls, I just use my brains differently, I'm a Heinz 57, and one day I shall find out where all the ingredients came from.'

'Go on, Sally,' asked a classmate, 'give us a hint, what do you secretly think is going to happen to you, are you really a Heinz 57? I always thought that street dogs were 57s.'

'They are indeed,' replied Sally, 'and the funny thing is there's never been a dog in our family.' Sally at all times loved to be the centre of attention, and in order to obtain complete control over the entire situation she would always speak extremely softly so that everyone had to shut up and listen.

'I think,' said Sally, 'that I shall leave the country, explore the world, become terribly famous, and oh so rich. Now, hands up everyone who believes what I've just said.'

Practically the whole class put their hands up.

'Right,' said Sally, 'then you are all formula Z, you nitwits; I made the whole story up while I went along.'

That's real mean, she told herself, truly, truly, mean. You told them your wishes, your ultimate goal in life. Be honest, and tell your chums the truth. They are all in grade A; grade Z only exists in our imagination. We're all going to perform together. We need to praise each other. Amen, Sally, Amen!

Sally had long ago noted in her book of secrets her wish to go to a school in Bishops Stortford, the grammar school nearest to her village and far away from London. She knew that cleverclogs from the villages always ended up in Stortford, and why shouldn't it happen to her? It sounds stupid but she never once doubted that it would truly happen.

Distances never had any frightening or unaccomplished meaning for Sally; if a bus, train, plane or car could get you there, then for her you could go, and that was that. Boats, no! She was petrified of water, horrible stuff, thought Sally, whoever invented it should be put away. It doesn't even smell and has no taste to it. Her scents and lavender water were an excellent substitute for water.

'We'll make our own perfume one day,' she had told her Aunt Jessie. 'One day you and I are going to be famous, mark my words. I'll choose the ingredients, you can choose the name. It must be romantic; it must make folks feel very weepy-weepy. In other words, Aunt Jess, they've got to wash themselves in it. Anything but water, Aunt Jess, anything but water.'

As young as Sally still was, the dollar signs were minutely entering her mind.

While Sally was dreaming her mother was scheming; she too had dollar signs on her mind. A little persuasion here, a little influence there: Gertrude Bone was convinced she could make a success of what she called her government project.

'What do you think, Frank, are we taking a risk moving everything out of London? We'll have to move house, but staff will be cheaper, and undoubtedly more loyal than the old Londoners. The lease won't be anything like ours; why shouldn't we take advantage of what the government is offering? They want young families out of London, there will be heaven knows how many women wanting to work. I'll have extra machines sent over from Italy; this generation still knows how to handle a sewing machine. In twelve months I'll have doubled the production.'

Frank knew his wife had everything worked out in her mind. She was determined to set up a new factory. She had an excellent reputation in the shoe business, supplies would be more than adequate, there was no need to lower her prices; in all fairness she couldn't go wrong. She had already asked Tom if he would move down south. Tom was their permanent driver, Jack of all trades, the type who knows nothing but can tell you everyone's history.

SCHOOL IN BISHOPS STORTFORD

There was an excellent school for Sally in Bishops Stortford, only three-quarters of an hour on the train. It had an excellent reputation, and if things didn't work out as predicted she could always enrol as a boarder. Sally's wishes were coming true. What absolute magic, thought Sally, the school will be great. One train went down to her parents' area, and in the opposite direction the train went down to Audley End, Cambridge. Why did I ever fear, thought Sally, that I would lose my village? In the future I can choose whichever train I want. She didn't dare anticipate living permanently in her village; that would be too good to be true. But one never knew what the future held in store.

Why is it that when we think the sun is going to shine it always rains, if we look forward to a party, it's usually a disaster and when we anticipate the disaster it's such a success we can't stop talking about it?

Sally's last and final grammar school was a complete disaster. There were too many emotions involved. Perhaps Bishops Stortford had been her wish for too long, perhaps her imagination had stretched too far.

The Bones' new temporary house in their new location was dark, damp and downright horrible. The school itself was stricter than strict. The uniforms were designed for three hundred and sixty days a year and three hundred and sixty years ago. In the winter one wore a brown felt hat, gymslip and white shirt and tie. In Sally's case it was a blue tie. In the summer it was a white and blue pleated check dress, white gloves, and white straw hat. When you walked on the street in your uniform, you were not allowed to have anything in your mouth and that applied to everything from a toffee to an ice cream.

If you were caught, you were punished. At lunch your table manners were checked. You stood up when a mistress walked into the class and you sat only when she told you to. All you ever heard was your surname, and Sally's wasn't all that attractive.

MAY

Their motto was: not good enough, then you will be expelled. Not that this worried Sally: she could give the answer before they asked the question. What is it? she asked herself, what does this school have that I dislike so much? The curriculum was superb, there was plenty of art, music, literature, language and sport, but why on earth did May Fletcher bring sandwiches with her every day? Why did she not eat with the rest at lunchtime? She didn't have a hockey stick or even a tennis racket, she was never on the list of trips to London to special music concerts in the Albert Hall, and her uniform was definitely second hand.

What Sally didn't discover with her 'I-spy game' wasn't really worth talking about.

'May, would you like to learn to play tennis with one of my rackets?' asked Sally. 'Go on and say yes. I'll give you a few lessons at lunch time, you'll be a champion in no time.'

May Fletcher was shy, she didn't know how to handle the situation. She liked Sally, she felt at ease with her, but how could she expose the fact that her father was a bricklayer, that she came from a very poor family, and only due to excellent results obtained from the entrance exam and the new law that such schools were obliged to allow a few bright pupils into their vicinity, did May find herself sitting amongst a bunch of children who were born with either a silver or a golden spoon in their mouths and who were not even friendly to each other, let alone to a bricklayer's daughter.

I must discuss the class distinction with Aunt Jess in the Christmas vacation, thought Sally. She used to be a teacher. It's disgusting that May has to look on and watch us making fools of ourselves with rackets, and eating ourselves sick in the canteen simply because we have the money to spend on a lunch and she doesn't.

While walking back from the chapel the following Sunday, she told her 'May' story to Frank. 'Why, Dad, do we make people unhappy, why can't we treat people like May as if she is one of us? The school should have a special fund for such families! Dad, would you mind if I gave May one of my rackets, and would you please treat her to concert hall tickets if only for the coming season? If you say yes, I'll bake you one of those plain cakes, you know, the ones you like the best. Three eggs and a little bit sticky.'

Before Frank could say no Sally was thanking him for being so kind. Her mother after all never visited schools on parents' day and she therefore saw nothing wrong in promoting her father. Most fathers were ugly and dull, and hers was Mister Charming himself.

May never knew who donated the tickets and train fares to London, and Sally never knew how May suddenly managed to sit every day in the lunchroom, but the wonder did happen and that, as far as Sally in her younger years was concerned, was what life was all about. The class distinction in the school obstructed Sally's flair for freedom. It never dawned on her that her good looks and *flair de bouche* created jealousy and anger. Why should it? She had no reason to be jealous; as long as her village remained intact, then her world could survive.

It was Friday midday. Sally had long planned that on this specific day she would walk over the bridge to the opposite platform, take the three thirty p.m. train to Audley End, use the school taxi to Chrishall, and spend the weekend with her true family. Her parents were so busy they never got home before nine in the evening. Saturday was always devoted now to the factory; she was sure no one would miss her and Aunt Jess could always phone and tell them that she had arrived.

'I've arrived,' screamed Sally, 'am I on time for tea?'

Everyone including Geoffrey greeted her as if she had been away for years. All except Fred: he could feel a storm blowing up. He waited until the table had been cleared, gave Jess a knowing wink, which in reality meant leave us two alone, took his jacket off and started to talk to Sally.

'Young lady, what are you doing here? This behaviour is going to annoy your parents, especially your mother. She will feel insulted, and without any explanation she will put a stop on your visiting us in the future.'

'But I . . .'

Sally didn't get any further. 'No, Sally, listen to me, we all love you here, we don't want to miss you, please do what I say. Be sensible, and while you're living in their house try at least to follow their rules.'

'But Uncle Fred, I'm so lonely, there's no one I can talk to. There's no one who gives me a kiss goodnight, please don't send me back!'

Fred phoned Sally's father and explained that Sally would return on Monday afternoon after school. He had spoken to her and he was sure it wouldn't happen again.

What I wouldn't give, thought Fred, to give them a piece of my mind. Never liked the two of them from the very start, real Londoners, they always think they are superior to us village folks.

Sally knew she had to take Fred's words seriously. She didn't want to take the risk of no more lovely holidays with Aunt Jess. She concluded that she would find a way to fill in the hours that she was alone; after all, she told herself, it's only a few more years, then I can fly off to wherever I really came from. Sally started to laugh. I know at least now I didn't come from a cabbage, or was it a cauliflower?

Late Monday afternoon arrived, Sally made her way to the station, or at least that was what she intended to do had it not been for a car that drove up alongside her, window down and a cheerful red haired man behind the steering wheel.

'Tom!' yelled Sally. 'What a lovely surprise! Have you come to capture me, put me in handcuffs or treat me to the biggest ice cream ever, before taking me back to the house of doom and gloom?'

It was of course ice cream plus all the trimmings, and Sally, for the very last time, preached her sermon, at Tom's request, on love, charity, loneliness, and interest in others. He knew the two female Bones weren't exactly lovebirds. He had known Gertrude for many years and had the greatest respect for her. He knew her background, her youth, the poverty, the utter will, and determination to succeed.

He was ready between the spoonfuls of ice cream to defend his employer but found himself listening to Sally as if he were listening to the radio.

'I know what I want later in life, Tom; I don't want to be surrounded by people who make me unhappy. Grandma has always told me life is so short, enjoy it while you can. I'm going to finish off this school, as soon as I can, I can easily skip a year, and then I'm going to fly.'

'Where to?' asked Tom, caramel ice on his lip and a stain on his tie.

'Anywhere, Tom, anywhere. I'm determined I'm going to learn what life is all about.' Tom knew from that moment on he was looking at a second Gertrude Bone. It may take time, he told himself, and Sally had not experienced poverty, but how many times had he heard her mother say, 'Tom, I'm determined.'

'Truly, Tom, I'm determined, so eat up and we'll have a singsong all the way back home. You take the high road and I'll take the low road and I'll be in Scotland before you.'

'Sally Bone,' said Tom, 'you're crazy, but I love you, don't ask me why but I do!'

GRANDMA

Sunday afternoon was often spent at Grandma Bone's. This particular Sunday Frank wanted to tell his mother that they were moving back to London, at least as far as the house was concerned. The factory was doing well with plenty of staff, but Gertrude missed her London shops, the retailers, their sense of humour. She felt like a foreigner in her new surroundings. Tom didn't mind driving backwards and forwards, and Sally had been enrolled as a boarder at her school. Not that Sally cared; she only had one objective in mind: study and pass, and then do something useful with her life.

Frank's mother was a good old stick, that is if you like the exception to the rule, and believe me, Grandma Bone was anything but average. She was really amusing. She always baked on a Friday, used a clean bowl for everything, and a scarf always kept her hair tidy and clean. She would clean the house to perfection; one could truly eat from the ground. She had a row with every domestic that was hired; they were frequently caught not picking up the milk bottles before scrubbing the floor. Now, did Grandma leave the milk bottles there intentionally? Of course she did!

She was from eight a.m to three p.m a professional trouble maker, but from four o'clock onwards everything was hunky-dory.

Tea was always at four sharp. Her tea tray was covered with a small lace cloth, a bone china tea service, and of course we must not forget the small linen napkins. Her cakes and sandwiches without the crusts were way above the standard of Harrods. Everything tasted like more, you couldn't stop; it was a fabulous treat to have tea at Grandma's. She always dressed for the occasion, her nose was powdered, and her beautiful diamond ring was a permanent feature of the domestic scenery. Today it would cut her finger off; in those days it was regarded as a status and a work of art.

Darling Gran always had the knack of saying something that would remain in your memory, where she got it from, one never knew. Perhaps it was her walk through life, her years in the war, she had lost so much during the bombing. Sally would have been pleased if Grandma had given her the chance to discuss and remember the ingredients relevant to the tea cakes. This subject, however, was never discussed. All Grandma's secrets were kept stowed away in the top drawer of her lovely old desk. What Sally wouldn't have given to obtain the chance to have a nose around in there. She was sure she would find more than cake recipes: perhaps a little story on her parents, a little juicy scandal, something to make your blood curdle. Really, Sally Bone, she thought, you are the biggest digger in the world, leave things the way they are; remember 'curiosity killed the cat'.

Rule number one from Grandma: 'When you are older and married do not forget to put money away for a rainy day.'

Rule two: 'Never start your married life in two rooms; you will never get out of them.'

Rule three: 'Never forget that when people cannot earn money on you, they are no longer interested in you.'

Sally used to secretly laugh about it all. She wanted desperately to say, 'Come on, Gran, don't be so morbid. I'm not going to get married and do not worry about the money business, tell me how to cook the cakes and handle the charwoman.'

For some reason she didn't dare. She always felt that her Grandma longed for a compliment so her goodbyes were always colourful. ''Bye, Gran. I wish I could put you in my pocket. You are a wise old owl, don't know where you get it all from.'

Sally always knew that the answer would be: 'Young lady, do not call me old. When you reach my age you will, I hope, still remember what I've told you. Life is hard, Sally, yours hasn't yet begun.'

Grandma was the first to hear about Sally's future plans. Her mind was made up. She was going to train to be a nurse in the hospital for all abandoned children. Why not, she had so much to be grateful for; now it was her turn to give something back to children who had received so little from their surroundings. Grandma thought it was a great idea. Aunt Jess was somewhat sceptical; she thought that Sally was too young. 'Such worldly dangers in the big city, Sally,' said Aunt Jess.

'If you go down to Cambridge we can keep an eye on you.' Fred thought it was an excellent idea. 'Do her good, Jess, hard work never killed anyone. She'll make a success of it, mark my words. I'll make sure she's got enough money in her savings account. She won't come to any harm; we both know where her heart is.'

Frank didn't like the idea at all, but anything was better than being an actress, and he was well aware that either occupation was going to cost him money. Actresses were poor but nurses were paid only enough to buy their toothpaste.

HOSPITAL

Matron Peterson was a figure for Madame Tussaud. She was magnificent. She had worked all over the world in army field hospitals where she had been involved in the amputation of limbs with a minimum of anaesthetics, in some cases with no anaesthetics whatsoever.

She was tall, had beautiful white hair and was immaculately dressed in her matron's uniform. Each garment: blue dress, white apron, white cap neatly fixed at the back of her head, was starched and ironed to perfection. Her 'waist' belt never missed Sally's eyes when she saw her walking.

The way she ran the hospital was above perfection. Sally adored her skill. The hospital consisted of three wards. One was for surgery: tonsils, appendix and so on, one for general medicine and one for the babies undoubtedly abandoned by their mothers. Each ward had a ward sister, and next in rank came the staff nurse. Both ladies frightened the daylight out of you; we'll come back to this later, but did they know how to judge and get the maximum of energy and discipline out of their junior staff? They most certainly did.

The rules of the hospital were quite simple.

You shared a room with a fellow nurse; if you didn't like her it was your bad luck.

You had to be in your room no later than ten thirty p.m. but if the concierge liked you or you were on good terms with the night nurse, then perhaps you could squeeze an additional thirty minutes into your programme. A twelve o'clock pass was given only by Matron.

There was an excellent kitchen and a laundry room. All the nurses' uniforms were kept extremely spic and span; the nurse had to make sure she had her black stockings and flat heeled shoes.

The tuition was free, except for the books of course. There were always two motivations: you either went on to the famous London

Hospital, though the chance was very small, for a further three year course; or you went on to the County General. If you went to London you were posh and well educated; if you went to the General you were in principle a nice person and a dedicated nurse.

The atmosphere was excellent ... The Irish didn't like the English, the English didn't like the Africans, the Africans didn't like anyone. The Welsh were always breaking the rules. They were never in on time; most of them were church ministers' daughters who came to London to enjoy the freedom. Do we need to say more?

Sally's first working day was in Ward 2. She had inquired the night before as to what she could expect. No one said a word, no one; did they feel sorry for the humble starter, or were they taking her down a peg or two?

Sister Rush, the ward sister, was sitting behind her desk checking the night log. She knew Sally was standing in front of her, but she totally ignored her.

'Good morning, Nurse,' said Sally, 'this is my first day, perhaps you could help me? I have no idea what I have to do, and my itinerary indicates that I'll be here for the next eight hours.'

Sister Rush continued to ignore Sally, and remained doing so until she had finished checking the logbook. She closed the book, looked up at Sally, and said: 'You will not call me Nurse, can you not read? My title is Sister and my name is Rush.'

'Yes, Nurse, sorry, Sister, I'm nervous, my apologies, it will not happen again.'

'Your sole task today, Nurse, will be to clean the bed rails and the wheels. Sheets from beds number ten and fourteen will be changed and made up for incoming patients. Nurse Jenkinson knows how to change sheets, watch her carefully. On my ward I do not want to see a single crease in the sheets and by the end of the day you will know what an envelope fold is and Nurse, do not forget it!'

'Yes, Sister, thank you, Sister.' Sally thought, I'll bash her. She didn't know what to think any more. Utter nonsense. I'll pack my bags and go ...

'Are you Nurse Bone? You look somewhat flushed. My name is Dot. Sister Rush has asked me to teach you some of the basic rules. Don't take too much notice of her; she can be quite pleasant at times. Start by washing the rails first then we'll get the sheets changed.'

Sally still couldn't believe this was happening to her: washing iron bed rails: good grief, nowhere could one read this type of chore in the advertisement.

By this time Sally had caught the eye of several of the young patients. 'Hello, young man,' she whispered 'how are you today? Are these your comics? There are more under the bed than on it; shall I pick them up for you?' A shy 'Yes please, Nurse' came from the bed and Sally crawled on her knees under the bed in order to pick up the child's comics.

'Nurse Bone, what are you doing under the bed? You are supposed to be cleaning it.'

Sally thought this can't be true, this just can't be true. If only Uncle Fred were here, he would give her a piece of his mind, but Uncle Fred wasn't there and Sister Rush was. Her Aunt Jess couldn't clean the beds for her either, and Pearl would certainly have put her rubber gloves on first.

Sally breathed extremely slowly, tossed her hair back as if she were Lauren Bacall and spoke a few words to herself. Sal, don't let them buckle you down, girl, if she wants her beds to glow, then we will make them glow, in fact they'll glow so much the old so and so will be able to see her nose in any rail of her choice, but before I plunge my lily white hands into this disgusting bucket of water, I'm going to pick these comics up and that, lady Sister whatever your name is, is that!

By one o'clock Sally was still to be found in the ward, and still at work. Sister Rush had told her three times not to talk so much; she could do all the talking in the world when off duty. At the third warning Sally decided to react. 'Sorry, Sister, talking just comes naturally to me. I can't help it.' Rush, in the first time for many years, didn't know what to do or how to react: nurses were never bold with her. She would discuss this little Madame with Matron. She had no desire to watch the discipline on her ward decrease; perhaps Matron should be more cautious with new applicants regardless of their backgrounds. Sally left the ward tired, no, exhausted is a better word. She was in a good mood, her hands were still attached to her arms, her Lauren Bacall hairstyle was still intact, but her feet were killing her.

'Dot, what are you doing this evening? Would you like to show me the nearby shops? I'll treat you to a fish and chip supper; you were great to me today.'

'We can have supper here, Sally. Save your money, you're going to need it.'

Sally knew her new friend meant it well and she didn't want to embarrass her. The two of them had supper with the rest of the staff. Sally couldn't believe the way the nurses were talking about their young patients. It all sounded so professional. They at least hadn't cleaned the bed rails and folded sheet corners the whole day. She told herself to be patient, to listen to everything going on around her and in particular to remember that a Sister is a Sister and not a Nurse.

She went to bed early, but what with the strain and panic of the day, she just couldn't fall asleep. She kept thinking of the children, how lonely they must be, no one to give them a kiss and a hug before they went to sleep. Tonight she had no one to chat to and the loneliness began to take its toll. There was a telephone box downstairs in the hall of the sleeping quarters. Why not, thought Sally, I've got some change. I'll phone someone up and tell them that I've had a wonderful, wonderful day, and that all is going well.

Sally in her famous red dressing gown descended to the nurses' phone box. Which number should she dial? She wasn't a child any more; she just wanted to have a quick down to earth chat before going back to bed.

She dialled a number and we all know who picked the receiver up. 'Is that London 4789?' said Sally. 'Yes, Sally, it is London 4789, and how was your first day?'

No criticism, no upsetting remarks, would she like to speak to her father? Her first day in the Bernardo's Hospital for Children was a day never to forget. It was an institution that would open many corridors of knowledge, and many, to her, unknown patterns of life. Sally returned to her room; her roommate was fast asleep. She sat on her eternal favourite spot, the window sill. Her thoughts went to the children and the things they missed in life. None of them were grumpy; they all laughed, chatted away, played with their simple ward games and chucked their comics under the beds. If they could be so cheerful with so little, why couldn't she be over the moon with everything she had? Her mother had, after all, paid for her expensive schools and hobbies. And although no one was comparable to her darling Aunt Jess, perhaps she should make an effort at least to get to know her.

Sally loved to dig; she always wanted to know what made people tick. Not immediately, thought Sally, but very soon, I'm going to find out what makes my mother tick. My father must know. I assume he must love her, but I still for the life of me can't fathom out why.

* * *

58

Sally's first month was geared to Ward 2 under the holy supervision of Sister Rush. Bone liked Rush and Rush was very, very cautious with her attitude towards Bone. Sister Rush knew that the Matron found Sally a very polite and humorous person. Within three weeks, Nurse Bone had already been invited to tea, on her day off, in Matron's cosy living quarters.

Sister Rush knew this was not a habit of the Matron and that Matron would never justify or defend herself to anyone; she was absolutely impartial to the thoughts of others. She could afford to be; her word was holier than holy. In fact if she had taken it into her head to literally discharge everyone, no one would have doubted her judgement. Sally's visit to Matron's quarters was a result of Sally still playing her favourite 'I spy with my little eye' game.

She delivered a report to Matron, all top secret stuff, of course, saw a book of Wordsworth's poetry lying on the desk and before Matron could return Sally's 'Good morning, Matron,' she was obliged to hear Sally recite:

> *I wandered lonely as a cloud*
> *That floats on high o'er vales and hills*
> *When all at once I saw a crowd,*
> *A host, of golden daffodils;*
> *Beside the lake, beneath the trees,*
> *Fluttering and dancing in the breeze.*

Matrons, like all folks at the top, are basically very lonely people, and that Matron slipped into the habit of asking Sally to tea now and then, with a view to chatting about poets and their lifestyles, was for both females, old and young, delightful and acceptable.

KEITHIE

Poets and daffodils never had the opportunity to reach Sally's mind when on duty. For Sally on Ward 2 there was something waiting for her that smelt like everything, but not like a flower. The smell came from a very little chap called Keithie Brooks. Now, every nurse, no matter how long they worked in the hospital, or which ward it was, they always had a favourite patient. They just couldn't help it.

Dot spoiled John because he was cross-eyed, Mildred gave Peter the latest comics because he stuttered and Sally, don't ask why, had taken

Keith Brooks to her heart. Sally called him Keithie; he was only two years old, and he had had at a very early age infantile paralysis. His left leg was strapped in a brace. The rails on both side of the bed were always pulled up which meant that the actual space that Keithie had to discover was extremely limited. The result was that you would always see him squatting in the middle of his bed sucking his fingers and making atrocious noises. Preferably the healthy foot was stuck through the opening between two railings, or he stood on both legs, his little hands grasping the top of the rail. There was only one word he could pronounce and that was 'PoPo'.

PoPo became a laugh, PoPo became a fragrance, PoPo became an alarm clock, and finally, PoPo became a nightmare for Sally. Perhaps our bowels do not work to an alarm clock but Keithie's most certainly did. As tiny as he was, he knew that his bowels wanted the PoPo at 7.55 a.m.

Night nurses went off, day nurses came on. The night nurses would always rush off before Keithie began his PoPo song and dance, and if Sally wasn't on the dot with the little white po, it meant a bedful, rails of a distinctive coloured substance. His blond hair was no longer blond; do we have to say more? God, what a mess!

Bucket, clean sheets, flannels and towels were rushed in. Keithie loved it; he had Sally's full attention for at least half an hour. That evening Sally discussed her Keithie problem with Dot. She couldn't go on forever playing the PoPo game with him. He had her completely in his grip.

Teddy bears will never cease to influence their environment and Pears, the bear purchased for Keithie, did the trick. He could hold the bear if he was clean and only if he was clean! Keithie was taught to sit on the po, hold the rail tight, and on no condition sway backwards and forwards. Prize for the completion of the PoPo project? one lovely cuddly grey bear whom everyone called Pears. Pears and Keithie became great pals, and when no one was around, Sally would always give Keithie a kiss on both cheeks, comb his hair and teach him some additional vocabulary.

Feeding time we will leave to everyone's imagination. Keithie's face looked as if he was having a facial from a well known cosmetic house. It was covered in mashed potato; he loved making himself dirty. What a promotional tool this could have been: 'Babies first, grown ups later.'

Sally's first pay packet was for her a chunk of gold. It was the first time she had ever earned her own keep. 'Four pounds, Dot, come on, let's go to the shops and treat ourselves to a little something, a weenie, weenie something, be a sport.'

Dot said no. Dot had no budget spare for anything but the basics and even that meant she had to be extremely careful.

'I'll tell you what we'll do,' said Sally, 'I'll pay the fares to Oxford Street. We can go window shopping, and from there on to the Odeon to see Humphrey. I know his latest film is playing there. You can pay for the cuppa and a sticky bun. Now, is that a deal or not?'

Dot more or less had her coat on. It was a great day out, excellent weather, film fantastic, the flavour of the sticky buns remained for at least two hours in their mouths; what more could the two Madames have wished for? However, Dot did notice that Sally purchased, without any explanation whatsoever, a very attractive powder compact. Dot's intuition told her not to ask why or who it was for. She was sure if Sally wanted her to know she would have told her straight out.

The day ended at the chip shop ten minutes from the hospital. 'Salt and vinegar, Dot, or just a little salt and pepper?' They were both hungry and Dot had very obviously enjoyed her day. So what, said Sally to herself, what are friends for if you can't spoil them now and then? 'Eat up, Dot, don't let them get cold! It's back to healthy food tomorrow.'

Apart from pal Keithie the rest of the children on Ward 2 were great. The poor little mites had broken bones or other serious sicknesses. One thing they all had in common was their need of attention. Now Sally, when it came to needles, bandages, steam baths or whatever, was a dead loss. She couldn't bear to put a needle into someone. If the child cried then she secretly shed a tear. The true born and bred nurses loved this weakness in Sally.

'Sal, can I take over your injections today? Sister doesn't have to know. I know you have something against needles.'

'You're on!' Sally would say, 'but I shall be watching you all the time.'

Did she watch? Heavens no, she held the child's hand and read either the lunch menu to them or some comic that was probably twelve months old. She knew she didn't have the making of a professional nurse, but she was superb in delegating to others, camouflaging her weaknesses and exhibiting the positive talents.

Yes, Sally was the bookworm in the hospital; she knew the names of every bone and muscle in your body. Latin was for her a second language, anatomy teachings were ABC to her.

THE BET

A visit home, for the very first time, was after she had completed four weeks of extremely hard work in the hospital. Her mother and father listened, to Sally's utter surprise, to every single word she said. Her father thought it was a great joke that she had to work so hard, and the PoPo stories brought tears of laughter to his eyes.

'I never thought I would see the day that my daughter would be cleaning potties and changing bed sheets,' said Frank. 'You're not going to bring this little chap home, are you, Sally?'

'Stop teasing,' said Sally. 'I truly love this work and what's more, you old so and so, I'll make a bet with you. If at the end of the course I'm the nurse of the year, I then win the first prize, you, as punishment for all the mean teasing, can give me a trip to any country of my choice, in the world.'

Frank turned to his wife and asked: 'What do you think, Gertrude, to this blackmail, shall we take her on?'

This type of conversation was right down her mother's street: the higher the stakes the more interest was shown. 'No, Frank dear, I'll take her on, as knowing you she would get her trip even if she ended at the bottom of the list.'

After eating enough for four days and with two bags full of goodies, one for Dot and one for the rest of the crew, safely in her travel bag, it was time for Sally to leave.

'Shall I ask Tom to drive you back, Sally?' asked her father. 'He won't mind, he always asks after you.'

'No thanks,' said Sally, 'I enjoy sitting at the top of double deckers, you can see for miles. Tell Tom I haven't forgotten him.'

She had her coat on, all ready to leave. Frank wanted to walk her to the bus stop. He had already slipped a pound note for the bus fare into her coat pocket, when to her father's amazement she walked back into the lounge, took a small packet out of her bag and gave it to her mother.

'Mum, this is for you. I bought it from my first salary. I do hope you like it. I think it's very pretty.' Sally turned to leave. She didn't want to be disappointed by her mother's reaction.

'Sally!' her mother called, 'for goodness sake wait until I have opened the parcel. It's so neatly wrapped there must be something very special in it.'

When the powder compact appeared her mother was speechless. 'Is this really for me, Sally? Frank dear, look, isn't it lovely, where shall we put it?'

'Put it? It's meant to be used.'

Her mother opened the powder compact and looked at herself in the mirror. 'You know, Sally, your choice is perfect, I do need to use it, it couldn't have come at a better time. Your friend Dot, why don't you bring her with you next time, that is if she is free; she is always welcome.'

The powder compact remained in Gertrude's possession until she retired, and she never stopped telling her staff: 'This is what my daughter bought for me from her very first pay packet.'

There was a piano in the ward, and, mostly after working hours, Sally would compose little sing-songs for and with the children, read to them from books of their choice, and teach them to imitate figures from their favourite pantomime stories.

Why Sally never got the sack for imitating hers, is something we'll never know. She called him Doctor Nugles. He was the non-resident doctor to the hospital, and was as ugly as one could make him. Her father would have said: 'Only a mother could have loved a face like that,' and what's more, the pompous John thought he was God's gift to all women. Sally and Dot used to talk for hours on these subjects.

'Sally, why can't you be just a normal human being, learn what we have to learn and perform like every other student nurse?'

'Impossible, Dot,' she would say, 'nothing can replace making people happy. You can give them all the medicine in the world, but if they are lonely and feel unwanted then you will never cure them. It's a pity this subject isn't part of our tuition.'

Dot told herself not to react, to say nothing, as knowing Sally, she was capable of writing a fifteen page essay on the entire topic and handing it to Matron, and Dot and the rest of the entire hospital nursing staff would be forced to read and digest it. Dot was an excellent nurse and she knew it. She loved having Sally as a friend, if only for the many hours she made her scream with laughter.

CHRISTMAS

Sally, or shall we call her Nurse Bone, stayed on duty at Christmas. She played her favourite carols and sang to all the children. Actually this is wrong; she didn't sing alone, they all sang together. All had hats on their heads, discovered in the crackers. Did Sally wear a paper hat on her head for the occasion? You bet she did, and what anyone said or thought was of no interest to her.

It was Christmas Day and the children deserved a laugh. A little book on Christmas had been purchased for each child. She was sure her Uncle Fred wouldn't mind her spending her savings on such a good cause. The hospital entertainment group never asked Sally to join in their Christmas choir group. Not that I blame them, Sally told herself, none of them can really sing. If I were in their shoes I wouldn't ask me either.

She phoned her Aunt Jess on Christmas Day, to hear that her presents were lying under the tree.

'What is it, Aunt Jess? Go on, tell me, I'm dying to know.'

'Nothing special, dear,' said Jess. Sally knew nothing special meant very special!

'I'll be coming to see you the first week of January. Could Pearl ask John to come; I'd love so much to see him. The males are horrible here, Aunt Jess, I haven't met a gentleman since day one, with the exception of Keithie of course. I'm starting night duty in a few weeks' time, not that I'm looking forward to it. Knowing me I'll fall asleep before the moon comes up, but we'll discuss it all when I see you. Give Uncle Fred a big hug from me. I still miss you all very much, oh, and Aunt Jess, I love you with all my heart, and can't wait to see you again.'

'I'll save you some Christmas cake, dear, and mince pies and we'll see if we can find John.' Sally placed the receiver down.

She felt homesick. She knew her village was crumbling. Aunt Jess was getting all of a sudden much older, her voice sounded tired. Fred didn't drive the car so much and Pearl was occupied with Geoffrey. Sal, buck your ideas up, she said to herself, there's a ward full of children who need their Christmas din-dins, and you, you sentimental Daisy Bloggins, are going to see that they get it! Your turn will come, there might be a Chinaman waiting somewhere for you. Good heavens, thought Sally, where do I get the nonsense from? China, who on earth wants to go to China? Do they have Christmas in China? If not, she ain't going.

'Nurse Bone, you're extremely quiet today,' said the Staff Nurse on duty. 'Are you missing your family on Christmas Day?'

'No, Staff Nurse,' said Sally. 'I'm enjoying being in a world so much different from the one outside these walls.'

Cleaning, thank goodness, was taboo on Christmas Day. Sally took

Keithie out of his prison bed, showed him the kitchen, and gave him a drum and drumsticks to play with.

Poor Matron blushed to the roots when she heard the beating of the drum, but the Christmas tree and its lights told her to restrain herself from any gloom and doom comments. It was, after all, Christmas and a little beating of the drum couldn't ruin anyone's appetite.

Father Christmas delivered his song and dance in the afternoon. And as far as Sally was concerned he could go back to where he came from. What a nutcase. He had obviously had a pint too much during lunch; however, his red alcohol nose did contribute to the Santa suit and white beard. The children loved him. He didn't realise what a fool he was making of himself. The more ridiculous he became, the louder the children screamed with laughter.

'Santa, can we offer you some refreshment?' said Sally. 'A nice cup of strong tea?'

'Later, perhaps, Nurse. I think however you're offering the medicine I need.' She saw him glaring at her, his eyes watery and distracted.

Poor Santa squatted himself down in the kitchen at the end of his performance. Staff Nurse gave him some strong tea and Sally, bit by bit, gave him the full Bone 'dig your history' treatment. She didn't find out what size shoes he wore but she did find out where he bought his underwear. He turned out to be a medical student from Malta, was alone for Christmas and wanted to earn some extra money. What could be nicer than playing Santa in a country like England?

'Nurse, could I take you out one evening? I'm sure the two of us have a lot in common.'

'Do we?' said Sally. 'I don't drink! I just like to smell of roses and nutmegs.' Nonsense, thought Sally, no one can smell of nutmegs, but he won't know. 'What's your name, before Staff Nurse throws you out?'

'Rodrique, but my friends call me Roddy, and yours?'

'Sally, and don't call me Sal.'

'Can I phone you, Sally? Can I take you to the theatre? How about the second Saturday in January and what are you laughing about?'

'Nothing really,' said Sally. 'Four hours ago I was thinking of China, now we are flying above Malta; is *Peter Pan and Wendy* playing anywhere? If so, I'll agree to that. I'm sure an ancestor of mine must have written it.'

Sally phoned her parents at the end of the day. She knew her father was waiting to hear something. He would enjoy the Malta 'one too many' story. I'll glamorise the whole thing, say the father is loaded, no, not loaded, filthy rich – that sounds even more inviting.

DANCING

Sally's introduction to the world of ballroom dancing never failed to intrigue Dot.

She purchased two special dresses, one black, one pink, both strapless, not that she had much to show, but we must be honest: when she took to the floor, the men liked what they saw.

The ballroom dancing took place in a special dancing hall some forty-five minutes away from the hospital; timing was usually from eight p.m to twelve p.m and with the occasional pass from Matron and a wink from the concierge our Prima Donna managed to enjoy all the hours available.

'Dot, why don't you come? You can borrow one of my dresses, our bras are the same size; they might see your knees but that doesn't matter.'

'Not for the world,' said Dot.

'But Dot, this teaches you what life is about; man looks for woman, woman looks for man.'

'But I don't want to look,' said Dot. 'Now shut up with all your nonsense and get your stockings washed out for tomorrow. I know you haven't any more in your drawer. I wanted to borrow a pair, but there's none left!'

Ward 1 was a complete disaster for Nurse Bone. Surgery, blood, instruments and too much imagination.

'Dot, have you watched Nugle's fingers while he is operating, they tremble, you know! I'm sure the man drinks. Watch my word, Dot, one day it will all come out.'

Poor Dot, who worked frequently on Ward 1 and in theatre, was taken aback by her own sudden obsession with Nugle's fingers. Were they moving all the time, did his hands really shake, was he on the booze? Sally Bone, you horror, thought Dot, now you've got me thinking. Before I know where I am, I'll be wanting to smell his breath.

Dot, probably out of sheer fear, never got to the latter stage and she never confided in Sally for fear of what she would get up to, but did she see his fingers tremble? She most certainly did and every time she was in the theatre she watched him like a hawk. Perhaps Sally wasn't such a nutcase after all.

She could also recite what Sally would say should she have confided in her. 'You are learning the facts of life, Dot, write it all down, and don't forget it!'

* * *

66

Ward 3 was for babies only, seventy-seven bottles of milk for every feeding time, seventy-seven bottles that had to be prepared, warmed up in an old fashioned machine. To be precise there were babies of all sizes and colours; take your pick, Ward 3 had them all.

Cheerful cases, heart breaking cases, some they even knew would die, but all received the most loving care one could bestow on any small patient. Ninety per cent had no parents, no future, only a world of loneliness.

There was something special about Ward 3. It was as if it was a privilege to work there. The Ward Sister was a gem. She knew from day one which nurse she wanted on her ward, and believe it or not they were all the same types that were chosen. There was no conflict of culture, no fear of misunderstanding because of a language problem. On Ward 3 Sally learnt what the feeling was to be responsible for someone's life.

She told her father: 'When I'm off duty I so desperately want them all to be alive when I return the next morning or night. They are all so alone; how many of them will find their own window sills as I did?'

The Ward Sister and Sally got on like a house on fire. There wasn't a case history that Sally didn't know backwards and it never worried her whether she had day or night duty, weekdays or weekends free: the babies were number one and no ballroom dancing or boyfriends could change her devotion to Ward 3.

She wrote frequently to Aunt Jess and told her that as soon as she knew when her holiday week was available she would rush down and see them. The odd day off in the week would be spent either with her father – the two of them would love to go to the theatre – or studying for her end of year exams.

'Men really are ghastly monsters, you know, Dot. I can't see what we women really see in them. They treat women, or rather females, as if they are the world atlas. Their hands are the ships and they are determined to discover every female harbour in the world.'

Dot thought, This is worth listening to. I'll put the kettle on, make some tea; knowing Sally this could be an extremely entertaining evening.

'It all starts, Dot, when they dance with you. The first dance is okay; they often tread on your feet, but nine out of the ten do say sorry. If you give them a second dance they hold you so close you are dancing on their feet, and as for the third dance, they look down into your bosom, press you to them and act as if they are making a carbon copy of you. It's all what they call body language. Think about your history lesson, Dot, it was all man to woman stuff. Either he wanted her in an apron or she wanted his bank account, but it all started with the carbon copy language. Just imagine, Dot, if Cleopatra had refused Caesar his photocopy act, you would be speaking Italian and we would all be eating spaghetti. When the men have finished their dancing and prancing, the wallet comes out for the alcohol, the male has his beer that stinks and you get your gin and tonic.'

'But Sal, you don't drink,' Dot replied. 'So what does he do with the gin and tonic?'

'Drinks it, of course. It gives him more courage and in his imagination he has already arrived in the harbour of New York while in reality the nitwit hasn't even reached the men's toilet ten yards away from him. You can tell them a thousand times, Dot: males are not allowed in the nurses' quarters, but they always insist on seeing you home. Take for example that idiot last week, he frightened the life out of me! Now I must admit, Dot, a kiss and a cuddle is okay but this chap had his hand practically in my knickers, his snake-like tongue in my mouth, I swear to heaven I could taste strawberry jam, and we're not there yet, Dot, oh no; he actually promised he would marry me if he made me pregnant.'

By this time Dot's eyes had nearly fallen out of her sockets and her mouth stood open. 'Sal, you're joking, you must be.'

Sally whispered, 'Dot, he nearly raped me and to make matters worse his name was Bill.'

Dot couldn't grasp the connection between rape and the name Bill but with Sally anything was possible. 'Tell me how it ended, Sal,' said Dot.

'Quite simple,' said Sally. 'I don't drink alcohol so I had my wits about me. I took his right hand and suggested that we could perhaps find our way into the nurses' quarters. Well, you know, Dot, how dark those lanes are, he couldn't see in which direction I was leading him ...'

'Don't say more,' said Dot, 'I've guessed already. The night porter's office, oh how lovely, Sally, brilliant planning, what an absolute scream! What did old Blackie do?'

'He took Billy's left hand and showed him the way out! No more ballroom dancing for me,' said Sally. 'I'm not an atlas looking for a ship nutter who wants to sail around my anatomy! I've long guessed where a male's brain can be found and it's not in his head. I think I would like to be a Matron, and if you pour me another cup of tea, you can be my assistant. By the way, my mother has invited you to our house, but please don't mention the Billy case, my father would have a heart attack on the spot, and I must remember to give dear Blackie a box of chocs for his wife. He gave me a cheeky wink yesterday; he really is a good old stick! I don't care how many free days I get for working nights, Dot, I fall asleep before the Night Sister does her rounds; if it wasn't for that foreign girl who heard Sister coming I would be in a good old mess. It's the quietness of the ward, Dot: the kiddies are all too young to snore, no one goes sleepwalking, and no one wants their potties.'

'What's the foreign girl like, Sally, is she nice? What's her English like?'

'Personally,' said Sally, 'I think she's great! Her English is out of this world, she's a right clever clogs, and talking about clogs, believe it or not, she is Dutch. She's here to learn English, or rather improve her English: some of the staff here could certainly learn a few idioms from her! Last night she brought all the family photos. Her Mum and Dad look so friendly, but does she have a brother, Dot, Cary Grant and Humphrey are nothing compared to him!'

'Go on with you, Sal,' said Dot, 'you're exaggerating as usual, he can't be all that dishy.'

'Dot, if I say he is fabulous to look at, then he is fabulous to look at, and that is that! He would like to write to an English girl, Dot, what do you think? Is it dangerous?'

'Sally, I don't believe a word of this, you're making it all up as you go along. Go on, Sal, be honest, you want to write to him. If he's all that dishy then he must have a few girls tucked away!'

'But Dot, he hasn't seen me yet, now has he? I think it's fun to have a try, he can't be worse than all these English bods with their everlasting blazers, pubs, cricket and stock exchange. His mother has a piano and his grandfather used to be a teacher, sounds all right to me, Dot. Maybe he has a nice cousin tucked away somewhere for you.'

'Sally Bone, don't even think about it! I love listening to your stories but leave me out of them.'

WOODEN SHOES

The letters did arrive, all very correct. His name was Dirk Jan van der Poel, and his English was unbelievable. In her imagination Sally saw him struggling through at least two dictionaries, and yet intuition kept warning her that there was something peculiar about them. They were too perfect, examination style. He asked for a photo and told Sally he would love to meet her. Unfortunately that would take some time, as he was doing military service and it would take twelve months more before his time was up.

He then wanted to study to become a teacher; he loved children, and teaching was in his family. He joked about the long school holidays, his love for boats and his desire, one day, to own one. 'Here you are, Dot,' said Sally, 'It all sounds okay to me. Read them, they won't bite you.'

Dot read the pages one by one. 'Too good to be true, Sal, all too perfect for my liking. You be careful, Sally, and for the time being don't tell your father.'

Dot had paid two visits to Sally's home and she was sure Sally's father would say, 'No foreigners in my family, thank you, young lady, there's enough Englishmen to go around. I saw enough of those French in the first world war, none of that foreign lot in my family.'

'Well, Dad does like flowers and Holland produces flowers, Dot, but let's see first what clever clogs Dirk Jan is really like.'

It didn't enter her mind that she would never see him, listen to his voice, see the colour of his eyes. She didn't know when, she didn't know how, but that she would meet him was a prediction that needed no further discussion. As for her father, oh, a few plain cakes, a new portrait photo for on his desk, a tear or two, who could say no to such female manipulation?

'He'll be putty in my hands, Dot, as long as my mother isn't around. I usually get my own way, within reason of course, and don't forget he can't play the piano, if you get what I mean!'

SAYING GOODBYE

Sally was back to day duties and enjoying her days on her favourite ward, Ward 2. Keithie was no longer with them; he had been sent to live with foster parents. Sally hoped he wouldn't shock them with any PoPo nonsense but somehow she knew he would be fine. He was such a lovely little chap, no one could possibly dislike him.

'Sal, isn't that Matron's secretary in the kitchen with Sister? We don't see her very often, there must be something wrong.'

'We'll know soon enough,' said Sally. 'She can't be here for the fun.'

Sister was suddenly coming towards her. 'Nurse Bone, Matron would like to see you, she's in her office waiting for you. Leave what you are doing, Nurse Jones can finish that for you.'

Sally felt her heart beating: there's something wrong, thought Sally, something very wrong, if it was good news Matron would come herself to the ward. She knocked on Matron's door and entered after she heard 'Come in.'

'Hello, Sally,' said Matron. 'Do sit down. I am, I'm afraid, the bearer of some sad news. I've just spoken to your father on the telephone. He phoned me, Sally, to explain a certain, shall we say family, situation which is very dear to your heart. You have, I believe, lived for many years with a kind lady who you called your Aunt Jessie.'

Matron had difficulty in formulating her words.

'I'm so sorry, my dear, to have to tell you your Aunt Jessie passed away in her sleep last night.' Matron leaned across her desk and placed her hand on Sally.

'Don't be brave, Sally, I've seen so many tears in my life you won't embarrass me, dear.'

Sally was shivering from the shock. All she could think was, it can't be true, it can't be true, Aunt Jessie was my whole being, she was the only person I have ever truly loved, please God let this not be true, bring her back, please, please, please, please bring her back. The tears were streaming over her cheeks.

Matron said, 'I'm going to leave you alone for a few minutes, Sally. I'll go and see if they can make some nice strong tea for us. It's always sad, my dear, when we have to lose someone we love so much.'

'Matron, my aunt was so wise, kind and tolerant, she taught me so many rules of life.'

'People that we love, Sally, never leave us,' said Matron, 'and our faith in God always gives us strength to carry on. I'm sure your aunt was extremely proud of you, and we both know you will never do anything to disgrace her memory.'

Matron had agreed with Sally's father to allow her to go down to Chrishall, to pay her respects and say goodbye in her own manner to her Aunt Jess. Tom would pick her up at noon, and they should arrive at Chrishall at three o'clock.

Matron had agreed to give her two free days off during the following week for the funeral. 'It's all right, Tom,' Sally murmured, 'you may talk, you would have loved my Aunt Jess. Do you know, I, or rather we, found each other by accident. I was only four years old when I ran from one train carriage to the other, and ended up in Chrishall. God won't take her away from me, you know, Tom; one day we'll be all together again. Do you believe in God, Tom?'

'Sometimes, Sally, but only sometimes.'

'Impossible, Tom,' said Sally firmly. 'My Aunt Jess always said you either believe or you don't; you can't play around with a religion, so make your mind up before you die.'

'You sound like the church minister, Sal. I've never heard you talk this way but I do understand how you're feeling.'

'Tell you what, Tom, turn the radio on; some nice soft music is what we both need.'

The car drove up the drive and Pearl came out to greet them. She looked tired and her eyes were red. Uncle Fred was sitting in his chair; it was as if he couldn't fathom what had happened.

'I'm so sorry, Pearl, I'm so sorry. Is she lying in her room, Pearl?' asked Sally.

'No, Sally, she wasn't feeling very well the last few days and wanted to sleep alone. She's in your bed, dear. She looks very peaceful. Now, would you like me to come with you?'

'No, thank you, Pearl, I prefer to be alone.'

Sally went upstairs to her own bedroom. She had promised herself she wouldn't cry; she was determined to be in complete control of her emotions.

She touched her aunt's cheek, and smoothed a hair back which hadn't fallen completely in place, stroked her hand and knelt down at the side of the bed.

'Thank you, Aunt Jess, for loving me. For teaching me how to cook, how to learn and appreciate music, for taking me to church and making me learn to respect others. I promise you I will do my utmost to make a success of my life, and I'll try to follow in your footsteps.'

Sally turned her head and looked at the window sill, and in a flash she remembered the many hours she had spent sitting there, looking up to the sky and speaking to her Mr Jesus. She couldn't resist it: she stood up, placed her hands on the window sill, looked up at the brilliant blue sky and whispered, 'Please Mr Jesus, take care of the most wonderful woman in the world. She is so special, she deserves a very special place in your kingdom!'

Sally touched Jessie's hand once more and walked backwards to the door. She couldn't turn her back on her aunt. She reached the door and realised that something was wrong. Her goodbye to Aunt Jess was incomplete; there was something missing.

Jessie and Sally had so often sung hymns together. She couldn't leave without filling the air with one of their favourite hymns. Downstairs Pearl and Fred could hear Sally singing. It was Jessie's favourite hymn.

The Lord's my shepherd, I'll not want.
He makes me down to lie
In pastures green; He leadeth me
The quiet waters by.

My Soul He doth restore again
And me to walk doth make,
Within the paths of righteousness
E'en for His own Name's sake.

Yea, though I walk in death's dark vale
Yet will I fear no ill,
For Thou art with me, and Thy rod
And staff me comfort still.

My table Thou has furnished
In presence of my foes,
My head Thou dost with oil anoint,
And my cup overflows.

Goodness and mercy all my life
Shall surely follow me,
And in God's house for ever more
My dwelling place shall be.

They had heard Jessie play it so often, in the chapel and on a Sunday in the music room. Fred got out of his chair and stood listening at the bottom of the stairs. When all was quiet he turned to Pearl and said, 'We've brought her up well, Pearl, your mother did a good job, God bless her. Let's make Sally some tea before she has to leave. That driver fellow said he'd be back round about five.'

Sally and her father attended the funeral. This was the end of a wonderful start in her life. How many children could look back on so much loving care? Sally knew she had been one of the lucky few during the war years.

She knew she would make a success of her life and that her darling Aunt Jess would always be with her. Sally returned to the hospital that evening feeling sad, but nevertheless mature and ready for what the future had in store for her.

THE PRIZE

She had been accepted for further training in London and try as she might, she couldn't think of any obstacle that would stand in her way to achieve her colourful goals in life.

Dirk Jan's letters continued to arrive; she asked the questions and he replied. 'Reminds me of a quiz, it's too methodical, Dot, he must be terribly well organised.' Whatever it was, it certainly aroused Sally's interest and desire to meet him, but how or when had yet to be planned. Money was also a factor. 'Any ideas on the subject, Dot?' asked Sally. 'Can you imagine me in clogs, but then clogs with high heels and a cute little lace hat on my head?'

'Sally, would you please shut up, we've got exams in six weeks' time. Don't you ever study, have you ever thought you could fail?'

Sally didn't fail. Was she number one? No. She was number two.

Her father was informed of the results.

'What are we going to do, Dad?' asked Sally. 'How can we come to a satisfactory solution, after all I did get a prize, not that I expected anything else. How about you giving me a ticket for a nearby country. A small ticket for a small prize?'

Sally thought, Well, that will at least get me to Holland. There is always plenty of time to get to America.

'I'm sure we can arrange something,' said her father. Two weeks in Holland can't cause any shambles in the family; a new environment, a fresh look on other folks' habits, it can only make her appreciative of the things she has. Frank was a confirmed believer that British goods were the best, and anything further than Dover or Harwich was inferior and totally uninteresting. It never entered his head that his daughter might have a totally different view on the matter. She wrote to her penfriend, informed him and his sister who was still working at the hospital, on the subject of prizes and tickets to Amsterdam, and lo and behold, the invitation arrived for a visit to their house.

Sally couldn't believe it. She couldn't sleep, she told Dot, she phoned Pearl, she wanted to tell the whole world she was going to Cloggie's land, Holland.

New clothes, sufficient pocket money, a handsome penfriend: to her this was an all-in-one safari adventure. She couldn't speak the language, but neither could Eskimos. She had read somewhere that Eskimos communicated with their noses; well, if Eskimos could find a way of communicating, so could she.

* * *

Prize Day, regardless of whether it is in a school, a hospital, the Olympics or the Boy Scouts, always accumulates a cloud of tension, pride and in some cases utter amusement. Sally tried so hard to remain serious, but be honest, try and imagine a panel consisting of a Matron, Nugles, Sister Tutor and a Bishop. A genuine dressed-up Bishop, with dog collar, purple waistcoat, and extremely, no highly, black polished shoes.

'I've never seen the man before,' said Sally. 'Dot, shall I give him a kiss, after he has shaken my pearly white delicate little hand with his hands that look like shovels. Go on, Dot, dare me. I'll bet you anything no one has ever dared to give a dressed up Bishop a smacker on both cheeks, and what's more, it will be the prize of the year for him.'

Did that poor chap blush? He blushed to the roots. It was, after all, 1954. Bishops avoided in those years any opportunity to blush.

'May I congratulate you, Nurse Bone,' said the Bishop. 'I see you are nurse number two of the year. Where do your talents lie?'

'I'm not sure yet, Sir,' said Sally. 'They still have to be discovered, but it is extremely kind of you to ask.'

She shook his hand, thanked him for the beautiful leather covered book on Greek mythology, stood on her toes, and kissed the old darling on both cheeks.

'Cheer up, Dot, it's not the end of the world, we'll continue to see and write to each other. You know you are always welcome at our house.'

Dot knew that this special prize day was the beginning of the end for the two pals and their nursing adventures with the orphans. One more month and off they would go, each one in a different direction.

'There's one thing I've learnt, Dot, in the last few months, or rather there's one thing perfectly clear. In life we are always saying hello and goodbye. I can't get used to saying goodbye, in fact I hate it! I'm going to miss these children. They gave us more than we gave them. They gave us trust, they believed in us; what greater compliment can one acquire? Promise me, Dot, never to say goodbye, and when we are old, grey and beautiful, we'll still be able to chat about old Nugles, Keithie the PoPo-boy, Matron and her daffodils, Bill and the strawberry jam, Blackie the porter, night nurse and the policeman . . . gordon bennet!, that really was a blue movie performance. You only had to peep for one second through the keyhole and your hormones went all of a dizz. It was a great time, Dot, I wouldn't have missed it for the world.'

'Stop!' shouted Dot. 'Stop! I know what you are going to say, I've heard it countless times. "You are learning the facts of life, Dot, write it all down and don't forget it"!'

'Well done, Dot, well done. At least I can say I was the best chum of the nurse of the year.' A statement that was true and undeniably deserved.

CLOUDS

Sally's holiday trip, prize, whatever, had a different character than it might have today. The select few went to Switzerland, perhaps Spain or Jersey, but on the whole the English were in those days fans of their own holiday resorts.

Her father insisted on seeing her off at Liverpool Street. 'Do you have enough money with you, Sally? If you don't like it, come back immediately; there are more places where we can go to.'

Her father knew nothing about the Cloggie penfriend, or did he? 'Shut up, Dad, stop being so dramatic. It's a distance of nothing. I'll bring you back a nice present, something I know you will remember me by for ever and ever.'

They both started to laugh. Frank loved Dutch cheese, and knowing his daughter as he did, he was sure she would bring back a sample of every brand available.

'Be careful, young lady, a bag full of cheese has a disgusting smell. I've known women to be jailed for less.' The whistles could be heard, carriage doors were closing. 'Take care, Sally, come back in one piece, I don't want to miss you for too long.'

Sally threw him a kiss. 'See you soon, Dad. I'll send you a card. 'Bye, we're off.' She closed the carriage window.

I must be mad, she thought, completely, totally out of my nut, now is this an adventure or a fairy story? Why do I always get myself into unforeseen situations? Always seeking, always digging, nosey parker stuff. Look out of the window, Sal, enjoy the beautiful scenery, count the number of cows. You can't resist it, can you? Any minute now you're going to dissect every passenger in this carriage. If any one of them asks you to join them for dinner you will say no! Sal, are you listening to yourself? You will say no! Although the tall dark, handsome mongrel sitting in the corner does look interesting; my guess is he's African Dutch if such folks exist. He reminds me of a mongrel, because I'm sure he growls at people, probably barks at them, but whatever he does, my guess is he does it to perfection. Why, for goodness sake? Simple, she told herself, perfectly simple: his hands are beautifully cared for, nails sublime. I know he's a doctor, no, Sal, he's a surgeon. Shut up, for God's sake, she told herself. The poor chap is probably the Queen's gardener, has a wife and ten children, has never barked in his life and is as big a softie as the pillow I sleep on. I'd love to ask him how he combs his hair; now would he comb it or brush it? Sal, take your eyes off the man; you know it's rude to stare! He's probably quite nice if you fancy that type. Fancy waking up in the middle of the night and finding that ghastly mongrel next to you!

Sally, by the way, had now focused her attention on the passenger opposite her: red hair, red moustache, typical English brogues, why are Englishmen so ugly? They have such little facial expression, too much cottonwool; jelly and custard – nothing meaty about them. That's it, they miss the manly touch. Somewhere down the line, I'm sure my Dad must be foreign. I've never associated him with a mongrel, or cottonwool for that matter.

The boat trip was above Sally's wildest dreams, Her love of water increased with the minute. It came out from below her toes, this was seasickness in all its shapes and sizes. The gods are punishing me, joked Sally, they're ruining the holiday of my life and all because I didn't tell Dad the truth about Mr Clever Cloggs and his methodical letters. Okay, you bunch up there, if Clever Cloggs turns out to be worth mentioning, I shall tell the whole community when I get back; no, even better I'll make a script for a TV serial. Now, will you please let me go to sleep? I feel so ill I wish the ship would sink. I can't believe anyone is worth getting so sick for! At that moment Sally would have given anything to have got off board and back to her familiar surroundings.

I've been in this country before, you know. Sally, who could talk for hours to herself, found herself sitting in the train, taking her from the boat to the promised land, for her the capital of Cloggie-land, Amsterdam. She told herself that what she was looking at was a repeat performance of generations ago. The landscape, the flower fields, they were exceptional, but not unfamiliar. Shut up, woman, come down to earth; before you know where you are you'll be dreaming of the days when you were a farmer's wife or something agricultural some hundred years ago. Her daydreaming ended when the train stopped at The Hague and then went on to what was to be for her, the city of no return. Unknown friends were awaiting her arrival. Their genuine kindness and hospitality was, putting it crudely, written all over them. They did not own a dog otherwise we are sure he too would have been one of the welcoming committee.

Cloggie's parents were there. Sally recognized them from the photo. Their son wouldn't be home until the weekend; he still had to finish his military service.

Sally, who was utterly spoiled, had no idea as to how these extremely courteous people had organised themselves in order to give Sally an unlimited amount of Dutch hospitality. Never will Sally forget her first impression of the apartment and the beautiful city.

It was the year of 1954. The buildings were at least twenty years old. The apartment consisted of four rooms: two bedrooms, one dining room, and one little room which, lo and behold, was furnished with a piano. Sally couldn't make head nor tail of it. There was no hot running water, just a little shower room containing a hot water boiler. No fridge, no telephone, but the most beautiful clocks and Persian carpets one could ever dream of. There was a carpet on the wall above the fireplace, on the floor, in fact these exquisite carpets were everywhere; at least that was the first impression Sally got.

A touring programme had been designed. What a thrill, what an experience for a young British citizen, who had been taught that the British Empire ruled the world and that what was left over was of minor significance.

The city, the lights, the canals, the architecture. The bikes, the food, and number one on the list, the divine policemen. Sally thought they were all so handsome; in those days they were! She sent a card to her parents: 'All is well.' She also sent one to Dot: 'Wouldn't mind living here.' Her penfriend 'Clever Cloggs Jan' as she secretly called him, had still to arrive; in fact she had four days to get used to the idea that she was actually going to meet him. The letter hero, the bod who had always given an exact answer to her questions, was only four days away from her presence. It was evident that he was his mother's little ray of sunshine. She loved talking about him, showing off with his photos. Sally had already seen him with his nappy on, with his bucket and spade at the seaside, his first pair of long trousers, his first cigarette, and last but not least, her darling son in uniform.

Right, thought Sally, after seeing that whole lot, what on earth do I say to him when I meet him? 'Hello there, stranger, I've seen you in your nappy,' or shall we be sensible for once and let him do the talking? Was Sal nervous when the final day arrived? She was so nervous she couldn't eat, and that for Sally was definitely a serious complaint.

One would almost have thought that her knowledge of suitors was nil. Anything but, she had the pick of the town, why the anxiety for a Dutch male, whose voice she had never heard, whose face she had never seen? The only tangible assets had been a photo and a few letters. Let's not be mysterious, or perhaps too hasty, but were those letters from Mr Cloggie, were they intended for Sally? The contents were anything but original. She knew what flattery was compiled of and the false impression that famous writers impose upon their readers. Yet all this didn't disturb her. In fact she found it interesting.

Her anxiety trailed backwards and forwards to her one incurable emotion, curiosity. In this incident perhaps curiosity would kill the cat; who knows, who can predict?

Tomcats can also be curious. Perhaps Mr Cloggs was also a curious tomcat. Tomcats can also be calculated, super intelligent. Tomcats are much stronger; they can open mousetraps, and watch while little curious mice or pretty little kittens walk straight into them.

SILENT ROMANCE

When someone walks up the stairs, it implies they have nothing of any specific interest to hear or tell, but if they dash or leap up to their destination, then you can expect either a shock, a surprise, or a caller who can't wait to see what's waiting for them. 'Talk to her,' said the father, 'she's not going to bite you. We understand every word she says, she plays the piano, she sings; for goodness sake, man, say something.'

Sally was aware that the situation was becoming a little embarrassing. The father kept talking, the mother was doing her best to finish the father's sentences, but our Mr Cloggie was dumbstruck. He couldn't believe his eyes: red shoes with high heels, a beautiful, in his eyes sexy dress, and what's more she was made up – he couldn't take his eyes off her.

Take over, Sal, take over, we must save this huge handsome hunk of a man from making a fool of himself, he can't look at me forever. The large velvet eyes found their way to his. Pity he has to wear spectacles, thought Sally, it always spoils the effect, but keep going, he'll melt; any minute now, he'll come back to earth.

'I've nicknamed you Mr Cloggie. I've given you two g's, hope you don't mind. I see you don't wear clogs but those shoes do look extremely heavy. Am I looking at the uniform of a military service man who can't wait to be back in his normal civilised world? You play in a band, you're the one who makes the most noise, you play the trumpet. Tell me, am I on the right track, yes or no?'

The ice was broken; Cloggie and Sally chatted non-stop, she the questions, he the answers. 'Will you play the trumpet for me tomorrow?' Before he could give a reply she bent forward and whispered, 'Be honest, do the neighbours not complain, do the cats and the dogs not join in the Armstrong melody? If I were your neighbour, I'd thrash the living daylights out of you, but to make it enjoyable for one and all, I'll personally squat my derrière on the piano seat, and as soon as the neighbours and their pets show signs of rejection, I'll take over with my version of good old Handel's Water Music. It's majestically soothing for one and all; oh, and take my word, Mr Cloggie, from this moment on your life will never be the same again.' Sal, she asked herself, where do you get the nerve from?

Cloggie didn't really hear what Sally was yapping on about; he still couldn't take his eyes off her. At last a female who wasn't shy; she knows what she wants. I've only been in the room for two hours and already she's telling me what to do, and by the look of things, she certainly doesn't need me to pay for her entertainment.

'Would you like me to take you to a Dutch cinema, Sally, and perhaps a boat trip to one of our authentic Dutch villages?'

Sal was in heaven. He was tall, broad, and very handsome. His accent was divine. Wherever they went, he didn't leave go of her arm for one single minute. We'll never know who made whose heart beat faster! They were two young people, both at the bottom of the ladder, he had a school certificate, and seven guilders a day for being an imitation serviceman who would have run a mile should danger have ever approached him. She was a protected young nobody who thought the world was hers and wanted one thing only, to learn what was in that world and how it got there.

Sally not only fell in love with her Cloggie, she adored everything she saw during her initial trip to Amsterdam. So much culture, she thought, in such a small place. Do these people realise how rich they are? They might not have fridges and TVs in all the living quarters, but their environment is just beautiful.

Now, today, Cloggie and Sally would have jumped into bed after the first, no let's agree upon the second, night out. They would have sealed their passion for each other by performing an Indian war dance in the parallel position, and the closing language would have been 'oh ah oh aaaah', an exact imitation of what the Indians chant when they have finally caught their prey. Nothing so hideously unromantic came into their daily menu. She fell for the first impression: the divine smell of his skin, he could hold her so tight, her lungs could hardly function, she had no idea whether the air was coming in or going out, and just fancy being spoken to every day with an accent that reminds one of Maurice Chevalier.

Sally wrote in her book of secrets, 'He creates butterflies in my tum tum. I'm sure he's no virgin. If he were mine I'd cook roast beef, Yorkshire pudding, roast potatoes, and gravy of his choice, every day! If he wants sex at night time, that's okay. I'm sure I would prefer it in the morning. Holland is poor. I'd like to be around when the explosion comes, for come it will. Their standard of education is much higher than ours and there's nothing more rewarding than knowledge. I think I'll shock everyone and come back and make my fortune here.'

Cloggie on the other hand knew he had found the type of girl he had always dreamed of. One who paid for her own sherry, independent, no nagging: he'd seen for years that his father had invested his whole income in his family, and luxury items for himself had been nil. His mother had given all her love and devotion to her two children. Her adoration for him was undeniable; to her he was the only male specimen who was blameless for all his deeds. Cloggie had however one critical problem . . . he didn't have one!

He had just two days left over to spend with Sally. He had no idea how to tackle the romantic issue, how could he ask her to come back? He had nothing to offer her, nothing but his desire and fascination for her. No, he thought, the whole idea is ridiculous. It would never work; she's spoilt and I can only buy two packets of tobacco in a week. The last two days of their luxury romantic exploration of each other was spent on the most expensive and technical device that Holland had in those days: Cloggie's bike. Cloggie did the steering, Sally's voice was the radio. She held on to him, her arms around his waist, frightened that he and his bike would take off from the ground any minute. She waved to all the policemen as if she were royalty visiting her people and sang the few French songs which had remained, owing to their simplicity, in her mind.

'What did you say, Cloggie, I can't hear you; do you want to sit here, and let me do the peddling?'

'Cloggie, I'm listening, what was it you said? A little louder please.'

'Sally, please come back to Holland. I love you, I've never felt like this before for anyone, please say you'll come back.'

'Stop the car,' screamed Sally, 'stop the car, Cloggs, park it here at the corner.'

Sally jumped off the bike, took no notice whatsoever of the traffic and the street walkers, threw her arms around Cloggie's neck, kissed him on his lips as if she was about to dismantle his entire collection of teeth and without one moment of hesitation and between sounds of laughter and joy, Sally informed her Cloggs that nothing could keep her away from him. 'There is, however, one thing, Cloggie, one very, very special promise you must make,'

'And,' said Cloggs, 'let's have it.'

'Promise you'll never stop loving me then I'll go to the end of the world with you, but not on the back seat of this bike.'

Their declaration of love was sealed with an Italian ice cream waffle and the purchase of two tiny silver clogs which could be worn as earrings. Sally wrote in her book that these earrings were to go with her in her grave; if the Egyptians dressed themselves up, why shouldn't she?

Cloggie was to be taken care of for ever and ever, no matter what happened from this day onwards.

'I don't want to tell you what to do, Cloggs, but if I were you, I would keep this declaration of love and adventure to yourself. My instinct tells me that your mother has a completely different type of female in mind for you. One at least who speaks your language, who cooks your potatoes the way you like them, who will give you four children, darn your socks once a week and last but not least, be a perfect juggler with your monthly salary.'

Cloggie couldn't help laughing; he knew Sally was correct in her assumption. He also knew that Sally wouldn't get further than the kitchen door, should she apply for the job. 'Is there one item, Sally, just one item that will remain in your mind, whilst you're back home?'

'Let's see,' said Sally, 'let me give the following some serious thought. At the moment I would bet on no children, potatoes definitely no problem, socks we'll throw away and buy new ones! Housekeeping money I won't need. Within five years I'll have a housekeeper who can clean, cook and iron your shirts, and we'll import our first car from

France. Be honest, Cloggie, it would be fun. Life could be a garden of roses; the occasional thorn of course will shoot up, not forgetting the weedkiller, but as long as we never have furious thoughts or anger in our minds, and lots of laughter and respect for each other, what indeed could go wrong?'

Now how's that for positive fantasy? After all, the worst has still to come. I've got to sell this double Dutch story to my father and I'm not so sure that he will be jumping over the moon. My guess is he will curse the moment for ever allowing me to come in the first place. Your luck is you are not French; if you were French, he would lock me up in a cupboard and let me out once I had come to my senses. I'll sort things out, don't worry, Cloggie, I usually accomplish what I set out to start.

The sultry, velvety evening fell around them. The air was full of the smell of warm dry grass, and the low grumble of traffic seemed to be everywhere. Sally wanted to stay. I'll come back, she told herself. I've had a little taste of honey and Sally Bone wants the whole pot.

The last Sunday was a dyke, boats, water and silence. Could they afford a boat? No, but they could both talk and dream of one.

Sal had curled herself up in Cloggie's coat on the top of the dyke. It was heaven to hear his heart beating. Would she ever see him again? Would this trip remain a bundle of fantasy, old fashioned morals, a brief friendship never to forget? Sally had not only felt butterflies for Mr Cloggie, but she just loved the atmosphere in Holland. It was 1954, it was beautiful and primitive, it was small; one could oversee and predict what the future could bring. The following morning the two of them walked to the lovely old fashioned tram which would take her Mr Handsome down to the station. He had to go back to his unit, she the same evening had to go back to England.

'Come back soon, Sally, life is going to be dull without you.'

They both stood waving, he in the open carriage, she in the little tram house, until the tram was completely out of sight. It was still very early in the morning. There were hundreds of bikes everywhere. She still had the whole morning for herself.

She decided to take a taxi into the centre of town and take a boat trip along the canals, then a tram back to where she had started. Presents still had to be purchased for her parents, and if there was time over, a letter to Dot. The taxi driver wouldn't or couldn't stop talking. Was she French? Did she like Holland? Sally leant forward and tapped the chauffeur on his shoulder. 'Please drive me back to the tram house, I'm not feeling very well.' She wanted to say, 'Your voice is driving me crazy. I'm missing my boyfriend, and I'm going to start to cry any minute now.'

All she really wanted to do was to go back home and tell her parents she had met the most wonderful young man in the world, that she was going back to be with him, and that was that. No discussion, no details, her mind was made up, it was her future, and not theirs!

The letter to Dot was typical of Sally. She spoke of Mr Cloggs as if he truly was God's gift to women, as if he was the most intelligent specimen she had ever met and she would cause him great pain if she didn't return. I know you will like him, Dot, there is something fascinating about him. I'm not sure what, but I certainly intend to find out. See you soon, Dot. I miss you! Love Sally.

P.S. They do wear normal clothes and shoes, and they eat their bread with knives and forks, tell you more later.

Mr Cloggs, as the new girl friend liked to call him, was extremely generous with his information to his fellow comrades. They had, after all, written most of the letters to Sally, and he would be in a right old plight if their desire to write romantic letters to a girl they didn't know suddenly came to a stop. Finky, his closest friend and chief editor, requested a detailed summary of Cloggs' very obvious fascination for a foreign girl who had either charmed his service pal, manipulated him, or suspiciously hypnotised him.

To Finky nothing made sense. This wasn't the way things go in life: passion, okay, but in moderation. 'You didn't by any chance . . .'

'No, no, no,' replied Mr Cloggs, 'she was after all a visitor to my parents' house.'

'Thank God for that, you had me scared. I'm not in the mood for looking up words on parenthood and morning sickness, and I truly think we both should stop this charade.' Cloggs knew he meant it.

'Fink, she is special, she's not like my family. I can't imagine her nagging or moaning, talking about the quality of cakes or holidays at the seaside.'

'To be precise you mean she doesn't need a budget, shall we say she's eccentric, and finally she could manipulate, in an extremely charming fashion, any judge into saying she is right and you are wrong.'

Cloggs wanted to think first before giving an answer to his friend's statement. It was too direct for his liking. 'Come on,' said Fink, 'give me an honest answer.'

'Fink, my friend, you are absolutely right. Your description is one hundred per cent and your sense of the situation is excellent. I can't stop thinking of her.' He paused for a second and then went on. 'Is she lovely? No, Fink, she's beautiful, definitely more French than English.'

'Great,' replied Fink, 'just great, then you have finally met your match. Now what do you want to say to her? I've got a train to catch and I want to spend my free weekend with my fiancée. She loves baking, enjoys getting sand between her toes, and can't wait to settle down and start a family. Be careful, my friend, your Sally is in for a tough time. We Dutch give the impression that we're hospitable, and we certainly are, when it suits us. Make sure she's not plunging into an adventure which could destroy her. Now let's get started.'

'*Dear Sally, It was so lovely having you here.* Good God man, even I'm becoming emotional about the girl and I've never seen her. Roll me a shag, pour me a beer and let's get this letter over with. Do I say good night to her, sleep well, what's the new version going to be?'

Sally's father was waiting at the London station for her. He was glad to have his daughter back in one piece; he couldn't wait to hear her version of Holland and the lovely windmills. He knew she would have amusing stories to tell, she always did, but something so ridiculous? No, this insane adventure she had in mind, this he had never anticipated.

In the train going home, she told him everything, well, almost everything!

'You don't have to think for me, Dad, I'm going.'

To her utter surprise he said nothing. He didn't have to: she wasn't twenty-one. She needed his signature to allow her to move out of England and become a temporary and working resident in another country.

'Your mother isn't going to like this at all. You've cost her a fortune. Your English is equal to that of the Queen's. I'm sure she has a little something more in mind than what you are relating. As pleasant as these kind people are and with all respect for their lifestyle, is this really what you want?'

'You're not taking me seriously, are you, Dad? You think I'm having you on, but I'm not. I just loved everything. I saw the people, their primitive way of life, and I want to be around when the explosion takes place. I'll bet you anything their standard of living will, within ten years, exceed ours; it's only the privileged few in this country who have a good life. So stop being so arrogant and give me a mint ring, and tell me what we are having for supper. If it makes you happy, your darling daughter did miss her fish and chips, all dressed up in the *News of the World* newspaper. Terribly common, Dad, totally out of your league, but so unique and oh so English.'

Sal gave him a quick kiss on his cheek. Poor Frank, he wanted so desperately to warn his only daughter. To tell her she would be heading for a disaster, loneliness, misunderstanding, and above all a religion that was not hers. Frank Bone had been down the same road. Gertrude, Sally's mother, was Frank's second wife, a family secret which Sally discovered many years later.

The last eight months of Sally's life in England was a mixture of irritation for everyone. No one, including Gran, could convince her not to go. Her mother paid no attention to the subject. 'Let her go, dear, let her go, she'll come back. Let her pay her own boat fare, and don't let me catch you, Frank, giving her an allowance. If she wants to create her own world then I suggest she invests in this so called new life style with her own energy and her own earnings. Maybe she'll come across your grandmother, have her name changed. Does she know that her mother's parents came originally from Holland?'

'No, Gertrude,' said Frank, 'and for the time being don't tell her. We don't want to make it more romantic than it is. I'm relying on your intuition that she will come back and that this so called Rudolph Valentino will have the courtesy to come and introduce himself to us. Truly, Gertrude, if he were French, I would lock her in a cupboard and pray that she would come to her senses.'

For the last six months Sally had worked in a pharmacy shop. She paid for her ticket to Holland and had exactly one hundred pounds in her wallet. She couldn't wait for her first adventure to begin.

Cloggs had negotiated with a hospital and Sally had her first position waiting for her two days after her arrival. Tom drove her down to Harwich; it was 2 February 1955. She wore a fur coat which she had taken from her mother's wardrobe and one of the two pairs of extremely high heeled shoes that good old Tom had stolen for her from the factory's stockroom.

'Sally, your parents are going to miss you. Now just listen to me carefully, if things go wrong use your nut and come back. Pride doesn't exist, Sally, in cases like this, intelligence does. I've been in Holland for a few weeks at the end of the war, it's not your country, believe me.'

Sally felt extremely nice and comfortable in her fur coat. She couldn't be bothered to give Tom an answer. She had no intention to make promises; she could see the sea and the ships in the distance and all she wanted right here and now was to breathe the sea air and dream of what her new environment had to offer.

'Goodbye, Tom, I love you, keep an eye on my parents.'

Tom stood and waved her out. What my children wouldn't have given to have had her opportunities, what an absolute waste. While Tom was doing his best to be mellow and critical, our sea passenger had already accepted the offer to have dinner with two American officers stationed in Germany. She was already flying; her thoughts were in the clouds, exploding with passion and energy to discover and understand the secrets of life and the unforeseen power that guides us.

The evening was great. Danger didn't enter her head. She wanted to know how the tax free goods worked, and did they get allowances for being abroad? If passion was on their minds it most certainly had melted by the time Sally had finished with them.

'Gentlemen,' said Sally, 'I want to thank you for a delightful evening. I hope you can both go back home soon to your families. If you don't mind I would like to retire to my cabin. I've a busy day tomorrow. I hope to rush into the arms of my supersonic Dutch boyfriend.' She put her fingers to her lips and whispered, 'My problem is, I can't for the life of me remember what he looks like. The Dutch are all so tall, blond, and handsome; knowing me, I could end up in the arms of the stationmaster. Goodnight, chaps, you were both great company.'

Had Sally forgotten what Mr Cloggie looked like or was she joking? She did, by the way, write the following in her daybook: 'There is nothing to worry about. Cloggs will remember every detail about me. I always use my nose and instinct so nothing can possibly go wrong. Please God let this adventure be a success. I've promised so many people that I will do my utmost to be successful, I can't let them down.

Please stay with me till the end.

THE ROOM

FUNERALS AND PHOTOS

People always say that when someone passes on part of us goes with them: we lose an arm, a leg, they always take our feeling of comfort away.

Cloggie and his wife Sally were man and wife for forty-seven years. The ship swayed now and then. Sally couldn't resist a little mischief, he couldn't resist spending a little money, but whatever the gale, both knew how to turn a blind eye and keep the temperature at a level that was more than pleasant to live in. Cloggs had been a sick man for the last twenty years of their marriage. Sally had experienced the front seat of the ambulance no fewer than thirteen times. At her husband's funeral, relatives praised her for her undivided care and loving devotion, her tolerance and patience throughout the years. Her old friend Dot had flown over for the funeral.

Sally herself gave a final speech in which she not only thanked everyone for coming, but also declared undying love for her long accepted fatherland and the true friend who had always been at her side when she needed him. Sally looked towards the coffin and decided it was time to say goodbye. Cloggs, my old dear, let's get one thing perfectly straight. While on earth, you always knew how to get your own way, I could never say no, and the two of us knew how to keep the home fires burning. Now you're on your way to Mr Jesus. I do not want any hanky panky up there. I shall not come up to you before it is my time, and I intend to remain down here for another ten to fifteen years. Thank you, dear Cloggie, for always being my true friend. For always being in your old chair when I came home late at night; for giving me the freedom to pursue my ambitions.

Sally walked to the coffin, bowed her head in reverence, and touched the beautiful red roses for the last time. Sally's husband was placed to lie one single footstep away from the grave of his parents, two wonderful people who had given him life and who had loved him as only loving parents are capable of doing.

Sally was alone. Her visitors had left. Come on, Sal, she told herself, let's make a strong cuppa. Cloggie wouldn't want me to cry. He was a very sick man, his life was full of fear and agony. Let's try and be happy for him, that he is finally at peace, no more hospitals, no more pompous doctors. Now get your photos out, you've got boxes full. Treat yourself to the past. Lock the door, pull the telephone switch out, put your easy clothes on, and try for one last time to put your life together.

You couldn't see the floor for photos. I'll select them, thought Sally. To start with, I'll throw the ones away that make me look ugly. No we won't, we'll start with the photos of when we were young and innocent. Darling Aunt Jess can have a quick peep around the corner. There's Dad cutting his roses. You know, Sal, Cloggie was a handsome devil when he was young; he always smelt like more. It was late afternoon, Sal was tired. She did her best to keep awake, but her eyes started to close. Too much had happened during the last few weeks, and try as she did, her ability to fight the tiredness was impossible. Surrounded by all her life photos and a mist that felt like a dose of anaesthetic Sally slipped away, into a deep and unknown space.

AMSTERDAM AND DISCOVERY TIME

It was drizzling, cold, and still very early in the morning. She recognised the station, would she recognise him? She followed the passengers out of the train. There was no porter, and her high heels were about to snap. Mum's fur coat felt extremely heavy and her lips were purple from the cold. Shut up, Sal, shut up, that's him, look, for goodness sake, I'm sure it's him. He's running, he's coming this way, so you start to run. Before this female idiot could get her wits about her, Mr Cloggie had tossed her up into the air; he hugged the living daylights out of her. He had to do something. He was so topsyturvy, he couldn't speak for the first three minutes. Sally who loved an exhibition, enjoyed every single minute of it. She didn't ask the poor chap where the flowers were, but knowing Sal I'm sure it was in her mind. He took the large suitcase, she the smaller, and as if the scene had been rehearsed our young excited female explorer looked up through her sexy green eyes and whispered, 'Cloggs, do we have to walk very far? Tom has stolen the wrong shoes, these are killing me. I don't think I'm going to make it. Bend down, I want to kiss you. I've just travelled sixteen hours to find you.'

Now, working in those days in an English hospital, when you could speak the language, was nerveracking enough, but gliding through the wards of a foreign institution was either the height of comedy, insanity, or an escape route to get your two feet deeper into foreign soil. For Sally it was all three aspects. The largest dose found its way to the comedy, followed by foreign soil and finally insanity. Can you imagine someone like our Sal wearing a garment similar to a sort of surgeon's apron – hers was creamy white – for two whole months? It was far too long for her. She looked like a ghost. She would trip over it at least once a week. An additional piece of string around her waist did have its effect for a few hours. It certainly caused laughter on the men's ward. Most of the poor men were suffering from arthritis and if you hardly touched them they would almost cry with pain. Sally was the perfect distraction for all of them. They all taught her Dutch words. Their game was 'What's this, Nurse?' and if Sal could pronounce the name of the product, then she was rewarded by receiving a sample of the chosen quiz product. It was truly unbelievable; even the wives came along with language material. The doctors taught her the fancy words, the patients also taught her how to swear – the basics. The nurses exercised their English, and her roommate took her home in order to enjoy true Dutch cuisine.

From the very start Sally loved Holland; she was fascinated by the Dutch. Cloggs was always waiting outside the hospital with his bike, no matter whether he experienced rain, snow, or sun! The back of that bike was a 'Rolls' replacement and Cloggs' waist the steering wheel. That she never fell off the bike was a complete miracle.

'Cloggs, will you please listen to me?' Sally begged. 'Cloggs, I want you to listen! I was in the lift today coming down from floor five to the ground, and standing in the lift was a dark gentleman, whom I'm sure I sat opposite to in the train bringing me to Amsterdam last year. I'm sure it was him, he had the same look about him, as if he growls all the time. At the time I had a bet with myself: he was either the Queen's gardener or a surgeon. Do you believe in coincidences, Cloggs, or could I be dreaming? If he recognised me, he certainly didn't show it.'

'Nonsense,' said Cloggs, 'if you've seen one you've seen them all.'

Sally took the hint and immediately dropped the subject. 'Cloggs, would you like me to tell you about bedpans, open wounds, pompous doctors who cannot make up their minds if they want sugar in their tea, yes or no, or the plain simple truth? Do you realise I still do not have a free Saturday or Sunday? I'm never free when you are. I can't force the issue, I'm never going to be Sister Nightingale, so I think in a few months' time I'll get myself reorganised.'

'Sally, please be sensible,' said Cloggs, 'don't mess around. Without a work permit there will be no Holland. Permits are only issued if there are sufficient grounds for employing foreign staff, and in your case someone outside the hospital would have to come up with a real juicy excuse for wanting to employ you. I can't help you, Sal, it will take another year before I start to earn a salary. Try and stick it out till then. I don't want to lose you, Sally.'

Sally decided there and then that being dependent on Cloggs' Rolls had got to stop. After all, Sal, she told herself, he is sitting pretty and I don't have to give up literally everything.

AMSTERDAM

One evening per week, she could have her dinner with Cloggs' family; apart from that it was hospital food and the comfort of a hospital bedroom. Slowly it began to dawn on her that she had no home, no domestic comfort whatsoever, in fact the only truly comfortable chairs available with cola and peanuts to go with them were to be found in the cinema. Now that was great fun when a good film was being shown, but on the whole Sally couldn't appreciate the Dutch taste for films. All those cowboys and Indians really was a bit old fashioned, and that people went to the pictures on a Sunday was absolute blasphemy, but gorgeous!

She just had to get her act together. Thus a letter was sent to England containing the request to have her Rolls sent over and if it was not too inconvenient would they please not forget the bike's shopping basket and finally her green mac and matching sou'wester. Sally had plans. Cloggs was her dear friend; maybe if he did his best she would marry him, maybe if she did her best he would marry her, but for the time being expansion and finance should remain entirely in her hands. If I get my two wheels here then I can discover every street in Amsterdam, find out where the office regions are, homes for the poor and rich and of course I must find out where the Lord Mayor lives. You never know, he might like to drink tea with me one day. With this plan in mind Sally began to feel her old self. Her curiosity was now well established in the Dutch soil, all it needed was a solid plan of action and for good old Sal, it was always food that started the engines going.

She was sitting in the canteen when her friend Miep nudged her and said: 'Sal, that young blond chap is constantly looking at you. Go on, reward him for his bravery, give him at least a smile. I bet you a croquette and a coke he'll be carrying your food tray and asking for a date within five days.'

'Miep, really, how can you say such things? I'm betrothed too.' She couldn't finish her sentence, the utter, nonsense: Sally, betrothed. She couldn't stop laughing; the idea was so ridiculous she started to choke. Everyone thought it was a joke but she really was choking. Our blondie-locks didn't have to wait five days. It took him exactly five seconds to cure the patient and ten to introduce himself.

'Do you always choke yourself,' he asked, 'when you're eating? Are you okay now?'

By this time he had squatted himself next to her, elbows on the table, and off he went in the circle of his own private interview. Sally thought: you an answer, me a request. 'Before you go any further, do you by chance have a book or a map showing the names of all the streets in Amsterdam? And before we both go any further, what's your name?'

'Maikel, Maikel Katz.'

Sal liked him, no pompous John type; if he had said Doctor she would have said Baroness Bone.

'See you tomorrow, Maikel,' Sally said, 'and try and have the book or map with you.'

Poor Miep was speechless; she looked as if she'd seen a ghost.

'What's wrong, Miep?'

'Sally, don't you know who he is?'

'No, should I?' Sally asked. 'He should feel honoured that I spoke to him. I'm not just anyone and neither are you. I'll bring your dishes and mine back to the counter and off we'll go to the ward to exercise our hocus pocus talents and our medical know-how! Only four more hours then I'm off to the pictures with my Cloggie. If it's a good film, we'll probably watch the film twice. In England they play the National Anthem at the end of each film, which really means wipe your eyes and buzz off, there're more waiting to come in.'

'Why are you interested in a map, Sally? Are you thinking of setting up a mail order company? You are not allowed to sell medicines over here, by the way.'

Maikel discovered Sally in the nurses' reading room. He was immensely curious as to what she wanted the whole list of streets for. She didn't resemble the rest of the nursing staff, that was for sure, and she certainly had her wits about her. Was she perhaps interested in dungeons, canal history?

'It's all very simple, Maikel,' said Sally. 'I want to know who's who, and what's what, and I am first starting with the streets. According to my itinerary I shall get up at six o'clock every morning and cycle through as many streets as possible. Now be a good chap and mark down where the poor and old buildings are. I'll discover them first, the rest can come later. If you want to come along,' Sally said, 'in order to protect me from the layabouts, sleepabouts and any other worms crawling around, you are more than welcome. I shall stop my Rolls now and then, to make the necessary notes. You may hold my bike and explain exactly where we are going.'

'Don't forget,' said Maikel, 'the cycle jams start here at seven o'clock and for goodness sake watch out what you are doing, don't get your wheels between the tram lines.'

'Please, Maikel, give me some credit. Do I look so nutty?'

He desperately wanted to tease her and say yes, nuttier than nutty, but try as he did the only response which come to his mind was 'I'll be here tomorrow morning, seven o'clock on the dot. We'll cycle all through the famous Jordaan, you'll love that, have lunch at an authentic Dutch restaurant that prepares steaks that melt in your mouth, and have tea in the afternoon at my mother's. How about it, Sally, would you enjoy my company?'

Now Sally never had to say yes or no, her eyes always did the talking. 'Maikel, would you ask your mother to cut a few sandwiches just in case we get a little peckish on the way? I'll bring the chocolate, then between us we should have enough energy to keep us going.' Sally looked in the mirror that evening. She was flushed and excited. A little bicycle flirt was just what she needed. The world is beginning to open, Sal, be patient, you can't expect everyone to bow to you. Speak their language, understand their movements, appreciate their way of thinking and life will be what you make it. Sally wrote that evening a long, long letter to Dot. She missed her old pal and she felt a bit homesick. Her father, the good old stick, sent her the Sunday newspaper every week. He always wrapped it around a huge tablet of her favourite chocolate and inside the chocolate packaging he invariably slipped three pound notes which in those days was a small fortune.

Window boxes filled with flowers, organ grinders, smelly herring carts, canals and historical buildings: 'It all reminds me of the theatre,' said Sally, 'you don't have to search for anything, it's all looking at you. Such a variety of unbelievable visions in such short distances. It's fabulous, Maikel, out of this world, no wonder the Dutch think they know everything. No wonder they feel superior. They have every reason to be proud. How come everyone can speak languages so well? Has the standard of education always been much higher here than in England? I know that on the whole, we English are not so bright, but what do you chaps do with all your know-how? How many rats do they catch per annum; there must be thousands in the canals!'

Maikel did his best between the traffic lights, tramlines, public crossings and finally the digesting of a two hundred gram beefsteak, to answer Sal's stream of questions. She, to his delight, didn't keep talking about herself, or her boyfriend, no embarrassing female gossip; he felt perfectly at ease with her. It made a change: most women got on his nerves; they always had something to nag about. Maikel was enjoying his day. Sally's chatter and display of cycling was an enjoyable contrast to the daily allocation of personal dramas and the indescribable loneliness of his patients in the hospital. He had almost forgotten that such humans as Sally still existed. His mother thought she was magical, charming and delightful.

'Maikel, you're a gem. What a wonderful day I've had,' sang Sally, 'can we do it again? Please say yes, an opportunity like this only comes once.'

'Yes, Sally! On one condition: you tell me what you are up to.' He continued, 'I haven't laughed so much in years. You falling on your backside, legs, or rather toes reaching up to the stars, looking at the buildings as if you're trying to guess when they have had their last coat of paint; now cough it up, Sally, what's this tour really all about?'

'Cross your heart,' she said, 'you won't tell a soul. I'm not really happy here, Maikel. Most of the nurses have a home to go to when they are free. I have nowhere, that at least is the feeling which is constantly with me. Now if I could find a company, preferably an English or American firm, who desperately require an English national who could bring the tea and coffee around, then I could rent a room, see Cloggs more often, and take it from there.' Maikel was secretly thinking, Why can't Cloggs, or whatever his name is, rent a little something? This current situation, he was sure, was destined to go down the drain.

'Ever thought of going back, Sally?' said Maikel. 'Don't be too proud; you might come to regret it.'

'Good heavens, no,' said Sally. 'I've only just arrived; we don't give up that quickly in my family and to me Amsterdam is heaven. I just love it. All I need is freedom to have a bed of my own, a regular job in the daytime, night school for a few years, absolute command of the Dutch language and in five years my own business. No one in our family has ever worked for someone else and I have no intention of breaking with the family tradition, regardless as to whether I live in Holland or in the middle of the Sahara. Now leave your map behind, please. The next spin will be to the rich areas, and from there on towards the new projects. I've heard you are building some lovely offices and flats in the west and Maikel, if you hear of somebody who wants an English jack of all trades, think of me. Before you go I've got another teeny weenie request and before you get the wrong idea I'm not nosy, I'm just inquisitive. Is there in this hospital an African doctor, six foot tall, with curly, curly hair and a look on him as if he is ready to growl, bark and devour you?'

'There is.'

'Great,' said Sally.

'At least twenty of them,' said Maikel.

'You're having me on, I don't believe a word of it. Okay, one last time,' said Sally, 'does any one of them travel frequently to England? Think, Maikel, please think! I know you, you're grinning, so come on and let the cat out of the bag.'

'You must mean Leslie, Leslie Blitz,' he said. 'His mother lives in England. He goes a few times a year to visit her and don't ask me anything more, I honestly know nothing about him. He is extremely reserved, comes and goes. If I'm not mistaken he's associated with surgery, but again, I truly do not know the details.'

'Thank you, Maikel,' said Sally, 'you've been most helpful. This can't be coincidence,' she whispered.

'What can't?' he said.

'Forget it,' Sally replied, 'I'm just dreaming. If you hear of any work that could be interesting for me, please let me know, and Maikel, it's our little secret. Thank your mother for her wonderful hospitality; I loved every minute of it.'

Maikel was about to leave but didn't have the heart to walk off and just close the door. This was a woman with charisma, who knew what she wanted. 'Keep me informed, okay?' said Maikel. 'I'll look around for you,

I promise. If you see me hanging around in the canteen, don't hesitate to join me. If my legs are not killing me by tomorrow morning, I'll repeat the performance perhaps next week, and if you are out there alone on that bike of yours, watch the tram rails. Keep the wheels away from them and remember, we are not island cave folks, we drive like all sane creatures on the right hand side. See you, Sally, it was all most inspiring.'

I wonder how old he is, murmured Sally to herself. Now, Gran would like him, she giggled: she always wanted a doctor in the family.

FLOWER MARKET AND FRIENDS

Every spare minute Sally was on her bike. The summer months had entered her dream world. The flower market was always on the list of spots to be visited. She didn't have any money to buy, but there was a darling old man who gave her a small bunch of roses every time he saw her. His name was Johan. He had a beautiful flower hut right in the middle of the market street and when Sal appeared on the spot, our Johan would truly leave his customers to his staff. Even the ones he was helping.

Like a young schoolboy he would give her a kiss on the cheek and take her to the little café opposite for coffee and Dutch apple pie. He knew Sal loved Dutch apple pie. She would eat it as if it was going out of fashion, and whatever the time of day Johan would always have his snaps. She would practise her Dutch on him and he exhibited his amusing knowledge of English. Johan was already a grandfather. He loved to tell Sal how Dutch families lived. Sally used to ask him about the religions and politics. What those two didn't discuss wasn't worth knowing. Sal would go off with her roses, Johan frequently with a bar of Sally's favourite English chocolate, which he undoubtedly gave to his wife. The dear man would always send Sally off with the same message in Dutch: 'Be careful, young lady, there's always danger out there, you can never be careful enough.'

To this day Sally can always hear his voice. Johan taught her the meaning of genuineness. There was nothing false or calculated about him. He loved his Dutch culture; he was proud of it. The war, the German occupation, all the subjects never discussed at the 'la-di-da' schools Sally had been to in England, were explained by Johan in every possible detail. The war years had been a paradise for Johan's young admirer, and the two chums, as indeed they were, never once ignored each other's opinion on the values and lifestyles which each felt should be free for all cultures.

'I've learned it the hard way, little Madame,' said Johan. 'You still have to learn what it's all about. We Dutch are Calvinistic, down to earth. Pomp and ceremony is all right once or twice a year; just be yourself, we always say, you can't get any crazier!'

Johan and his dear wife Laura became, as Sally used to quote, her 'secret service guardians'. Johan had been in the flower business his whole working life and Laura was in those days the typical Dutch housewife. They were Catholics with a large family and one more seat at the table gave no problem whatsoever. It was from Johan and Laura's house that Sally got married.

Their support of Sally and her activities was unlimited. Johan didn't like Cloggs and Laura would frequently tell him to shut up. 'How often have I told you love is blind; look in the mirror if you dare, you'll see exactly what I mean!'

Sally didn't have to find Maikel, he discovered her.

'Sally, I've got news for you. How's your English grammar, medical language etc.? There is a publisher I know who produces worldwide medical journals in English and they need experts in the English language to correct the typing before it all goes to print. The pay is excellent, let's say secretary level. Are you interested? Here is the number, phone them yourself.'

Within twenty-four hours Sally had her first taste of freedom, and she couldn't wait to tell Laura and Johan. Maikel had to promise he would never forget her and Cloggs was saddled with the task of finding her a respectable room and use of kitchen. She knew she wasn't going to cook, so why waste money on unused space? Cloggs' mother donated the generous offer of confirming to her son that Sally could eat every Sunday with them.

On her bike trips she had already discovered the basements where students regularly gorged, and among others, a few cheap Indonesian restaurants were also on her list. She had to promise Johan that she would visit or phone once a week and as long as they existed, Sally knew she would never starve.

The hospital staff were sorry to see her go. She was always good for a laugh. It didn't matter if it was the cleaner or Matron, to Sally they were all the same.

THE SMELL OF MONEY AND HOME SECRETS

Five weeks later the medical publishers welcomed Miss Sally Bone to their extremely, especially for those days, elaborate offices. She had her own desk, her own internal telephone. Two of the typists in the typing room were allocated to her and to top everything a grand overweight Dutch lady brought her anything she wanted: coffee, tea, bics and cakes. She phoned Maikel and told him he'd found a paradise for her and as soon as the first pay cheque was delivered she would take him out to dinner. 'An offer, Maikel, I know you can't refuse.' Cloggs found her a room near his home, believe it or not with a German family, and the distance, dwelling to office, was short enough to cycle. Sally on that bike was becoming almost a tourist attraction. The huge Dutch bikes gave the impression that they had given birth to Sally's and it didn't take her long to learn and adopt the appalling selfmade Dutch traffic rules for cyclists.

The two pairs of extremely high heels came in very useful. Everyone heard her coming. Everyone heard her going. 'Sally,' asked one of the men, 'how on earth can you walk on them? Have you no fear that you could break your neck?'

'Well, if I do,' said Sally, 'it means the whole female population is going to break its neck. I'll bet you a month's salary that within two years, this country will be showered in modern shoes, TVs and fridges and you, young man, will be choosing the right colour tiles for your bathroom in your fancy new house. Once the Pope has less influence in everyone's daily routine, you'll see the whole bunch of you will get richer and richer and for those who haven't got your brains, there'll be enough dosh left over to make even their lives worth living.'

Sal enjoyed her work as an English corrector. The pay was excellent. She could help Cloggs buy some new clothes and she knew he desperately wanted to buy a German scooter.

'Sal,' said Cloggs, 'in a few months time I shall be earning too. Now, I've worked it out. If I pay one half of the monthly instalments, you the other, in one year we'll have our own scooter. I can show you the whole of Holland and we can stay away for weekends. What do you think?'

It didn't enter Sally's mind to say no, why should she? Her mind was full of plans and as long as Cloggs was happy she knew life couldn't be better. Things could not go wrong. Someone once told her that if you can't share success with someone, then you have no success, and Cloggs was definitely someone she wanted to share with.

Her second pay packet was destined to take her to London. She wanted so much to surprise her parents, especially her father: a full weekend, a healthy English meal, see Dot, get Mother to buy her a new suit and last but not least let poor Cloggs have his scooter. We don't want jealousy and competition in the family. Share, share, share alike. I'll surprise him with a handsome donation. He's going to buy it anyway, Sally told herself, so the sooner the better.

Poor Dad, he was always accused of falling over things, dropping things, but when he saw his daughter walking down the street towards him, he didn't fall, he didn't drop just anything, he just gazed into space and let everything fall. Tomatoes, bread, the whole lot, and to make matters worse, he tripped over them when he made one dash towards her. The poor man was crying: his Sally was standing in front of him.

'Sally, my dear, I've missed you so much, so has your mother, give me your arm, my feet are killing me, couldn't you have warned us, Sal? Mother will have the fright of her life when she sees you.'

'Dad, do you expect the vegetables to find their own way home? Let's pick them up first and then get cracking.'

Between the fish, chips and tomato ketchup Sally told her parents about her Dutch experiences: Maikel, Johan, Cloggs, his parents, the German landlady. Johan received the most attention. 'You must come over and meet them, Dad. They are the most wonderful bunch of people and as far as Holland goes, I love it, I love it, I love it.'

Frank loathed the idea of his daughter living abroad. He listened patiently to all the details. Gertrude, on the other hand, already smelling her daughter's appetite for business, decided that the time had come to pay more attention to her. Nothing Sally was telling them surprised her. The scooter chapter certainly didn't meet with her approval but for once she told herself not to interfere. Sally popped down to Chrishall to see Pearl and Uncle Fred. Her little village was the one thing she still missed; no canals or Cloggs could ever block her love for her little kingdom.

'Stop looking so sad, Dad, be honest, did you really expect me to be back so quickly? I'm earning good money so I can fly over to see you often. Dear old Johan says you are always welcome to stay with him. I've also discovered a lovely hotel for the two of you, so buck your ideas up and stop being so stupidly British. Remember, Dad, you taught me that the world is a rainbow and without all the colours around us, life would be extremely dull.'

When her mother had left the room, Sal quickly put her arm around her father's shoulder.

'Thanks for the weekly paper, Dad, the chocolate and the money in the packaging. Knowing you, you put it all together late at night, when Mother is in bed. Go on, Dad, be honest, am I right as usual?'

'No, Sally,' said her father, 'this time you are wrong. I save the newspaper, I buy the chocolate and your mother slips the money into the wrapping. Come back to England, Sal, be part of the company. I know Mother gives the impression of being a tough cookie, but she's had a hard time. She never talks about it. Her father, who was a military man, left her mother with ten children. Mother was the eldest and as a young girl she went to work in a shoe factory in the East End. She and Uncle Percy brought up the entire family, put them all on their feet. Not one of them has ever worked for a boss, all have their own businesses, and to this day no one has ever said thank you. Not that Mother ever needed their thanks or their help. She surpassed them all. What she as a woman has achieved in this generation is above anyone's wildest dream and to this day I've never stopped admiring her.'

'Give it a rest, Dad,' Sally whispered. 'Without you in the background, Mother would never have reached the top. She only has to look at you; you're like her Wizard of Oz. You make all her wishes come true. Now be my wizard and make one of your famous cups of tea; four choc bics on a tea plate and I'll love you for ever.'

The two of them, perhaps owing to the smell of China tea, started to reminisce about the past.

'Remember that boy ten houses away, who used to pass by the house at least eight times a day with his dog in the hope he would be asked in? When you finally allowed him to inspect your garden, Mother poked her nose in, as usual, by telling him, behind my back, that I had so many boyfriends, he was just wasting his time. Now, don't stick up for her. The only problem was, I'm sure his old man probably had more money than Mother and she wasn't having that in the family. Do you remember him, Dad? His name was Mac. He came to see me while I was working in the hospital. He told me the whole story. I'm sure Mother secretly executed them all behind my back, that's why they came and disappeared so quickly. And there was I thinking that perhaps my teeth weren't white enough, my backside was too protruding or was I perhaps short-sighted? I'm sure there must have been at least ten male specimens who saw something in me.'

'Be honest, Sally,' said her father, 'were any of those young lads up to your standard?'

'Well, if I have to be honest, Dad, no, but it's the thought that counts. They all did their best and Mother sent them packing before they could take their shoes off. Is there any more tea in the pot? You must admit, Dad, when you think about it now, it was a scream. Charlie came, Charlie went; Dennis came, Dennis went; Graham came, Graham went; Ivan came, now he was a real smasher, but even he went. The only one who reached the tea table was Charlie Brooks' son. Didn't they have the huge garden centre about ten miles away from where we were living at the time? Wasn't his name Peter Brooks? I can remember he sniffed constantly, got on my nerves, sniff, sniff, sniff. I always wanted to hand him a handkerchief and knowing me I probably did.'

Gertrude, who couldn't restrain her curiosity any longer, wanted to find out where the hilarity was coming from. She opened the kitchen door to discover Sally imitating Charlie Brooks' son and Frank red in the face from laughter.

'Mother, sit yourself down; we're recapturing all the tricks of the trade you exercised to eliminate all possible Bone spouses in the past. Be honest, who were you waiting for, Bonny Prince Charlie?'

'Frank dear,' said Gertrude, 'is there any more tea left in that pot; if not, make a nice fresh one. Sally, when will you learn? I didn't get rid of any of your suitors, I felt sorry for them! It was your father who did the wheeling and dealing and told them all to come back in three years' time.'

Now, there is an expression 'it was so quiet you could hear a pin drop'. The kettle started to whistle and so did Sally, but with a different tone from that which was coming from the kettle. 'That, Frank Bone, is going to cost you money, serious down to earth money, no bits and pieces in between chocolate wrappings. I'll take one lump sum and settle your punishment here and now. If you give the money with a smile, the subject will be forgotten. Anything that smells like rejection, the price will increase with five per cent, thus ten times twenty equals two hundred pounds, please.'

'Gertrude, dear, do I have to take all this seriously? Help me before she skins me of every penny.'

'Well, dear,' said Gertrude, 'let's look at it like this: Charlie Brooks' son probably doesn't sniff any more. Their garden centre is a huge success. Personally I think Sally is letting you off very lightly. If I were you, I would pay up very quickly before she changes her mind. Goodnight, you two. It's nice having you here, Sally, if only to hear your father laugh again. We'll go out tomorrow and buy you a new suit. Something red, red always suits you.'

DOMESTIC PLANS, MORALS AND ANTISEPTIC

Sally couldn't wait to get back to Holland, back to her new friends. She just loved the atmosphere in Holland. The Dutch could never do anything wrong in her eyes. They never failed to amuse her: their politics, their religions, their meanness, and their jealousy of each other. If you asked her, 'What are the English sicknesses?' she would always say, 'Homosexuality, the English created it. I should know, we have a whole biscuit tin full of them! Males, females, one can take one's pick. However, we as a family have been extremely consistent. Every generation produced a minimum of two. Mind you,' Sally would say, 'they have always been the most intelligent and colourful members of our family circle.'

I'm sure someone, at some time, was so active he even reached for the Sunday newspaper. All very hush hush of course. At this point Sally would look oh so innocent.

'Or was it the chap next door? It was such a long time ago, times have changed; so many men wear earrings today, one can't segregate one from the other. Secondly, the English are so hopelessly polite, they say yes when they mean no and no when they mean yes, and as soon as they use the word "pleasant" then we are all in trouble!'

Cloggs came to meet her at the airport, his face as long as a cucumber. 'I've failed my exams,' he said bluntly.

Sally thought of the two hundred pounds sterling burning in her handbag. She had every intention of giving it to Cloggs as an extra donation towards his scooter. However, owing to the present domestic situation, she decided to leave things the way they were.

'Cloggs, sweetie, it's just bad luck, no good crying over yesterday. I've missed my Chinese food, so let's have a good nosh this evening and we'll discuss everything from A to Z. You know me, there's nothing like a good meal to make one think positively. First my baggage back to my room and then down to the nitty gritty. I'll have two of those pancake things, white rice and chicken in peanut sauce, a simple cola, and you can push your knee romantically up to mine. I've missed your old knee these last few days and we will, as two sensible young nitwits, discuss the future.'

Once in the restaurant Sally opened all the doors for a positive debate. 'Go on, Cloggs, you go first; I'll fill in the gaps. Oh dear, why can't we have this lovely Dutch food in England? It tastes like angels doing weewees on your tongue. Cloggs, what is that Dutch expression angels and weewees, any idea who made it up? The creatures I see here doing their weewees all over the place are dogs of all shapes and sizes. Any idea why dogs have so much freedom here? Are they holy or something, you know, like the cows in India?'

Cloggs did not respond. 'May I now start to say something? From now onwards, I have decided I am not ever going to say one more word to you in English, it's going to be Dutch all the way.'

'Okay, Mr Clever Cloggs, get on with it, let's hear your version of the future. Just give me a little more rice before you start and I'll be as quiet as a mouse.'

'I've passed in four subjects,' Cloggs whispered, 'failed in three and it will take another six months before I have completed the entire programme.'

'Thus,' said Sally, who had promised to keep her mouth shut, 'you have six months to go in the daytime. Why not get yourself enrolled right now for the evening handcraft course that interests you so much. When that has been completed, you will by then have a job, then you go and take the two years' night school study for headmastership, and if all goes to plan you'll be a headmaster when you're twenty-eight. You can then go off to University and study to be a Professor Doctor in the jack of all trades. You're spoilt, Cloggie. If you shot down the whole street, that dear mother of yours would find an excuse for you, and I, dear friend, believe it or not, am not your mother. You want scooters, cars, boats? Then we have to work for them. The heavens have made many wonders but up till now they, for some unknown reason, do not manufacture our wishes, and have them transported down to earth.'

'Sally, let's get engaged.'

Sal, who was just about to put a spoonful of rice in her mouth, plus all the trimmings, saw the humour in Cloggie's romantic request. She mentions scooters, cars, boats, and studies and he finalises the conversation with an engagement.

'Be a sport, Cloggs, and tell me first what a true Dutch engagement means. What do we do? What do we have to buy? Then when you've finished the entire protocol, I, Sally Bone, will say yes or no. Take it all slowly, please, if it's all going to be preached in Dutch. I want to digest every single word. I am after all English and could easily say yes when I mean no, and no when I mean yes.'

The fiancée to be couldn't help secretly laughing at him. Poor Cloggs looked and sounded like the church minister about to perform the service.

'We will go to a jeweller's,' he explained, 'and buy two rings. The same rings are used later when we get married. If you're a Catholic the rings are worn on the left hand. If you are of any other denomination, or rather what's left over, you then use the right hand.'

By this time Sally had forgotten her food, her elbows were on the table, her eyes piercing right through poor old Cloggs as if she was scared to death she might miss something.

'We usually send official little cards to all friends and family. They all arrive on the actual day with a present. A little wine, cookies, and delicious Dutch pastries will be served. You will love it, Sal, you'll be the belle of the ball.'

'Can I ask Johan and his wife and all my friends?'

'We'll see what my parents can cater for,' said Cloggs. 'I'm sure we'll find a way to make everyone whom we invite welcome.'

Sally's immediate thoughts were, if my Johan isn't there then I'm not coming either.

The engagement took place three months later. Two lovebirds looked at each other as if all they needed was a knife, fork, salt and pepper to eat each other up. The rings were engraved with the date. It was a perfect old-fashioned Dutch engagement happening. It all started at two o'clock and went on until seven. Sally's immediate thoughts went to Christmas. She hadn't seen so many presents since her schooldays, many years ago. Friends and family came with cutlery, pudding bowls, kitchen utensils, pudding bowls, Chinese soup cups, and again more pudding bowls. 'Wonderful, wonderful, how kind, how kind you all are,' sang Sally. Sal wanted to say, 'Did someone say we're going into the restaurant business?' but no, she kept her poker face intact and told each and every one of them that their choice was most original and that she knew everything would be more than welcome.

Cloggs' mother did everything to make the day perfect. She was a very smart, well-dressed lady, the perfect hostess at all times. The entire day was unforgettable in more ways than one. Johan and Laura arrived with a beautiful teaset, teapot, the whole lot. Maikel and his mother had flowers delivered. Friends from her office gave her her first Dutch clock; three Dutch restaurants that had taken Sally into their hearts sent flowers and cards. On one of the cards her favourite waiter had written in English, 'Dear Sally, please don't ever learn to cook, we do not want to miss you. Good luck, Marco and team.'

It was a selected stream of kind generous people coming and going, all with large or small parcels under their arms. Sally could recite even years later who came, at what time and which pudding bowl came from which friend. The funny thing is, not one of those bowls ever got broken. But of all the bowls, six remained extremely historical. Two young men, unknown to Sally, rang the doorbell at exactly three o'clock. The visitors were still sitting, standing, all chatting and laughing, thus the sudden appearance of two unknown male visitors startled practically everyone. They were very obviously friends of Cloggs. For the rest no one knew them. With all the charm in the world they introduced themselves to everyone, approached Sally, and handed her a huge box. It was obvious they were service friends of Cloggs. Both were eager to know if she was enjoying life in their country and continued to tease her by asking if their friend was looking after her.

'Let me first open probably the last present of the day, and then, sorry what was your name again? Oh yes, Peter, I'll answer all your questions.'

There was something about the parcel that made Sal feel uneasy. She first read the card wishing them both the very best. Was it the colour of the ink? Was it the signatures of the two attentive young men? She knew that the card was telling her something, but what? Cloggs took the wrapping paper off and Sal took the first peep into the box. Good heavens, thought Sally, not another set of glass pudding dishes. I know, I'll decorate them, paint windmills and Volendam ladies on them, use them for pouring my jelly into.

'Gentlemen,' said Sally with a mischievous sparkle in her eyes, 'how thoughtful; you know we English just love our puddings, we can't live without them. I shall undoubtedly think of you both every day.'

The three men took over the conversation. How great it was to be out of the services. Yes, Peter was on the verge of getting married. Ian was still a free man. Let's have a little fresh air, thought Sally, it's a bit warm in here. I'll vanish for ten minutes to the balcony. No one will miss me there. I'll decide what to do with all those Dutch pudding dishes. Sal didn't have to guess who was going to join her. It took exactly nine minutes for Peter to appear. His English was perfect. 'I've often wondered what you would really look like. Are you truly happy here, Sally, do you really feel you're one of us?'

The speed at which he threw the questions made Sally even more alert. The handwriting on the engagement card; she didn't have to analyse her thoughts any deeper. 'You wrote those love letters to me, didn't you, Peter? I recognise the writing, and the stream of questions. Dirk Jan as you call him, hardly ever asks questions; he is an expert at making statements. Please don't be embarrassed, I loved reading your letters. As a child I always believed in Santa Claus and this time last year I couldn't wait for the postman to deliver mail from Holland. It never entered my silly little head that Santa didn't exist, and when one is romantically involved one never treads on the path of doubt or make-believe. No one needs to know that I have caught on to the past procedures. I'm sure you'll make a wonderful, wonderful husband, and I wish you all the happiness in the world. Remember me as the romantic girl you so often wrote to and I shall always remember you when I read through those lovely letters, which gave me the confidence I needed to start on this wonderful Dutch adventure.'

The guests had left. The day ended with Sally's favourite menu. She had been allowed to choose what she wanted to eat. Her choice was *zuurkool*, stewed beef, biscuit and yoghurt, with jam in between. At the end of the day Cloggie walked her to her room.

'What a fabulous day. I love you so much, Cloggs, however I do have a small little question. Something I'm sure we can both solve. You don't by any chance know of anyone who could use some pudding dishes, do you? Do you realise we have thirty-six small and six big?'

'You could copy our Dutch tradition, Sal, and save two sets, at least, for giving to friends who have wedding plans.'

'Was my Dutch good today, Cloggie? Do you realise I didn't speak one word of English? I love it here, Cloggs, I really enjoy every minute. Perhaps I shake hands with too many people, if I'm not careful I'll be shaking hands with the postman, but on the whole I find the Dutch so interesting to talk to. They love telling me what to do. They ask you anything and everything. I think they're great.'

For the next two years life was a complete tumult. Cloggs passed all his basic exams. Sally found herself with three jobs: in the daytime at the publishers; in the evening she gave English lessons at an Institution for Dutch students; and in the early morning hours she would translate Dutch children's books into English. Cloggs worked in the evenings at the post office sorting letters. It was one fabulous crazy exciting rush that belongs or should belong to everyone's youth. As Sal had previously quoted: wonders do not get manufactured in heaven; roll your sleeves up and work for them. And thus within two years their dream of all dreams came true. Jacob the scooter was born. Sally gave a name to everything and for some unknown reason the scooter, although of German manufacture, was christened Mr Jacob 2000. Life was miraculous. No more bikes, at least for Cloggs. Holland in all its glory could now be seen from a height of eighty-seven centimetres, Sally looking like Miss Marple and Cloggs resembling the TV personality of the year. He was all dressed up for the occasion.

Cloggs was a speed maniac. He never actually took off from the ground; let's be kind and say he was just searching into space. Perhaps for something he missed in his youth, perhaps his bicycle brakes never worked. Who knows, once seated on his scooter fear was never part of the speeding; he loved it! He was intelligent enough to know that he was playing with death. He knew that Sally was terrified but it made no difference, no influence whatsoever. Speed was almost a sickness. He had to get to the final destination even before he had started the engine. Speed or no speed, countryside or towns, the two Mad Hatters, regardless of their age, were instructed in those days to be home by eight o'clock. Cloggs' parents felt responsible for Sally, and there would be no overnights until they were married. Sally wanted to see Zeeland, a delightful small Dutch town in the south of Holland. Cloggs wanted a romantic night in a luxury hotel. Maps were purchased. They had planned their tour of romance at least four weeks ahead. The last evening at home arrived. Pa sat reading his newspaper as usual at the table. The mother was sitting in her beautifully embroidered chair knitting away as if the sheep were about to go on strike. Sally and Cloggs were whispering the ins and outs of their oh so longed for adventure. Pa, who was as healthy as a fish, started to cough. To be polite he cleared his throat, closed the newspaper and decided to let everyone know that he was in the same room.

'Rie, are you giving these two lovebirds sandwiches and a flask of coffee to take with them? What time are you leaving? If I were you,' he looked towards his son, 'I would leave early. It could be very busy tomorrow, the weather forecast is excellent, and it will take you at least three hours to get back.' Sal gave Cloggs a kick under the table: in other words, 'Say something, I haven't had my hair done for nothing.'

'Pa, we're not coming back tomorrow, we're staying in the . . .'

Poor Cloggs didn't have the space to finish his declaration of sexual desire. Any hopes that were up went down and stayed down. For years Sally could scream with laughter when she told the story to young and old. It's almost as ridiculous as life today; however, her story always expresses one major memory, the respect that she had for the father in his hour of concern for his family. He meant well and after all these years his words were never forgotten. Did they stay overnight? Good heavens no. What time did they arrive back? To be precise 7.55 p.m. on the dot. Did they have a good time? Fabulous!

Cloggs was now working as a teacher. His interest was geared towards retarded children. They need me, he would say, the rest only need books and a brain. Sally never forced the issue. If he was happy with his work and it gave him the satisfaction that he needed, who was she to manipulate him in other directions? She could, however, never associate speed maniacs with retarded humans: was it that neither feared death, both had an urge to fly into space, or primarily that neither party knew exactly what they were doing and left therefore the consequences to fate. Fate was hospitals, fate was operations, fate kept Sally occupied day and night, and finally it kept her a prisoner.

'Sal, telephone for you; I have a feeling it's your future mother-in-law. They've put her through to me.'

'It's okay, Kees, I'm coming, what on earth does she want?'

'Sally, this is Dirk Jan's mother speaking. There's been an accident with the scooter. A garbage truck drove off without looking, scooter total loss and Dirk is in hospital with two broken legs. They're operating on him now. One leg has serious injuries. I'm not sure exactly what. We can see him this evening. I'll see you outside the hospital.'

Sal put the receiver down. She was angry: garbage truck my foot, he was speeding! The poor truck driver didn't have time to see him, let alone avoid him.

'Kees, do you mind if I phone someone? I feel a little creepy. I want to talk to someone, someone with some brains in their head.'

'Take the rest of the day off, Sally, he'll be all right. Thank God you weren't sitting on the back of that thing. I don't want to interfere, Sally, but if I were you, I wouldn't sit on the back of that machine if you paid me. If your fiancé loves speeding, let him do it alone. If you're not careful we'll be shipping you back to England in a box.'

'May I have a pink silk lining and mahogany wood, please, Kees, and for goodness sake make sure I've got no hairs on my chin; it runs in the family.'

Sally went rushing off to her dear friend Johan. She needed someone to confide in. At times like this the excitement of foreign adventures and romance disappear. One's native language is oh so far, far away. You want someone near you, a shoulder to cry on. You can say a thousand times 'everything's okay,' but deep down you know there is something missing. The core of the problem is you don't know what is missing, you can't describe it, you just have to learn to live with it. One cannot be a little bit Dutch and a little bit English. It just doesn't work. If one can complete one's goal, thus ninety-five per cent Dutch and five per cent English, then the chances of smooth sailing are in the air. One can retain one's sense of humour, one's accent, preference of interior, but that's where one stops. The rest of one's existence belongs to the culture of the country itself. If you're not prepared to accept such a formula then life will become extremely secluded. As Sally would say so often to Johan, you're either one of them or you're not! What little Madame really needed was a gossip partner, someone who would help her to sharpen her intellect and make the right decisions in a culture that for some years had not been hers.

Now why does it always rain or snow when we have to visit hospitals? Poor Cloggie was in a right old mess, one leg up, one leg down. Tears in his eyes, he certainly didn't look as if he was going to play with snowballs for a long time.

'It's okay, Cloggs, you don't have to say anything, I know the poor dustman was extremely negligent. You poor boy, you were moving so slowly you almost needed someone to push you.'

'Shut up, Sal,' said Cloggy, 'don't make me laugh, it hurts.'

'There is nothing left of the scooter,' answered Sally, 'and your cheese head made a great big dent in the garbage truck. I don't want to think what would have happened to mine if I'd been sitting on the back. I'm going to leave you now,' she could see he was tired, 'then your mother can come in. Don't get upset, those legs will survive; we'll all have you back to normal before the summer sets in. I'll have a look around for a few car magazines. There's a new little French car come out, a model just down our street.' Sally knew this was just what Cloggs needed to cheer him up.

'Now, no more tears, I still love you even if you do look like Pinocchio dressed up for a midnight party. I'll be back tomorrow evening. Try and sleep, I'll be thinking of you.'

'Where are you going, Sal?' asked Cloggs.

'This evening I'm at your parents', it's your father's birthday, remember? You know me, Cloggs, I wouldn't miss a Dutch birthday for anything and knowing your family you will be the topic of the conversation during the serving of the coffee, biscuits, and cheese bits.'

'Sal, please shut up, you're doing this on purpose. I didn't bash into the lousy garbage truck on purpose. The truck and I, we both met at the same time, same place and by the look of me it'll be some time before I can look at a dustbin without swearing at it!'

'I'll be on time tomorrow. I promise,' said Sally. 'You'll see, every day you will improve; chin-up, kiss kiss. Come here, you speedy nutcase. I love you so much. Let me nibble your ear, the rest I'll leave to the nurses.'

It was snowing like mad when she left the hospital. There was nothing romantic about the tram that evening. A horrible smell of wet coats, deodorants weren't in fashion, everyone looked gloomy, curtains drawn in the houses, it all looked so different. Even the street lights looked as if they were going on strike. It made her realise how meaningful her relationship was with her Dutch friend. She couldn't bear to think of him being all alone in that sterile and sickly ward. She wanted to hold his hand, tell him not to worry, tell him she would be there every spare moment, if only to pep up his spirits and try to chat away his fear. He was in a right old mess; perhaps this is why everything looks so morbid. I'll get out at the next stop then I'll walk a little, cry a little, converse with myself a little, sing a little, and finally pray a little. My intuition tells me this is going to be the test to my entire existence in this country.

She knew the tram stop well. She knew she would walk past her favourite antique shop and the divine flower shop with its superb flower arrangements. How often had she not told herself, When I get married I'm going to save and buy all my furniture in that store. My wedding bouquet is coming from this flower shop and later, when I'm rich, I'm going to have flowers delivered every week to homes for poor elderly people, give them some colour in their lives.

DREAMS, WONDERFUL, WONDERFUL DREAMS

Sally was looking at a beautiful Dutch cupboard, one that the Dutch called a *buik*. It was so beautiful she couldn't take her eyes off it. It made her forget her sadness, her loneliness and the fact that her salary was almost exhausted. The lights were still burning in the shop; someone was obviously making room for new pieces. I'm sure that comes from China, said Sally to herself, must be, those colours aren't European. The tapping at the window brought her back to earth. She was being invited to come into the little shop. Sally shook her head, pointed to her watch as if to say 'it's late'. The shop was closed, but the proprietor had obviously seen Sally before. Her adoration for his furniture had obviously been registered with him. She said no, he said yes and yes it was. Sally Bone, who trusted everything that smelt like Dutch, found herself sitting in the middle of the lovely, smelly, overcrowded antique shop, a mug of hot chocolate in her hands, discussing the beauty of the furniture, asking a thousand and one questions and talking about her gran as if Gran with all her knowledge of antiques was sitting next to her. She forgot both the time and the birthday.

'When I'm married,' Sally said, 'I'm definitely going to stay in Holland. You may furnish our house; it will have to be piece by piece, we're still short of cash, but I'm sure this is only temporary. This little country has so many opportunities. I love it as much as I love your furniture. Every street has its own history. The same applies to your antiques. I want to live with history and beauty around me. It helps to drive all the ugliness of life away.'

'Young lady,' the proprietor said, 'you are always welcome in my cave of history as you so beautifully call it. I haven't discovered where you come from, but something tells me that it won't take long before I do. I want you to promise me: no more dreaming through the window, the door is always open for you.'

Little did our proprietor realise that on the evening of 2 February 1955, he had entertained the best customer ever. Not only did Sally purchase regularly, she enjoyed helping him to sell to the Americans, a market which gave him not only wealth but an additional push in the right 'local' direction, thus obtaining, shall we say, a little tiny crown glowing above his doorway.

When you're young you always wants to skip. Sally wanted to skip when she left the 'history cave', as she called it, on that particular evening. It was still snowing. She was confidant that her Mr Speedy would be okay. We'll talk cars and books, no more scooters, until he is completely recovered. You'll see, she told herself, my medicine is magic, it never fails. I'll never forget dear sweet Keithie and Pears the bear, Mum and her powder compact, Johan and his English chocs. A little something to keep the mind going, something to look forward to: it's the best medicine in the world and no one could convince Sally that she was wrong on this subject. She was now five minutes from Cloggs' home. She found herself standing on the bridge, the bridge she always enjoyed walking across. 'Why can't we have little bridges in England,' she whispered, 'that open and shut? It's like *Alice in Wonderland*, absolutely exquisite.' She bent over the rail and looked down into the circling water. She imagined she saw Cloggs' face. 'Cloggs,' she whispered, 'you're going to be all right. We have so much to do together. Sleep well, my dearest friend, and may all your wishes come true.' Sal wiped her tears away and marched on to the birthday circle.

This was the fourth Dutch birthday she had experienced and what an experience it always was. Sally had to force herself to eat slowly, the reason being the guests always had a decisive evaluation of what they were eating. The procedure took time; it was not something to laugh about. Birthdays were, in those days, serious occasions. It all cost money, and money was not taken for granted. They chatted constantly on the quality of the food being devoured.

'There was definitely more alcohol in the cake last year than there is now! Too much sugar in the whipped cream; the butter cake, delicious,' said Grandma, 'but personally I prefer it with ginger on the top.'

'The chocolate cake is first class, lovely and light! Aunt Mabel made it, no wonder, you can't beat her home made stuff.'

'Where did you buy the wine? There's a special offer at the supermarket. I wouldn't buy it if I were you; there's nothing like good French wine. After all, it's only once or twice a year we need it.'

This chatter used to go on for at least an hour, from Aunt Ria, Aunt Connie, Uncle Peter and Aunt Betty. Grandma was the worst. Everyone dreaded her judgement. They were their own private consumer panel. They saved for it, and the hostess made sure that every Dutch cent went to a good cause. Palate, conversation, entertainment and finally an acceptable return for the amount of finance invested in the presents. On the whole the food and the beverage budget were equal to the gifts, which meant that everyone, including Grandma, left the family gathering happy and satisfied. They had received value for their money and, as Sal's father once quoted, 'They're not mean, they're just extremely careful.'

It took our hospital hero exactly two years before he could walk. Two whole years free to converse, two whole years free to predict the future, two whole years to learn each other's personalities and values. I would say Cloggs was the winner. He was calculated in the positive sense of the word. He knew Sally a hundred times better than she did him. This was his country; he didn't have to use his energy to define why this or why that. He could listen, compare, become overwhelmed, become excited, but still place her thoughts in his culture. As long as he could have a warm meal such as he, his parents and his grandparents had had at six o'clock every evening, then what more could one demand?

Under the strain of two years of plaster, walking sticks and hospital beds, one couldn't envisage a period of passion, love making or singing songs around a midnight fire.

One thing Sally did discover in those two years is that Holland had more crossword puzzles per square metre than any other country in Europe. Crossword puzzles in books, newspapers, jigsaws. Retail promotions in all its segments. They were always filling in answers to everything. Sal could never grasp the objective of it all. Was it because they answered a question with a question? No! Impossible, declared Sally to herself. Only Jews answer a question with a question and I'm sure a piece of Jewish culture has long been registered elsewhere. She decided that the answer was quite simple. The Dutch just wanted to be clever. They wanted to be superior to the surrounding countries. The Belgians were nitwits; the Germans had no sense of humour, most unintelligent; the French were never on time and sloppy; the Italians couldn't be trusted. The English, poor lot, they all live on an island, too simple to speak any languages, but on the whole a mentality that could be appreciated by this mini country of water, frogs, windmills and miles and miles of pancake landscape.

'You arrogant bunch,' said Sally, chatting into space, 'no wonder I love it here. I'm not simple, I'm arrogant, just like the rest of you. Holland and I are going to have a beautiful relationship, a relationship never to be forgotten. But please get rid of those disgusting dogs. They leave their mess everywhere and that really is taking Dutch arrogance too far!'

Sally and Cloggs were married in true Dutch style four years after her arrival in Amsterdam. Her father came. He cried all through the registry office service. Her mother did not attend. She said no and no it was. Her new mother-in-law looked sad. After twenty-seven years she was losing her son and who would clean his glasses every morning and clean his shoes? Grandma had a face like a thunderstorm. The chair allocated was not in keeping with her status. Johan and Laura were witnesses for Sally; the rest she no longer remembers. All she could remember was that she wanted to do it all over again sometime. They rented an apartment near town, exclusive, but worth working for. Cloggs went to night school; he wanted his final papers for his headmastership.

Sally, who already had four Dutch diplomas in her hatbox, decided to study marketing: a new phenomenon for Holland. There were eighty males and two women in total enrolled. It was after all 1959 and none of us at that time were sure whether to spell marketing with one 't' or two. Sally, when asked what she thought about the material, replied, 'Plain common sense. Read every book on this subject that ever originated from the States and you can't go wrong.' She knew that, in that era, if as women you wanted to enter the world of commerce, then you needed the American companies and their influence and recognition of a woman's qualities in business. The majority of Dutch companies in those days employed women only until they married. Their contract was then terminated. Sally experienced the same procedure. At the time of her marriage she was working for an accountant's company with international customers, but the employer was Dutch, so the rules remained Dutch. Sally just had to go! Was this a cause for tears, anger, and fear of not being able to pay the family bills?

On the contrary, the accountants used their employment rules and regulations as means to service their own customers. They gave her the information that one of their customers was looking for a secretary. The president of an American pharmaceutical company was desperate for someone completely in command of the English language. Thus Madame found herself still at a very young age almost at the top of the ladder. Her boss once asked her, 'Sally, what is your objective in life?' She replied without batting an eyelid, 'You off that chair and me on it.' To the day of his retirement he never forgot her bluntness and he followed her career for many years to come.

The two of them got on like a house on fire until the end of the first year. He had planned a birthday lunch for her, something special. He thought Sally had deserved it. There is no doubt the man was extremely fond of her. He had visited her parents during one of his business trips to England and always came back with perfume for her. He was undoubtedly so sure of his feelings towards Sally that a hint, or rather subtle advice, from him in the right direction would be sensibly accepted.

'Sally, it's almost the end of the year,' said our generous admirer, 'time for Christmas presents, an increase in salary, and of course, the annual bonus. I have made a decision and I hope you will agree. Believe me, it's all for your own good. I'll put you on the list for an extremely high salary increase if you promise me you will open your own bank account. An account solely in your name, one signature only, yours!' He was so confident of himself that he made a final blunder by insinuating that two cars purchased by her husband in one year was a sheer waste of money.

Was this Dutch? Did they interfere to the extent of Sally's future bank account? The Americans always say that if you want to know your business, ask a Dutchman, but really, this was going too far! Sally was anything but amused. It didn't take her one second to conclude that bullets were being fired at her Cloggs and no way was she going to allow a perfect stranger to crucify her Cloggie. If anyone was going to crucify him then it would be Sally herself. The utter cheek, now, where did I go wrong?, she asked herself. Just because he went to the same school as Cloggs doesn't give him the freedom to run our lives! By this time her glass was empty. Purr at him, Sal, she told herself, look him in the eyes, and tell him where to go.

'I'm going to take your advice extremely seriously. I want you to know I appreciate it, but what I would appreciate is the freedom to sit in at the meetings with the marketing chaps. I always read their reports before we mail them to head office. I'd love to discover how they really operate.'

Not in Sally's wildest dreams did she envisage that her boss was another guardian father. He had long concluded that Sal's hubby was, more times than not, in the cinema every Friday evening. If it wasn't the cinema, then it certainly was a location elsewhere. He would willingly have placed a bet revealing that in no way was hubby-dear anywhere near an evening school or a place of teaching. The educational background of his secretary's husband was such that he, of all people, certainly didn't need to follow a course for two years just to get the diploma he needed. But who was he to interfere? So long as she had her own bank account he felt he had done his best. He was sure the day would come when she would wake up and be grateful for his decision.

HORROR AND CRAB ROLLS

Cloggs was tall, slim, and had a moustache that resembled a paintbrush, and yet somehow the moustache didn't hide the nearness of illness which he always seemed to carry with him. He avoided restaurants as the temperature was too high; when possible he avoided people. The atmosphere in which he worked gave no problems, he was like a fish in water, and yet he had that certain something about him which automatically created a response to spoil him. Sally could never say no. She always said he was the best salesman in the world and she, trying to be more Dutch than Dutch, had long taken over the role of the mother. His first illness made history in the life of Sally. The young, curious woman, who thought she had her life well planned, experienced that day, or rather night, the most startling shock ever!

Cloggs was in bed; his temperature was going up and up. Even his habit of smoking like a chimney had come to an end. Sal was scared. He said: 'No doctor.' She ignored him! They didn't have a doctor, who the hell should she call? I know, keep calm, Sal, she told herself. Knock next door, she's a nurse. She'll know someone. Not only did she know a doctor, she influenced him to come straight away.

'He's new,' said the nurse. 'Don't worry, your hubby will be in good hands. This doctor is good, really good, so just take it easy. We all get ill sometimes.'

The doorbell downstairs made Sally shiver. She was so scared, she completely forgot to put the light on in the porch.

A quiet knock at the door of the apartment resulted in the loudest scream Sally had ever made in her short life. Cloggs nearly fell out of his bed and the whole street must have thought she was being murdered. Sal opened the door to complete darkness. She saw nothing, looked up and saw a set of the largest, whitest, and most regular teeth one could ever dream of. As for the rest she still saw nothing, only darkness. She took three steps backwards, screamed as loud as her lungs could take, and ran as fast as her legs could take her into Cloggs' clammy arms.

'Cloggs,' whispered Sally, 'there's something peculiar going on. I'm literally petrified.'

'Shss,' said Cloggs, 'shss, Sal, there's a doctor standing behind you.'

She didn't turn her head to look at the medical visitor; she knew, without any doubt or hesitation, it was her Mr Trainman, the Liftman, the man who had never escaped from her fantasy and imagination. Compose yourself, Sal, he won't eat you.

Leslie Blitz stood in their bedroom laughing. 'Tell me,' he asked, 'which of you two is sick?'

Sally walked out of the bedroom; the presence of her Mr Trainman made her feel slightly uncomfortable. She closed the door to the apartment and waited in the kitchen for Doctor Leslie Blitz to release her from her fear and agony.

'Nice place you have here, very nice indeed. Do you enjoy living here in Holland? Do you like their food?'

It was a non-stop stream of questions. The bastard, thought Sally, he does know who I am, he must have recognised me in the hospital, in the lift, doing my shopping here in the neighbourhood.

'Tell me, doctor, is my husband very ill?' said Sally, looking up to him as if she desperately wanted to ask him how he brushed and combed his hair.

'Do you want the truth now,' he said, 'or shall I come back tomorrow?' Sal knew he was having her on; she knew he had the courage to tease her. 'Well, he has a slight touch of flu. I'm sure he'll be sitting in his chair tomorrow morning. Don't worry, he'll be okay.'

'I'm sorry I called you out, doctor, I really am,' said Sally. She knew he wasn't listening, She could feel he was exploring for imperfections in her face and she knew he wouldn't find one.

He saw himself out. Sally heard the front door close. She drew the kitchen curtain open. The street lights were still burning. For some hideous reason she didn't want him to disappear; she wanted to feel that she would see him tomorrow and the next day and the next. He was on the verge of getting into his car; one leg had already disappeared when to Sal's almost childish joy he was standing, waving up to her.

'Thank you, Mr Leslie Blitz,' whispered Sally to herself, 'thank you. I feel oh so much better now.' Long after he had left, she stood gazing out of the window dreaming of what was and what could be. Her dream was to have her own business, her network of very special friends; she must phone Maikel, who was still working in the hospital, and his mother this week, they were both still her very dear friends, and tell them the joke about Leslie Blitz. Johan and Laura wanted to go holidaying in England; I'll ask Mother to let them stay at our place. Ron can show them around.

'Goodnight, Cloggs, I love you,' whispered Sal as she slid into her bed. Tomorrow is another day. Tomorrow you'll be better.

As much as she tried she could not fall into sleep. Everyone has a history book, Sally always told herself, and I have a mischievous feeling my history book page number one has just flown in through the window.

FATHER'S JEALOUSY

'Dad, when will you accept,' said Sally, 'he's just a nice, solid, down to earth man.'

'But Sally, he doesn't even put the kettle on, let alone make you a drink. How often haven't you seen your old Dad spoil Mother, and don't tell me that all Dutch women work the hours you do. There's not one woman who works in this avenue. I know because I chat with them every morning when I go out walking.'

Sally's father was the guest of Sally and her hubby for one whole week. Not that he saw much of hubby; he disappeared, one day after his arrival, to his boat and the excuse that the English language was tiring for him resulted in long periods of heavy discussion between father and daughter. The two relatively newly weds had purchased a beautiful house just outside the city, with an office downstairs for Sally, who by now had her own marketing bureau and was travelling to most of the European countries for one of her American textile customers.

She had yet to reach the age of thirty and her network already consisted of a super, down to earth Dutch secretary, who loved the freedom Sally gave her to earn money and drive in her car; a domestic who was allowed to run the household as if it was hers; and a bookkeeper who knew too much, but who kept her trap shut.

There was also the bank manager whom she lunched with, her accountant whom she loved arguing with, and last but not least, her one and only lawyer who until the end of time saved her from various legal scrapes. He was God's gift to the legal profession: a man of justice. A man who was always slightly curious to know exactly where his female customer came from, and why; but who nevertheless defended and protected her from evil devices until the bitter end.

'Can you imagine me,' Pa replied, 'behaving in such a disgraceful way, young lady? And don't tell me it's Dutch. I've seen his father, poor man; he passed away far too young, a perfect gentleman. Now, be honest with yourself, would he have behaved in such an atrocious way? And what's more, it's not the first time. My first visit to your apartment resulted in the biggest shock ever. I couldn't get it over my lips to tell Mother, but if you think I didn't know what was going on behind my back, then you are wrong. A dockworker would have had more respect for himself, and this man is so-called educated. Does he help you with anything, does he go anywhere with you? Has he in the past few years ever taken you away on a holiday, saved up to surprise you?'

Sally could hear from his tone of voice, his red cheeks, his fingers scratching away at his ring, that he was, poor man, reaching the point of explosion. Harsh words were never part of her father's vocabulary; this just wasn't him. He always saw the good in everyone. He's going to regret this, thought Sally. Take action, before it's too late!

'Stop, Frank Bone, calm down immediately. Put all those expressions which are flying out of your mouth, your nose and your eyes, away; far, far away. Please, Dad, don't spoil your last day here. I know this isn't your idea of a marriage; it isn't mine either. Of course I dreamt of a man who would spoil me like you spoil Mother. Of course I wanted passion in my life, a man who would be part of my existence, who would support me in my thoughts and in my actions. People are never robots, Dad; you simply cannot programme them to change their attitude and emotions to your desires. He is brilliant at his work. Neither you nor I would have the guts and patience to work in such an environment. His mother still thinks that the sun comes out of his arse – he's a super egocentric man. He wants nothing whatsoever to do with the world and its inhabitants. When necessary and only when required he can be extremely charming, but not for too long, and finally, he functions superbly when he's one hundred per cent alone with me and when the pair of us are walking around a showroom which has the latest car model on show.'

Sally didn't say it, but her thoughts chanted, 'Speed, man, speed!'

'There is however one huge advantage to such an evaluation. I know what makes my hubby tick. I have no expectations and no surprises. Most husbands go to their graves leaving a trail of questions behind them. In our case, I'm sure the shoe will be on the other foot.' She took her father's well-manicured hand in hers. 'Are we, Mr Silly, feeling a little better now?' She knew she had brought so much sorrow to so many loved ones, by leaving them all for this adventure, a journey in life which had been transparent to so many, but not to her.

'Sally, I'll say no more. These are my last words on the subject.'

By this time Frank had tears in his eyes. 'This man will be the death of you, Sally. I know what I'm talking about. Let no one feed on your energy, my dear, unless they too are prepared to give. Always remember, your mother and I are both so proud of you. Mother tells the bank manager you're in Switzerland before the plane you're in has had the chance to land. I mustn't forget to take your present back for Dot. I'll treat her to a plane ticket to come here, she'll love that, then the two of you can gossip until the cows come home!'

The last evening of Frank's stay was spent at Johan's. Laura had prepared a typical Dutch dish, *hachee*, meat with lots of onions and plenty of it. Both of them arrived the next day at the airport. They wanted to wave their English friend goodbye. Sally was not allowed to go back to an empty house, first she should go to them and when she felt like it back to home.

'I wonder,' asked Laura, 'if he'll be there when she arrives. He knows the father is leaving today; surely he won't stay away until tomorrow?'

'Laura, stop it,' said Johan. 'I'm sure Sally is sitting behind her desk, will work through until the early hours and when this husband of hers walks in tomorrow, she will say with a smile, "Did you have a wonderful time? Coffee or tea? Are you hungry, would you like me to fetch you some Chinese?"'

'How on earth,' asked Laura, 'do you know all this, Johan, where do you get it all from?'

'Well,' he replied, 'remember those photos on the television and in the lounge. They, if you looked carefully, Laura, told a thousand and one stories from the past. Didn't you see the photo of Sally and her grandmother? Frank told me that his ancestors had fled from Russia, found their way to Vlaanderen York; some stayed in England. Five families went on to Australia. Frank's father owned a large chunk of Covent Garden, so there must be wealth still floating around above some of their heads. Her background is so different to his. Believe me, Sally wouldn't know how to tackle such a domestic situation, and between the two of us I wouldn't like to be around if she ever did.

'She comes from a line of survivors. She's not going to let anyone buckle her under. I can still laugh when I think of her for the first time standing in front of my stall, and then to think she's now one of the family. I told Frank last night, I'll keep an eye on things. He knows our doors are always open.'

'Did you have a good flight, Dad? Did Mother like her present?' There was a silence. Sally was sure it was her father on the line. 'What's going on at your end? Say something, please, you're scaring me.'

It took at least thirty more seconds before she could capture his voice. 'Sally, my dear I'm so sorry for the way I spoke to you in your house. Please forgive me. It's just that I want so much to see you happy.'

'Forgive you, don't be ridiculous. I've long forgotten what you said. I love you. You're the best Dad ever; now shut up, get to bed early, you must be tired. I'll phone you tomorrow. I promise.'

SERIOUS BUSINESS

'Excuse me doctor, are you listening to me? Do you mind putting that cigarette away! I have a chain-smoker at home. I've never seen him without a shag thing between his fingers and I need advice. He's a bundle of nerves,' Sally explained, 'constantly tired, there's definitely something wrong. He won't come to you; please help me, and make a trip out to us. Charge me whatever you like. I trust your judgement and I only want the best for my hubby.'

Leslie Blitz walked her to her car, stood and waved goodbye. We assume he didn't blow a kiss, but apart from that, no one could conclude that we were dealing with a routine exercised by someone with a room full of patients waiting for him. Did Sally search for a reason? Good heavens, no! To her it was a most normal thing in the world. It wasn't the first time he'd walked her to her car. No problem whatsoever, she muttered to herself, most delightful. Makes my blood go warm in my veins, makes me feel young. I'll have my hair cut tomorrow. No I won't. I'll have it coloured. We'll change the Lancôme mascara to Rubinstein. Makes my lashes look longer. By this time the little Mini had found its destination, its driver relaxed and certain that all black thorns would turn to roses. That Cloggie would once more turn into the super trumpet player, the handsome young Dutchman whom she still loved with every fibre of her existence.

She was desperate. Too many business contacts thought she wasn't married. Try as she did with all the patience of Job she could not get Hubby to budge, she could not move him to place one foot in her environment, the world which produced the richness and independence which both enjoyed. Was it a question of poor health, upbringing, or that godforsaken fear and jealousy that so many males have, and still have, for successful businesswomen? She knew the situation wouldn't change. It was no good dreaming that pigs would learn to fly. She loved him. She interpreted her task as a role. She had a short time ago repeated the famous two words: 'I will.' She always prayed the day would never come when she would say: 'I won't.'

Blimey, thought Sal, he's a man of his word, he's not wasting any time. 'Is he in, Sally? I'm in your neighbourhood late this afternoon. Round about five thirty. I'll try and sort out what's wrong.' Leslie Blitz's voice sounded like thunder and damnation on the telephone; it always did. One had to look at him in order to define what was going on in his mind. Perhaps he's always got toothache. Maybe his wife never cooks for him, such women do exist, you know. I know, she told herself. She spends all his money. Of course she does, that's it! She does the bookkeeping, she exhausts the bank accounts. His suits come from C&A and his shoes from ... before further absurdity could be created Blitz was sitting upstairs talking and prodding. He wanted to know why his patient was such a bundle of nerves; had the man never learned that to say 'Yes' is sometimes a far easier task than to say constantly 'No'? What was behind it all? He had everything a man could dream of. Why did he feel so much at home in the world he worked in, why the solitude? This man should have been a hermit, Blitz told himself, a monk. What the hell was he doing with a wife like Sally? One didn't have to be a doctor to define that they were as different as chalk and cheese, black and white, Mickey Mouse and Goofy.

The two men occupied the empty chairs in the office downstairs. It was the end of a day full of rain and miserable distorted clouds. Two men, both puffing at cigarettes, both as tall as lamp posts, one acknowledging his own language, the other the language of Sally.

Blitz glided over the English words as if they had been with him since birth. 'Your husband's going to have a few blood tests,' he said, 'and spoil him with a few Dutch herrings. What's more, he's going with you to America, a week in New York. Theatres, the whole treatment, you're going to enjoy yourselves; most of my patients would give their right hand to have the freedom you two have. Enjoy it. It's there for the taking.'

Blitz knew he was wasting his time, but what else could he do? He was, after all, their doctor, but the course that he knew, in all honesty, that should be taken, wasn't for whatever reason to be defined in his medical journals. He took a quick look at the time. 'Have you anything to drink, Sally? I've got thirty minutes to spare then I am off to a football match, the one and only love in my life.' This was Leslie Blitz, without the music of thunder and damnation. In fact Leslie was beginning to feel well at home, perhaps we should say, extremely well at home, in Sal's office. 'I'm not on duty any more today,' he remarked, 'so yes, I will have a sandwich; on second thoughts, make it three, no ham, just cheese,' he chuckled. 'Tell me, Sally. What do you really get up to in this office? And where do you get it all from?'

'My mother,' she answered. 'I couldn't stand her when I was young. I am now the living image of her. Would you be interested in hearing my plans for the coming five years?'

What a gorgeous treat, she could speak in her own language. No restraint, no fear of being misunderstood. A listener who could appreciate her desire to accomplish and help other women find their way in a world that was at last, slowly but surely, accepting females in their establishment. It was the time of the Beatles, the flower girlies, as Sal called them, the pill, mortgages, the car, no, two cars, preferably a Mini or a Fiat with four gears in it. It was an explosion that swept through Holland like a whirlpool, a tornado: a new lifestyle for women, regardless of their education, background, or age.

The speed or direction of the football that evening, the cheers and whistles of the crowds filling the grounds, had no immediate impression on our football fan. Was he still enjoying the taste of the cheese, the atmosphere of the house? Or was it his patient's passion for her work together with her desire to protect her husband? Whatever, she intrigued him; the entire situation intrigued him. Football for the first time in his life simply went out of the door. Who had scored what? He, Leslie Blitz, had no idea. There was, however, one young female player who had unintentionally scored a goal, a goal that would remain in his system for many years to come.

Life took its course, life went on. The vibration in the shops, in the streets and the markets with their foreign goods; the new fashions, hair designs, and specifically cosmetics: it all thrilled her and the Dutch population immensely. The politicians amused her. They were always so contradictory. They said A, they meant B. They said B and back they went to A. Her friend Dot was over for a short stay. It was yap, yap, yap, for twenty-four hours a day.

'Do you know, Dot, they ... '

'Who's they, Sal?'

'The politicians, silly, they have a legal way of doing illegal business. It takes you months to work it out, but as God is my judge, this is the most fascinating and complicated little country in the world.'

Dot had soon discovered there was a diabetic in the family. She saw books on the subject; they were all over the place. 'Sal, are you thinking of setting up a production line or are all these books specifically for the kitchen?'

Dot's intense curiosity towards Sally's Dutch domestic lifestyle resulted in many hours of probing into her friend's attachment to her new surroundings and acceptance by the residents of the country she now lived in. Were the Dutch truly friendly? Did they make her feel welcome? Could she communicate with her neighbours? Dot was not nosy. She just wanted to know everything! Did her hubby want her to continue working? Could she express herself in the third most difficult language in the world? Dot knew her friend loved the English classics; she also remembered her friend hated water. She knew she was petrified of it. Try as she might, she couldn't inspire her imagination to the degree of visualising Sal and Cloggs on a boat. The poor woman must be out of her mind with fear. She couldn't swim. Water, Sal would say, was for making tea with. How on earth had her friend got herself into such a whirlpool of contradictions? Why this absurdity to be one of them, why couldn't she retain her own identity, remain herself? A bulldog is a bulldog and not a terrier. Fine, okay, if Sal wanted her own business, naturally she needed to know the laws and language. She needed to know the elementary objectives and desires of staff. Her luck was that she had heard nothing else in her parents' surroundings.

People, Dot asked herself, were surely the same the whole world over. We all need a goal, a system, a path to walk down, a temptation to survive. But surely one doesn't have to bend back twice just to get a warm meal on the table at two o'clock instead of six! Sally must be out of her mind, Dot told herself, to give in to all these domestic traditions. She must be bonkers, crackers! Or was she just frightened to take the bull by the horns, scared of the consequences? Even while I'm here, Dot concluded, Cloggs still talks solely in his own language to Sally. Friends, let alone man and wife, should be honest, straightforward with each other; and with this declaration in mind, Dot, who regarded herself as being a true and loyal friend, decided she would take the bull by the horns. She would warn her friend of the sheer stupidity surrounding her, and if necessary kick her up the backside, anything to wake her up and get her back to her usual self. She was, according to Dot, becoming more Dutch than the Dutch; before we knew where we were, she'd be shaking hands with the milkman!

Breakfast over, Cloggs off, Dot was sitting in the attacking position: mouth empty, the last spoonful of cornflakes in the stomach. She had successfully rehearsed her prime speech of the century. Her thoughts in bed that night had swept through *Gone with the Wind*, *Brief Encounter*, and all the other nonsense that we mortals dream and write about in the hope that someone will be stupid enough to believe it. Even worse, they influence us that it's always greener on the other side: that the next door neighbour earns twice our annual salary, while half the time the poor bugger is up to his neck in debt, cheats on his wife as if it's going out of fashion, the kids are playing around with drugs and last but not least the house belongs to her mother!

'Dot, don't even think about it.' Sally wasn't in the mood for sermons. 'I mean it, you can start to nag when and only when I give you permission. He's not well, Dot,' Sally said. 'Remember in the hospital we used to say I could smell it! Well, I don't have to be a fortune-teller to read in the cards that my husband is sick. I no longer leave the country except for one or two days to visit my parents, neither do I come home late nowadays. If he feels safe and secure in his own environment, plus his boats and water, with his own traditional blankets around him, who am I to force the issue? Who am I to challenge his lifestyle of so many years? We're all a product of our own upbringing. You, as no other, should know that and unless we can both go back, which we can't, and relive our lives together, each in the harmony of his or her youth, there will always be that curtain of misunderstanding, mistrust, always looking for proof and evidence. That one dangerous little pin-point that falsely reminds you of your own happy memories is miles and miles away.

'Have you ever been back to look at a house you once lived in? The fantastic house with its huge rooms, fireplace with logs burning, tennis courts and two cars in the drive? Everyone beautifully dressed: in a nutshell, Dot, the concept of domestic perfection. Until you return, after twenty years. Believe me you first have to drive down the street twice before you can find the wretched place. It looks like a matchbox. Tennis courts: we must have made our own rules up to play tennis on that size lawn. Cars? One at the most! In these past twenty years my memory gave birth to choirs, Sunday lunches, and at least twenty public gardens. It was all so beautiful; one could always smell the home fires burning. Those memories which in our moments of loneliness have the habit of bewitching us into homesickness. An absurd longing for love and affection in one's own language, conversing with others in our own native language. All emotions which create the existence of our curtain, our thin, almost transparent, wall, which will always be dangling between two people, two crowds, two foreign nations.

'Now, if everyone were to read Shakespeare's *Midsummer Night's Dream* and the peeping through the wall part, life for all would be so much easier to understand. Shakespeare, Dot, wrote everything there is to know of life, from the darkest vice to serene innocent beauty.'

Sal glanced towards the kitchen window. Dot could read her thoughts; it wasn't very difficult. Here was a woman who had given so much energy, so much time and sincere interest in the history of her new homeland and what was she doing? She was chanting, reciting verses, taking her memories back to her prophet of world history, Willie Shakespeare.

'Before I get myself washed, Sal, tell me,' asked Dot, 'could your friend Shakespeare save the world today?' Good old Dot, she really was the best! Her hair was getting just a little bit grey, but her mystified glance on life remained her charm.

'Dot,' said Sally, 'when we come back to this world, I shall personally arrange that we both sit next to each other: same class, same street, same everything. Then you can read that Shakespeare did attempt to save the world; unfortunately, only a few know how to experience his readings. Now shut up, posh yourself up. I'm taking you to meet a very special friend.'

'Is it a man, Sal? Go on, let me in on it, you always had tons of boyfriends. Nothing serious of course, you just played with them, tickled them crazy, and then dumped them! The odd one usually onto me!'

ALADDIN'S CAVE – THE ROOM

Leslie's room was, how shall we say, cosy. Without doubt it was difficult to describe, very difficult to describe! A huge man, with big ear lobes, hairy wrists and a thick neck, sitting in a chair two sizes too small for him. There was a red hand made rug under the desk. Photos everywhere: his grandfather, his mother, his sister, two daughters and their dogs. His wife for some reason could never be found amongst the collection. She was Australian. Where he met her, where he found her, they never found out. The subject was clearly taboo.

Not that 'other women' were Sally's close interest. She had sufficient working for her. She had enough female problems to solve, such as why they couldn't work because the cat had been out the whole night, the canary had flown out of the window, or the daughter had trouble with her relationship. The excuses that part-time women could sell to avoid working were humorous, childish, almost pathetic, whereas the thirty-eight hour a week team could, accordingly to Sal, out-rate any man.

Their interest in their results was genuine. When a woman is good, she is good! There's no messing around. She's always on her guard, always does her homework, hates failure, but is smart enough not to imitate the male colleagues, and remains a sexy unapproachable female at all times! It was always the so-called domestic love disasters that Sally had to listen to, disasters which moved everyone to laughter and tears. 'Does he gamble?' Sally would ask. 'Does he hit you? Does he take you and the kids out to the films? Or off once a year for a lovely holiday? Does he come home every night or is he sleeping with the widow at the end of the street who undoubtedly cooks better than you, irons his shirt collars better than you, and tells the poor hard working sod that he is the best ever or whatever he wants to hear?' Sally always knew she didn't have to go any further.

The female response was for ninety per cent identical. 'Sally, there isn't a widow at the end of the street, of course my Ian doesn't gamble; hit me, where do you get that silly idea from? We had a lovely holiday with the whole family in France this summer.' Not that Sally had expected any other reaction. The women were enjoying their freedom. They wanted to spend a night out with some would-be Romeo, a cosmetic representative who had chatted them up, told them they were what he had always longed for. His wife misunderstood him and his mother-in-law sat in his chair every Sunday.

'Now I ask you,' Sal would always say to anyone who would listen, 'who could resist such temptation?' Her advice was a cliché: spend some hours with the moron, let him do all the paying, then you'll know your first choice was the right one! A few extra vitamins now and then is never harmful, as long as we're not causing pain to those we love. Now get your backside off the chair and your feet on the ground. If you want a taste of honey, make sure the whole pot is for sale; just a taste of the stuff will get you nowhere!

Perhaps Dot was thinking honey pots – women can never resist a little romantic gossip, a smell of danger, a minute sniff in a strange kitchen – when she agreed to meet her friend's Mr Mystery. She was quick to detect there was no photo of his wife: his family, yes, but no 'Mrs'. She knew Sal liked him – she talked about him too much. He doesn't growl, thought Dot, where does Sally get the nonsense from? He speaks perfect English. His voice is soft, there's something kind about the man, caring, and I bet that suit cost a few bob. Dot decided the suit and car were enough to tell her that she was sitting in a successful practice, talking to a man who loved not only his profession but the scatterbrain sitting next to her. His eyes never left her; at least that was what it seemed like to Dot.

He apologised: 'I'm sorry I can't offer you coffee, Dorothy, but I'm truly delighted to meet you. Do you enjoy watching football? I'll get us some tickets, if you let me know on time, when you're coming back to Holland.' It was indeed football weather when the two would-be patients walked back to the car. Neither said a word, not even a giggle. Dot was chewing on her thoughts and observation.

'Sal, that desk of his – I'll bet you anything it must have belonged to the father. I saw the ink spots on the leather; we don't use ink in these times, you know. Mind you, one has the feeling he practically lives there. The walls could do with a coat of paint. The clock, have you had a good look at it? It must be worth a fortune. I can't make up my mind as to whether we were sitting in a surgery or a hotel room. One thing is certain, Sal, his patients will not experience a feeling of being on their guard. I'd probably take a teapot with me, bake a cake for him. It's a room, Sal, a nice comfortable, friendly room. It makes you think when you leave it. It's full of history. He's nice, Sal, I like him. I'm glad you've found someone whom you can converse with. All that yap, yap, every day in Dutch, it must be a strain; it's relaxing to talk in one's own language, if only to have a jolly good laugh now and then. Do you tell him the jokes about the girls and the honey pots?

'Sal, are you listening to me? You're miles away. Go on, spill the beans; what's on your mind? Are memories bobbing to the surface? Do you miss the fudge, the silly hats we used to wear, your father spoiling you? Attention that everyone needs, which brings me to the obvious: Is he, he?'

'There is no "he", Dot, there is no "he". Would you like to knit one for me? Nice round face, five foot ten, reasonable bank account. His legs must be long enough to walk to a flower shop. His eyes sharp enough to see when I'm tired or sad, his arms long enough to reach for the tins of carrots on the top shelf in the kitchen.'

'And,' said Dot, 'well, how about someone who will chat in my language when I get a little watery and the tears fall together with the last clashes of the National Anthem?'

'Honest, Dot, I always have a little weepie when I see all the poppies on Poppy Day, and the Queen on Christmas Day. Not that I ever let anyone see the tears; no one would understand. Why should they, the

Queen isn't their Queen and Poppy Day isn't their remembrance of the dead. But it is mine, and the older you get, the stronger is the effect these moments have on your life. I can recall a history teacher once telling us: always remember, there are no gates or walls when leading your thoughts back to the past. Time has no gate, time has no wall. I always give myself the time on Poppy Day to think back to my youth and the loved ones around me in those days. But have no fear, it doesn't take long to get myself back to normal. Now what were you talking about? If I'm not mistaken, the charms of Leslie Blitz. Well, I'm sure he would comfort. I'm sure he would buy the flowers, the whole shop, if it came to that, he has indeed got a nice round face, speaks super English, but I'm sure he never eats carrots; in fact methinks he's never even seen one. Now, let's stop being a pair of hooligans. I've got to pop into the office. You in the meantime can do something for your keep, cook! Tomorrow's your last day, so let's make the most of it.'

'Anything special, ladies?' Sally inquired. 'All stands occupied for tomorrow, reserves ready for any last minute illness, emotional or physical?' This line of inquiry always made the office staff laugh; when she mentioned the word emotional they knew only too well where her thoughts were.

Sally had, twelve months previously, discovered a niche in the market, as a result of which she expanded her current activities by offering trained cosmetic staff to the cosmetic world. It was unique, at the time. It was a challenge. It kept her on her toes. She was dealing with a bunch of women at the top, not her idea of heaven, in fact, anything but!

She kept them all at arm's distance; she knew they could break her and the less they all knew the better! The men had respect for her; they admitted she knew what she was talking about. The females were jealous, and rightly so. If I were in their shoes, Sal would say, I'd have the hump too! No boss, day and night on the go, no time to spend the money you're making. Responsibility for everyone's salary, telephone day and night; there was always some moron who forgot to place his order, and who woke you up in the middle of the night, half drunk and desperate for staff the same morning. Yes, Sal would repeat, I can truly understand their jealousy.

Would she have missed it? Did she ever anticipate stopping? Never! She lived for it. It was her world, her company, her staff, her achievement; it kept her mentally sane. It occupied her loneliness, it camouflaged her true self.

In that period of her life she scribbled in her notebook: 'I'm so lonely, as frightened as I am of dogs, I long for one to pass by, then I can stroke it, and hopefully feel its heart.'

ALADDIN'S TELEPHONE

'Sally, I've got a little secret to tell you. Come on, sit down and take it all in. You love mysteries. Work this one out, while you're watching tele with Dot and your hubby. No, I mean it,' said Paula. 'It's all getting a bit too obvious. There's someone dialling this number frequently.'

'What do mean, frequently?' said Sal, frowning at the same time, as if she could smell trouble.

'Frequently, just frequently.' Paula wanted to say 'Silly', but the look on her boss's face was more than sufficient. 'Nobody says anything,' said Paula, 'but it's the way the telephone falls, that's what gives the game away.

'Falls? Falls? What on earth are you talking about, Paula? How in God's name can a telephone fall?'

Sal thought, this poor kid was never very bright, but she means well.

'It's the noise it makes,' said Paula triumphantly, 'when they put the receiver down.'

'Like a lid on a dustbin?' replied Sal, 'Bang, bang, dustbin closed.'

'That's it, boom, I'm sure it's a boom,' said Paula with a look on her face as if she had discovered the latest device in the world of telephones. At that specific moment Sal thought of her mother. She would have said, 'Where do we meet them, Frank dear, where do we meet them?' and the two of them would have roared with laughter.

'Tell you what to do, Paula, next time you hear your boom, boom. Make a note of what time the nutcase is dialling our number. He doesn't make any naughty noises, does he? Breathing heavily? Sucking a sweety noise?'

'No, Sally,' said Paula indignantly, 'it's just a heavy boom.'

Sally walked off to her office. She was desperate to have a laugh. She sat down in her chair behind her desk. She could hear Paula singing her boom, boom. Blimey, she chatted to herself. I pay the girl for this nonsense, this nutcase better be good. If not – I'll – oh no, she's got me on it now. I wonder who he is?

The telephone brought her back to earth. 'Trouble, Sally, one of our girls has got her fingers stuck in the till, good luck! Do you want to bail her out or shall I send someone down there?' It was John on the phone, one of her make-up artists, a gem with magic in his fingers and charm oozing from every movement in his body.

'Leave it, John. I'll pop down tomorrow and apologise. In the past we would always try and turn the clock back for them. Unfortunately, John, when women steal, there's usually a man in the background. It's either to impress him with the extra present they really can't afford, or to resell for family debts caused by the hubby's drinking problems. Some even do it for the kick, whatever, but nine out of ten times the product is never stolen for themselves. There's always an emotional tie somewhere and that emotional tie is far stronger than their guilt concerning the disgrace branded on the company. I've lost count how many times I've tried in the past to help. It just doesn't work. Put it out of your mind, John; believe me, I know the feeling. What's the hot new autumn colour going to be? What? You're joking! I'll look like a Christmas clown,' said Sally, 'all dressed up and nowhere to go!'

'What shall I tell your mother?' Dot asked. The two chums were on their way to the airport.

'Tell her my left arm is falling off, we've had a fire in the kitchen, burglars have been in twice for tea. She's not to worry, the business is just fine. Now you're longing to say something to me, so I suggest, dotty Dot, you say it now, get it off your chest, and make it quick!'

Dot began rummaging in her bag, looking for something she knew was not there. She felt clumsy, out of place; she was about to interfere in the life of her dearest friend. They had shared so many secrets together. She knew her friend's utter disgust for defeat, imaginary sentiment. Perhaps it would have more effect if she kept it short and sweet. On second thoughts, she told herself, I'll say it the way her mother would say it. Now let's see, she would say 'Sally', and then there would be one second of silence, 'that husband of yours is ill, be careful,' and, 'that man, Sally, don't hurt him, he's obviously very fond of you.' She would then leave the room, leaving Sally to guess who 'that man' was. The only difference was that Dot couldn't leave the room. She went up into space and flew back home.

PAULA

'I know who dials our number, I do, I'm sure about it. Oh Sally, it's so romantic. Why can't these things happen to me?' The poor, kind hearted girl wanted so much to say, 'You've got it all! A wonderful husband, cars, all the luxury in the world.' She memorised an impression which her employer's attitude suggested. No one in or around the business was ever granted the time or space to discover the ins and outs of Sally's private life. One could only guess. A stage further than guessing was definitely off limits!

'What on earth, woman, are you chatting about? You look as if you've been pushed through a hedge backwards. Stop dropping your breadcrumbs on those papers. There's some nail varnish in the top drawer of my desk, use it!'

Sally, bursting with curiosity, rapidly threw a chair down opposite the company's mastermind, placed her bag on the desk and whispered, 'Go on, let's both have a giggle. Is he tall, dark and handsome? Could he be a pervert? Do we have to call the police? Who is this nutter? No beating around the bush. Just get cracking!'

'Well,' replied the company's female Poirot, 'my guess is . . .'

'Come on, woman,' responded Sally, excited like a child just about to receive her first party dress. 'Spit it out! Don't keep me in suspense any longer.'

'It's your doctor. You know, Sally, the one you arranged for me to see. Do you remember? My eyes were giving me trouble, constantly infected. You said if this doctor doesn't know what's wrong, no one will! So, off I went, Sally; a lovely kind man, he needed exactly one minute to diagnose my problem and twenty to discuss you. I'm sure he dials our number, hoping he'll get you automatically on the line. When you go next time, Sally, take him something nice, something special!'

'Are you finished, can I go?' Sally asked. She wasn't happy with the verdict. It was too personal. Too close to home. It made her remember why she had so often ignored the green light indicating that it was the next patient's turn. To be more precise, it was her turn! Her route was, invariably, from the waiting room to her car.

She couldn't handle her emotions; inasmuch as she was attracted to his personality she was also frightened of him. She knew that once he took over, there would be no turning back. He would devour her from top to toe! He would go completely over the top.

Was this the answer to her loneliness? She had her doubts. There were too many moths eating holes in the butterflies. Too many doubts to handle!

Her evaluation of romance via the telephone was interrupted by the noise of the window cleaner. A handsome young star with bucket, leathers surrounding his legs, and ladder, he had a certain something about him. They call it chemistry. In his case, it was a combination of chemistry and youth! Sal was sure all he needed was one little wink from a woman and he would push open the window – ladders, leather and water would go flying into space. Our extremely good looking window lad would take the afternoon off to enjoy and extend his knowledge on the art of sex. Sal could envisage him asking for tea first and a glass of whisky after he had put his pants back on. Whether it was the whisky, the pants, or just the old comforting tea, Sally without further thought picked up the telephone and dialled.

She hadn't a clue what she was going to say. She recalled that at this time of the day he would automatically pick up the receiver himself. She heard his voice, the silence; she could see the furnishings around him and the empty chair she loved to sit in. She was too nervous to talk. She felt an utter fool, how could she be so childish? She was on the verge of placing the receiver back when to her utter surprise she heard him talking. 'When are you coming to see me again? It's been so long. I know time flies; don't keep me waiting too long.'

It took her two minutes before she realised he was talking to her. The idiot thought he was talking to a patient. How could any woman not love a man like him? He was so natural, he never embarrassed his friends. He took everything in his stride; he didn't create an issue from her silence. Why should he? His frequent visits to England had taught him how the English suppress their feelings. He was so confident that Sally knew he was always there for her.

It might take time, he had the time, but one day, he knew, she would fly through that door. Talk; talk; talk. She would sit in her favourite little chair, look at him as if he was the next best thing to sliced bread; life would be oh so different.

It never once occurred to him that the combination of scalpels, vomit and faeces was not exactly an immediate choice for cosmetics. What's more, it didn't even interest him. He wanted her even if it meant a bath full of champagne and roses from a desert.

Poor, dear Leslie! Not in his wildest dreams could he have foreseen that thanks to the erotic help from some sexy looking window cleaner, Sal was on her way to the champagne and roses. It all sounds so infantile, she told herself. So *Alice Through The Looking Glass*. Executives, gold diggers at the top of the mountains, can't afford to have emotions. They are the cream of working society. They should set the correct example for the staff and the youth around them. Now, what would Aunt Jess have said? No, even better, what would Mother say? The traffic lights turned to red, giving Sally sufficient time to make up her mind.

Aunt Jess would have said, take the poor man a nice box of chocolates, preferably plain. Men always prefer plain to milk. Terry's Gold is the best brand. I'm sure he'll enjoy them. Aunt Jess's imagination would never have travelled further than the skill of eating chocolates.

Mother would say, thank God, my prayers have been heard. Frank dear, put the kettle on and fetch that chocolate cake out of the freezer. At last my daughter is using her brains.

There were no other cars in the parking lot, only his. No patients to be seen. Blitz had obviously completed his calls. His light was on above his desk, the door slightly ajar. The outside door was still wide open. Sally walked tiptoe down the corridor. She could hear her heart beating. Her mouth was dry. She was excited, terrified and inquisitive all at the same time. She knew: one step in that room and her visions and morals on life would change forever.

She reached for the open door. She could hear his pen scratching over his writing pad. She could smell disinfectant. His back was turned towards her. She didn't know what to say, should she cough? Should she let him know she was there?

He twirled his chair around; the expression on his face was one of someone who was looking at a picture for the first time. There were tears in his eyes. Neither he nor Sally spoke a single word. She closed the door softly. He stretched out his hand and drew her to him. His eyes were closed, his hands gliding over her face, her body. She was, at that precious moment, a delicate, beautiful china flower. He was terrified he would frighten her, force her into an intimacy she was not ready for.

The only comments that found their way into Sally's book of secrets were, 'I still cannot decide whether I raped him, or he raped me, but it was heaven on earth. I know now that most people have never been in love. They think they have. I certainly wasn't. This was the most beautiful moment of my life. Never will I forget the way he helped me button my shoe. Our eyes were glued to each other; the silly button wouldn't go through the loop. I want so much to share this secret with someone. I'll phone Dot. She will understand. Many years ago, I glanced at this wonderful man, in a train. Please, God, let the train keep churning, I never want it to stop.

'I'm not stealing, neither am I cheating.

'We are two lonely humans who are desperate to survive.'

LOVE

The feeling of wanting to be tucked inside him, a zipper each side, just to use when you felt like taking a peep outside to see what the weather is like. A feeling of safety, intense warmth, someone who had travelled into her system, took away her fear, and transformed the loneliness into love and attention. A listening ear, a shoulder to cry on, they were living in each other's worlds; they were both deeply in love. Sally Bone was for the first time in her life 'in love'. The butterflies were dancing and prancing through her veins; she felt alive, or rather, she was alive. She could talk without snapping. The world did exist, her emotions were still alive, she had found her natural vitamins to complete the rest of her journey, and no one was going to deprive her of this excitement. Blitzie, as Sal called him, had finally reached her heart. The man from the train, the lift, the encounter at the front door: it was all reality. He had entered her life, and his genuine motives were to stay. Her book of secrets found after many years an extensive purpose. She wrote: 'Without this devotion, without this undemanding love, I could never continue to play my required roles, both here at home and in the company.'

Pack her bags? Run? Desert everything she had worked for and loved, and still loved? Never! It did not enter her thoughts to leave her husband. Many years ago, when both she and her hubby were extremely young, she threw a promise into the air: 'We must always look after Cloggs,' and that promise could not be forgotten. She spoilt him like a child, she understood his fear; if she could she would have kept the wind away from him. She was his nurse and his mother, and as such she loved and cherished him. Her husband suffered from cardiac failure. Sal always tried to tease him by predicting they should both be mentioned in the *Guinness Book of Records*. Thirteen times she had sat next to the ambulance driver praying that the traffic would give way to the blue lights and that they would make it on time. Twice she had spent two nights in a hospital bed. The medical staff were convinced he wouldn't make it, but he did!

Sal wrote in her book of secrets, 'It's always Christmas in our house; hubby has always got something to look forward to. I can't take away his fear, but he knows I'm always there for him. I hate the nights. I never go to sleep until I've crept into his room and can hear him sleeping. Often he catches me out, and I find myself sitting in a chair until two o'clock, reading the newspaper to him. He's too frightened to sleep. We could both hear a slight fluid in his lungs; thank God I didn't have to call the doctor. I dread tomorrow night. Clogg's sickness is a fortress. He, I, and even dear Lenie my faithful housekeeper, are prisoners of these walls. The sicknesses dominate our entire freedom, they manipulate our mind. The air is polluted with tension, fear and darkness. I know I will have to miss him one day. He's a good man. Please God let him stay with us for a long time.' These were the last notes relevant to hubby that Sally confided to her book.

ALADDIN'S PARTIES

It was someone's birthday every month. The weekly female visitor to the room always made sure there was something to celebrate. A teddy bear's picnic that was always her favourite! Children's day in China: where the nonsense came from, no one knew. The result? The enjoyment between the two in 'the room' was for those brief moments the only issue of importance.

'Clear your desk, Blitzie, that's right. Put all those papers in the drawer. There we are, little tablecloth, we can't have any stains on the desk.' And out came the napkins, the paper plates, the coffee flask, the beakers. She even took the teaspoons with her. She knew he loved his coffee extremely sweet and, yes indeed, she had counted four lumps per beaker.

'I've purchased the most gorgeous fish today,' said Sal. 'Rolls with crab, shrimps, herring, everything I know you like. Please, Blitzie, put this linen napkin around your collar, we don't want a repeat performance of the last crab party. Remember, you took one bite, you greedy old so and so, and the crabs went floating all over the place, behind your ears, all over your pullover, between your legs and on your shoes. What a mess.' What absolute joy. A five star restaurant couldn't have produced a higher degree of service. If she discovered a new bakery, then the menu was plain cakes, cream cakes, fruit cakes and chocolate cake, which was definitely their favourite.

'Do you think all the family ghosts in this room can taste what we're eating? Do you think your Grandpa Blitzie approves of our menus? If we knew where he was, we'd despatch him a cake or two.'

Dr B. said nothing. He always sat and ate in a trance. The beaker would be raised, emptied, and placed down in utter silence. The beaker was a goblet of gold, the food caviar, eaten with a golden spoon. She chatted. He couldn't take his eyes off her. The only patient who had intrigued him, who had fascinated him from day one, was enjoying her grub, as she called it, in his room, plus an exhibition of photos revealing the climate and culture from which he had originated. He had travelled, as a young boy, to study in a country that was never his. For hours he would feed Sal's never ending curiosity on all the enchantment of his place of birth: the repulsive chicken slaughter, but above all the openness and hospitality of the families.

In reality, try as he might, and of course with the occasional exception, he disliked the Dutch. He thought they were mean, penny-pinching. You're never welcome when it's their time to eat, he would say, heaven forbid they share their meal with you. He was a brilliant doctor; he was an artist with the scalpel. He required no books. He knew what was wrong with you before you could have the chance to sit down. Did he have a weakness? Yes; God help you if he didn't like you.

'I'm sure you've got Jewish blood in you. You argue in a silent, extremely clever style,' Sally chanted. 'You must have, Jews always argue, that's why they're so superior. I should know; my old Gran used to argue, she would argue with the devil!'

Slowly but surely, every centimetre of that room came to life. He and his memories were the room. Sally brought in the decorations, the laughter, the eccentric atmosphere. Together, they created a hideaway which today we would have to see to believe. His wife and children never came into the conversation: why should they? Why should Sally ever mention them? She came for him, so why invite the energy of others by talking about them? She mentioned in her secret book: 'He never lets go of my hand for one minute and every time I walk out of the room, I want to cry. I start the engine, and by the time I approach the first bridge, my eyes are always filled with tears. This man is so wise, so knowledgeable, he makes me feel sane. He gives me energy. I adore him.' It took some time before she accepted that our Dr B. was the boom man. She wasn't romantic enough to visualise that someone could be so intoxicated, so possessive, that they were perfectly happy with your telephone number, but would never take the risk of talking to you, embarrassing you or bringing you into danger by creating questions from others. No, Leslie Blitz had lost so much in his life, he was taking no risk. A call indicated 'I'm thinking of you. I'm here. You're not alone!'

The room was, one minute, a fashion parade. He told her what to wear; he changed her style of clothing. The hairdressing salon followed.

Her long hair changed to short and the brown was mixed with blonde. Lastly her business; every aspect of her company moved slowly into his room. He translated the foreign brochures for her and helped her to understand the trading history of Holland. He gave her hints on how not to handle the customer. Sally would hang on his lips, listening to him say, 'Give it to them straight, don't be polite, don't spare their feelings, it's far too complicated for them; just keep to the point, to the subject. They don't have to like you, they don't have to marry you, just make sure they understand you enough to respect you. Then you can't go wrong!'

No one in the company ever dreamed of asking Sally where she was or where she was going to. They saw her leave, they saw her come back. There wasn't a week that went by, in fifty weeks of the year for fifteen solid years, that the room closed its doors. Be it for thirty, sixty, or ten minutes, a week could never pass without them seeing each other. Sally wrote: 'We grew old together. When my parents died, he was the only one who comforted me, who told me my father was waiting for me to visit him again in hospital. "Go back, Sally," he told me, "take a plane again tomorrow, hold his hand, he's waiting for you."' Her father passed away one hour after she had arrived in London, his well kept hand in hers. He knew his daughter had found some happiness in her life and he died a peaceful man. Standing alone at his grave was one of the saddest moments in her life. 'When I have time,' she whispered, 'perhaps next year, I'm going to find out where the old darling really came from.'

Looking out of the window of the plane on her return home she had one last glimpse of London. The city her parents had loved so much! This city was no longer a dwelling for her parents. Her mother had passed on two years previously. There were speeches; the mourners and members of the city council all paid their last respects. Only then did Sally realise the strength and achievement of her mother. Way above the clouds she murmured: 'Goodbye, you two. Let's hope there will be no war next time, no dictator to part us, no bombs to banish our hopes and dreams and tear our families apart.'

HOPE

Greeting someone in public is no offence, not if you do it in a normal everyday style. She jotted down: 'I screamed my head off when I saw him standing there at the airport. He must be my twin soul, or whatever they call them. My sadness vanished, his arms were around me. "Promise me you'll never die," I whispered, "I love you so much. Now let's eat".'

'Blitzie, is this not asking for trouble?' Sally asked. 'We live in a modern world but not so modern as we pretend; aren't you taking a risk meeting me here?'

Her Mr Handsome on his white horse had decided the world and time was passing too quickly. If only for a few minutes he wanted to hear her voice, hear her laugh and watch her crazy impressions. He wanted a good looking, well groomed woman next to him. Was this asking too much? Surely the time had come when they could think of themselves. There's nothing dramatic about being selfish now and then. How often had he told his patients, if you don't think of yourself no one else will.

'Are you enjoying that salad, Sal?' he asked. 'Didn't they give you anything to eat on the plane? Can you find the time to listen to me?' The knowledge that she was out of the country had made him restless.

'Let me first check,' Sally replied, 'if there are no spots, food droppings, whatever on my bosom, my bosom always attracts food droppings. Okay,' Sally grinned, 'I'm listening; my eyes are fixed on yours. I'm not going to miss a word. Start the engine and take off.'

Sal thought, He's going to ask me what I want for my birthday, or if I want a new car for Christmas. With this utter stupidity in mind, she listened to him announcing his coming trip to Sweden. There was a conference he wanted to attend; he would love so much to take her with him.

'Think it over, Sal, the clock isn't standing still. To be together for just three days, or at least to have you near me, would be a wonderful dream come true.'

'I don't have to think,' Sally replied. 'I'm not going to think, thought doesn't come into it. I'm coming! Discussion closed! I've just buried my father, I am all alone.' She closed her eyes, she placed her hand in his. 'No one, only the unforeseen, can stop me. I'll even push the plane, I'll be there.'

She could think of nothing else. The conversations in 'the room' were like that of a child going off on her first school trip. What shall I wear? I'll buy everything new, take no memories of history with you, she told herself. The little fur coat can come along. The rest will be new, totally, unquestionably, new, and of course, my perfume. I think I'll wear Infini, the eau de toilette from Caron. For her it was Christmas, Easter, everything rolled into one. Lenie would take care of the fortress. 'It's business,' she told everyone. 'I'll be back before you know I've gone.' The tickets were dated Monday the 11th, flight 9.55 a.m., return Wednesday 8.15 p.m. Leslie had the tickets; she would take an early taxi to the surgery which was closed until the 14th and from there to the airport in his car. She memorised in her book of secrets: 'Never have I longed so much for a moment of warmth. I can't wait to escape, close my eyes and dream that nothing exists.'

It was cold and crispy, lovely fur coat weather, and still a little dark as the taxi sped to its destination. 'Drive down here, please,' said Sally to the driver. 'My companion should be here by now.'

It was still so early in the morning they had the street and pavements to themselves. Both she and the taxi driver could see there was no Mercedes parked; there were no lights coming from the surgery. Everything was dark, unoccupied. He just wasn't there. Sally began to feel slightly upset. Something was wrong, it didn't feel right.

'Let's wait here, if you don't mind,' she asked the driver. 'Perhaps his clock didn't wake him up. I'm sure we agreed to meet here.' While she was talking, it suddenly dawned on her that she hadn't heard him using her telephone number. He never failed to let her know he was thinking of her on a Sunday, and the longer she recollected, the more certain she was that her telephone hadn't rung at all. Time went on, the streets came to life; still there was no sign of Leslie.

'Don't you have his telephone number?' asked the driver.

'No,' replied Sal. 'I only ever use the surgery number. I'm lost as what to do.'

'Tell you what,' said the driver, 'we'll go to the airport and inquire if there's a message at the airline info desk. Who knows, he could be there waiting for you. I'll stay around with your baggage until he shows up.' The taxi driver had long guessed what was going on; it didn't smell very healthy to him. The lady next to him wasn't a cheap so-and-so, anything but, what the devil was the chap getting up to? 'Bloody doctors,' he murmured to himself, 'they think they're God himself.'

'Let's drive back to the office, there's no message or reason to be found here,' said Sally. 'We've waited long enough. He's not coming. Would you be an angel and put my luggage in the corridor.'

She paid the driver. Where the hell is he, Sally was frantic. This wasn't like him. He was a brick, as solid as a rock. They used to joke that only death could part them and when they returned they would meet each other at school, study together and no more meeting in a dirty old

English railway train. Sally was choking; she couldn't cry, smile or speak. She had to get through the day somehow. The business trip had been cancelled at the last moment. As usual, no one doubted her word. Don't panic, Sal, she told herself, keep calm, he'll phone. I'm sure he will. The surgery was, after all, closed; of course he intended to go, how could you doubt the man? She phoned the surgery, no reply, she could do one thing only, go home act as if all was well.

Lenie, who at that moment was preparing the evening meal, saw on her face that something was wrong. 'No one has phoned,' she whispered. 'Tea, Sally? It's cold outside, you should drink more.'

The curtains were closed, the night had fallen. Lenie was cleaning up the dishes, hubby was reading the newspaper. As the English would say, all was quiet on the western front.

'I'm just going to take a walk,' said Sal, 'into the village. I've got a birthday card I want to mail, it won't take long.' Sally wanted to get out of the house, she couldn't breathe, she couldn't think, where oh where was he? She had reached the door of the hall, when suddenly she heard her husband call her:

'Sally, have you read this? It's in today's paper, Dr Blitz is dead, tragic accident, looking at the date it must have been Friday night. He was older than I thought. Was the man married, Sal? There's no mention of a wife here.'

Sally gave no answer. She walked out of the house and into the little village, tears streaming down her face. She wanted to die. This couldn't be happening; no longer his car parked in front of 'their' room.' No more dreaming of what perhaps could be. She wanted to stretch out her hand and touch him, his hair, his face. She wanted to feel his arms around her; she couldn't believe it was the end.

As cold as it was, she sat down on a small wooden bench and wiped the tears from her face. Her heart was breaking. 'Please God, give him back to me. I can't live without him, tell him I'll be waiting for him, if not in this life, then in the next.' Sally sat for at least an hour on that old bench, a bench that had heard so many love stories from young and old. A bench that was seating a gentle lady who had lost a love she had once found, a love so strong and pure it could never, never die.

The chimes of the clock woke her up. She saw a light burning in her little office at the back of the house. 'Blimey,' she said, 'Has Cloggs come back from the dead? I wouldn't put anything past him.'

'It's me, Sally,' said Lenie. 'I've been here since five o'clock and you've been sleeping for hours.'

'Sleeping? I've been dreaming, never dreamt so much in my life. Make me a strong cup of coffee. I'll pop down to the grave tomorrow. I want to see what has happened to all those beautiful flowers.'

'Would you like me to come with you, or do you want to go alone?'

'No thanks, Lenie, I'm fine. Those hours of sleep, just me and my dreams, were just what I needed. I predict the years to come will be quiet, pleasant, and uneventful. The sun will shine on us, music will give me joy, no demons or pickpockets around. Life is going to be straightforward, I know it will be. We'll make a fresh start. We can't undo what has been done. It's nice to dream, but in life we have to live with our mistakes. Tomorrow's another day, my friend, let's make sure we're ready for it. Go home. Sleep well. These photos can remain on the floor until tomorrow. Who knows, they might want to exchange a few secrets. Take it from me, these photos contain a fortune of surprises. When I've got nothing to do, we'll dig them all up. Write a book, make a film.'

'Sally,' said Lenie, who by this time was wearing her coat and hat, 'I thought you said everything was going to be quiet in the years to come, remember?'

Sal looked again at all the photos, photos resembling years of history and emotions. 'I remember,' said Sally, 'of course I remember; you were not listening. I didn't say which year, now did I? Buzz off, my friend, I'll see you tomorrow.'

PHOTOS FROM THE GRAVE

'Lenie, I can't for the life of me understand why I can't find that photo. I've looked everywhere; there's not a drawer, a book, an old or recent wallet that hasn't seen my fingernails at least twice.' The wallet that had housed the photo for at least twenty-five years could give her no satisfaction whatsoever. 'Where can it be? Photos don't just disappear, now do they? If someone had a photo with him, every minute of the day, then it must be traceable now. It can't just die a quick death. Torn up and thrown away!'

Lenie decided to be discreet. She knew Sally was dying to say, 'Something fishy going on here, Lenie.' What's more, she knew her employer well enough to understand that Sally B. would go to any extent:

143

the photo must and would be found. This sort of mystery was right down Sally's street. It's never what you think it is, she'd tell herself.

Be prepared for a shock. Cloggs wasn't an impulsive man, he was calculating. If that photo had to move house, then it was a deed to comfort his fading emotions. But what was he up to? He never lost anything. Even the thought that Cloggs could lose any specific item was ridiculous.

'Give it a rest, Sal,' she moaned to herself, 'your photo is without doubt part of an emotional jigsaw. Perhaps Cloggie had more than one photo flossy. Maybe a juicy, fruity, blondie had been showering her commodities around. Maybe he'd gotten his wallets mixed up, thrown the wrong photo away.'

It was eleven p.m. and Sally was tired. There had been so much that had needed her attention. Insurances, cars, boats: his personal administration was perfection. The man should have been an accountant; he was a sublime juggler with figures. Why, oh why, in all these years didn't I take the trouble ever to look or even ask to look into these books? She even had to admit to herself that she had no idea as to how much he had ever earned. Probably, she told herself, because it never interested me!

As long as he was happy and the bailiff never stood in front of the door, what was left to create domestic torture and sleepless nights? Nothing! Money gives freedom. It helps to create peace, a feeling of security. How often had Blitzie and Sal not laughed and argued on this very issue? How many times had Sally heard herself say, 'If I've got to be ill, then I'd rather suffer with money and independence, than reach death quicker by begging for help!'

The weeks passed. The house was beginning to regain its energy. Everything which resembled or even smelt of hospitals or pain disappeared. New furniture and curtains, new colours, new energy, Sally wanted so much to enjoy her house, but try as she did to create a new atmosphere, that wretched photo would not leave her mind. Her thoughts glided to the grave, the coffin. She had made sure his watch and rings were with him, all part of his goodbye glance to this world.

People always say he or she looked so peaceful. If so, this certainly didn't apply to Cloggs. He looked angry, an expression which expressed he wasn't ready to go. Would someone please turn his computer off; there was still some mail he wanted to send. 'A quick peep in the coffin was enough for me,' Sally told a friend. 'There was certainly something he wasn't happy about. Perhaps I'd given the wrong suit to the undertaker. Heaven knows, I did my best at the time, didn't think twice, just gave what I knew, or thought, would apply to his wishes.' Sally was getting used to being on her own. Friends were always kind and generous. But never on a Sunday!

Sally started to hate Sundays. What could she do? Walk, bake, phone, knit? She could never wait until Monday morning.

'Thank God,' she would say, 'life is back to normal.' Only this particular Sunday she made a definite promise to herself that the envelopes that were lying, untouched, from the cemetery, would be opened and sorted out! She had dreaded opening them. The ribbons freed from the beautiful flowers, the book containing the names of those present, the loving and well meaning words of comfort, all aspects the widow had put aside. She wasn't ready for it. No one would have been surprised if the rather large parcel had remained intact. But on that morbid Sunday afternoon five months after the funeral, Sally, hands shaking, took a plunge into the past of a man she had known and cared for for many, many, years!

The ribbons were beautiful. What an immense work for a florist, I must save them, the explorer thought. I'm so glad I waited before opening this parcel. I'm stable enough now almost to appreciate and admire what its contents are.

Sally read the kind words from her friends and business associates. She was deeply touched by all the sincere messages. Under the pile of colourful and highly respectable items, Sally discovered a white unsealed envelope. This can't be an invoice, the most obvious answer that would come into anyone's mind. What, she asked herself, could possibly be left over? Perhaps we forgot to pay for the cake!

With a feeling of slight hesitation, almost fear, Sally withdrew the valuable secrets which were destined to stay in this world and not the next. Three photos had found their way to the one place in the house where Sally and Cloggs always seemed to meet. In fact they called it their meeting point. The dining room table had absorbed enough debates to furnish any city's library, and now it was supporting the final secrets of its owners. Three photos which should have gone with Cloggs in his grave were back in the hands of his wife! Why? How did they get to the undertakers? Why these particular photos?

'How can they now be decorating my table?' Sally asked herself a thousand times. Pity they haven't got Internet in heaven, then I could send him an e-mail: will bring the photos when I come – Love, Sally. For the next two hours Sally B. chatted to herself. She made notes on everything she could remember from the past.

Anything and everything relevant to the person or persons shown on the photos. Remember your magic words, Sal, it's never what you think it is; your name means 'blindness' and for some reason methinks you needed a pair of glasses years ago!

She had found her long lost photo. There was a photo of the family, and photo number three revealed a chapter out of Cloggs' life which Sal had suspected but never thought it worth while her putting her glasses on for! Her husband knew he had only a short time to go and, knowing Sally as he did, he gambled on her giving the undertakers his latest grey suit and blue tie, not forgetting his new white shirt. He had slipped the envelope into the inside pocket of the jacket. It obviously had never dawned on him that one of the undertaker's staff would take the envelope out of the suit and place it along with the items which were automatically returned to the widow.

I was meant to know, Cloggie; those photos were not allowed to go into the grave. In her imagination he was sitting opposite her, dressed as he always was, distinct, his favourite red waistcoat buttoned from top to bottom. You gave the game away when you started to talk about her. When people are emotionally involved with someone, they can never keep the secret to themselves. You brought this woman to life, here at this dining table.

You told me about her problems, her stupid husband, that she was leaving. You even picked her up from the railway station. You, Cloggie dear, sorry, my friend, but those sorts of gestures simply did not belong to your repertoire! She obviously adored you. The handsome head, smartly dressed, top of the market cars and boats. When her childish picture postcards arrived here during the school holidays, I knew I was on the right track.

We had some love-stricken young woman who was willing to give and you, to please her, were willing to take. Did I know when? Of course I did. The whole play was identical to the cinema affair, many years ago. Did it ever enter my head that you would leave? Of course not! Men never give up their empires for something less than what they've got. The poor woman was a loser from the start.

Rest in peace, Cloggie dear, I miss you already.

I'll put the photos in the safe. Every house has its secrets. It makes us stronger, it keeps us alert. It ensures that we humans look forward to tomorrow!

THE WALL

ACCIDENT

Sally B felt like talking. When didn't she talk?

'What a jerk! What an absolute honeysuckle. Yet he was nice with it. He was a pervert.'

'Sal, how could you?' moaned Dot. 'You don't know what a pervert is, so how on earth can you use the word!'

Dot, for once, was in command.

Not that the situation lasted long. Sally B. was longing to tell her good friend all the ins and outs of the last few months. Although Dot was reasonably aware of the morbid, almost stupid, situation Sal had got herself into, there was one aspect which remained an unsolvable puzzle. Why hadn't she thrown him out? Why had she allowed the situation to reach such a climax? Her know-all friend who gave endless advice to the staff, she, the one who could always smell a rat!

'It was completely incomprehensible,' Sally admitted. 'He could have told me the world was square. During that period of time, I would have digested anything the Moron had prescribed. I was for him an open book. Unfortunately I realised all this when it was all too late. The bastard had even read my correspondence to our family solicitor in London. Come on, Dot, be honest; imagine your brain isn't working a hundred per cent. You are dependant on everyone around you. Some Little Lord Fauntleroy appears from the past and he comforts you with his long skinny arms and his thin white lips. Give me a break, Dodo, you too would have fallen for it. He swept me off my feet. End of story.

'To me at the time he was the greatest benefactor ever! Someone who was willing to brew and pour so many beautiful emotions, piles of tenderness, poetical words of love; he was indispensable, and just think, Dot, all that for rock bottom prices!'

When looking back I'm sure the patient was visiting the patient. 'If you promise to keep your mouth shut, and not interrupt, not even to go to the toilet, I shall condescend to unveil the entire incident. Remember, he was a nice man, and undoubtedly as sick as a dog.'

'Sally, for goodness sake get on with it! Sure you don't want me to dress for the occasion? Can I close my eyes now and listen to the last chapter? No porkies, please,' requested Dot, 'give credit where it's due, and chop 'em to pieces when you feel like it!'

'I've never been in hospital before,' said Sally, 'let alone in an ambulance. I was never the patient, it was always someone else. Now I know what it is to be scared, terrified I'm going to bleed to death,' said Sally to two worked-off-their-feet young doctors in the hospital. They probably thought, for God's sake shut up, or you will bleed to death. Neither of the two required instruments worked, and poor old B.V. Philips got the blame. Now, that one instrument didn't work, okay, but two, that really was taking it too far.

'Want to stay and help me stitch her?'

'It's deep.' Before the comrade in arms could even think of a yes or no, in marched the ultimate degree of superiority, a down to earth modern nurse. One glance was enough from her; there was no beating about the bush or messing around while she was on duty.

'Gentlemen, two doctors in one cubicle is one too many, there're more patients waiting. I'll give you another five minutes, then I'll help, and you, Doctor Hoekstra, are needed elsewhere.'

In all her agony, fear and amazement, blood still being the topic of conversation, Sally just couldn't keep her mouth shut.

'Ray, please tell the doctor I want to pee. Tell him to get a move on. I'm doing it in my trousers.' Ray knew she was in a mess. Her chatter came from sheer fright, her forehead was covered in small and deep wounds, and blood was still oozing from somewhere else.

'Stop squinting at the doctors,' he said, 'close your eyes, Sal, check your compass and go floating on a fluffy cloud.'

Not only did she lose a lot of blood, the blow to her head against the glass wall had broken her right shoulder and arm. Ray never found out which of the two needed the most repairs, the wall of glass or Sally. He knew she was in pain and the worst was still to come. She looked like a boxer who had lost the fight and wouldn't return to the ring. He took her home in a taxi. He didn't tell her that he was sure she should have stayed in that hospital. To him it was as clear as a bell that anyone with such head injuries must have concussion.

'I'm not going to leave you alone, Sal,' he said. 'We'll get you to bed. I'll make a little something. I'll phone Lenie, see if she can spare some time to come and look after you. We can't possibly leave you alone; you can't even take your dress off, let alone blow your nose.'

She felt awful; all she wanted to do was sleep and plunge into a fabulous dream. 'Ray, please help me get my clothes off. I can still taste sticky blood in my mouth. Could you come up with an idea to clean my teeth? Spray a little flowery perfume on me; we must get rid of this endless hospital smell.'

Ray helped her upstairs. 'Lie down for a minute,' he said. 'I'll take your shoes off.'

'Throw them away, Ray, just throw them away; throw all my clothes away, anything and everything that reminds us of today. Just throw it all in the garbage bin, please. I'll try and focus my thoughts to frost-covered Christmas trees, streamers of holly and mistletoe. Try and guess what your present will be and how you are going to get me back downstairs again. My hometown for the next few weeks is without doubt going to be a space of three by two square metres, on the ground floor, and someone to help me pull my knickers down and pull them up!'

Sally did indeed end up in a chair downstairs. She couldn't lie down; everything was as painful as hell. Painkillers didn't work.

'Ray, do you remember anything about that flight I made, tell me how it went, don't exaggerate, just the raw truth.'

'Sal, have you ever seen a swan take off on a flight?'

'No!'

'Well I have, you!'

'Don't overdo it, Ray, you promised not to tell porkies.'

'Sal, you honest to God took off! Your heel got caught in the matting that was still rolled up outside. Some idiot had forgotten to install it correctly. You were half walking, half running; your heel got caught and off you went, through the sliding glass doors. The force was so immense, the motor up above that regulates the opening and closing of the doors, broke down. So as usual, Sal, you had to cause an exhibition.'

He tried his best to be humorous, but it didn't work. He knew that if those glass doors had opened, she would have landed head down on the cement floor and that would, without any doubt whatsoever, have killed her flat out.

'All I can remember,' said Sally, 'is us arriving at the wholesaler, me saying to you, be an angel and get a trolley, and a child screaming its head off. The poor child was obviously terrified at seeing all the blood everywhere. Your lovely suede coat was covered with patches of blood and I must have looked like Frankenstein's monster. There was also a young energetic girl with blonde hair. I can still remember her rushing in with her medical box in her hand. There were no flies on her; with quick decisions she took command of the situation. You know, Ray? I've always had respect and admiration for ambulance teams. I'm sure they save more lives than we onlookers can ever envisage. The noise of the ambulance door closing is the last thing I remember.'

THE PHOTO

'If my memory doesn't fail me there's a camera in my desk. Be an angel, Ray, and take a photo of me. My intuition tells me I'm going to need it. I know I look a right mess, but that's exactly what I need the photo for! No one suggested taking photos of my head or my neck, so let's make a private file on my misfortune. Those doctors were extremely pleasant, lots of laughter, lots of wisecracks, but somehow I feel we are in for a series of mini nightmares and if we don't evaluate the situations ourselves no one else will. Now I'll be Watson, you Holmes. You take the photos, only this time, don't expect me to say cheese.' Little did Sally know what she was predicting. Between the pain, the painkillers, and the utter fear as to how this unforeseen nightmare would end, her photo, her potion called luck, would rescue her from a lifestyle you would not wish on your worst enemy.

'You must admit, Ray, our local doctors really are great. What I love about them is they never surprise me! They have all acted so correctly, so gentlemanly, so humanly. They must know about the accident, they know I am alone, they have earned a bloody fortune in the last twenty years on my dear old Cloggs' illness. I don't want to think what they earned on his medicine; they have their own pharmacy, you know. One little sign of recognition, let's say a personal visit or a telephone call, if only to say, "It is your own fault, or how is the head?" but to ignore the situation is really below any of my expectations.'

'Forget them, Sal,' said Ray, 'they are not worth talking about; their time will come. I am taking you to have your arm and shoulder checked in the hospital. Just put your trust in those guys, they should know what they are doing. You have always said, "If you want to stay alive, dig deep, and find only the best," and knowing you, you will find a way to survive.'

Ray took the photo the same day. Sally looked as if she was standing at death's door. Her eyes were lifeless, her face puffy. It was a total stranger who was looking at him. That someone could transform into an entirely different person was a confrontation he had never experienced in his entire colourful life. There was something about the photo that scared him. The photo could have been taken in a coffin. It gave him the creeps. It paralysed him with fear. He advised himself to hold the photo in his own wallet until it was asked for. He felt guilty, but decided it was for the best! He would give it to her when, and only when, she could digest the shock.

'Lenie, go home tonight. I am not going anywhere, you cannot leave your hubby alone every night, now can you?' Lenie, who had been her faithful housekeeper for years, knew more about Sally than she knew herself and had watched over Cloggs while Sally was at work. She was a darling who everyone could trust and respect. For two months Sally's chair and television downstairs were her living and sleeping quarters. She certainly couldn't move around. When she tried to tackle the stairs it was all too much. She felt tired, two steps and then a chair. It was her humour, her determination to get back to her everyday style of living, that kept her faculties working, or as Sal would say, 'kept her grey cells going'. The bones knitted together, slowly but surely, most of the stitches were removed from her forehead. She had complete belief in her recovery.

'These photos are horrifying,' muttered Sally to Albert. 'Take a look, Albert, have you ever seen anything so ghastly? I look like someone from another planet. In my youth I would have asked my Mr Jesus to make me pretty. Now I ask God, every night, to make sure I wake up the following morning. Now let us look what the cards tell us. I only want to hear nice things, nice people, please Albert: money back from the tax bods, a surprise visit from someone handsome, someone I have not seen in ten years.'

How many years had Albert been predicting the future? More years than Sally wanted to remember. Sally loved him. He was tall, slim, with white hair and a huge magical moustache. He looked slightly like a wizard, but then a well behaved wizard. He articulated each word that he spoke. His cards were years old; they were sticky and for some unknown reason they always reminded Sally of salty butter and marmalade. 'Albert,' she would say, 'shall I buy you a pack of new cards, new colour,

151

modern design; go on, throw these away.' Albert was always horrified, almost terrified!

'Sally, my dear, these cards are history, these cards contain more messages than all the telephone wires put together.' Then without the smallest change of expression, he would request her to choose eight cards. An hour with Albert made you forget the time. One was never affronted with suspicion. He was pure, no fancy nonsense whatsoever. She never allowed his words to rule her life, but she always knew he was on the right track! Sal only had to look at his face to get the message.

'We are not there yet, Sally, but have no fear, you will be. Stop looking at that television all the time, it is not good for your head. Get out into the fresh air, try knitting: knit me a scarf. I know it is difficult being alone, but try to believe in yourself. Your cards are still good, they are always good. There are thousands of people alone, Sally, who don't have the means you have to repair themselves. Who knows what will result from all of this.'

'Please, Albert,' Sally asked 'just one little prediction, just one little bit of romantic nonsense; a white horse, please, a handsome owner and a couple of millions to buy a house in Brazil, or to help all those thousands of people you keep reminding me about. I have known you long enough to know you are not making such statements for nothing!'

Albert took one last look in the cards.

'You are going to meet someone you have not seen in a long, long time. He has always been an admirer.'

Rule number one, keep your purse closed. You are too generous, keep the safe closed. Be careful who you trust, never doubt your intuition. A legal document could cause trouble, let no one read it.

Albert knew she was vulnerable. The face he was looking at did not belong to Sally. There was no expression in her eyes. The way she took her money out of her purse: she didn't count it, she left it to the receiver to count; she had no idea as to whether she had given enough. He knew there were many dark clouds coming her way; he didn't want to frighten her.

'I'll keep in touch,' said Albert. 'You know you can always phone me. Be sensible, Sally, keep your purse closed, just do what I'm telling you.'

As tired as Sally felt, she nevertheless thought at that moment of dear Johan and Laura: Johan and his everlasting warnings about danger. What she wouldn't have given to have had such people around her at this moment. Unfortunately they had all passed on. She knew Albert was right. The future was inevitable. She was alone: no Cloggie, no Leslie to control everything around her. He, the only doctor she had ever trusted and truly believed in, was no longer with her. Keep your wits about you, Sal. Your adventure hasn't ended yet, she told herself, and remember, you told Cloggie you were not joining him for at least another ten years, and less than ten years it will definitely not be!

With these thoughts in mind, she did her utmost to concentrate on her staff, her daily routine, the general bits and pieces, but she was hopelessly tired; too tired even to drive. A visit to her local GP resulted in a friendly chitty-chat, while he was taking the last stitches out. 'Patience' was his message to his patients, stress you had and patience you needed. 'Do you know, Lenie, the man is always picking his nose; no, honest to God, I am going to ask him what's he searching for one day. I'm sure he's going to get his finger stuck up it one day, and to make things worse he never washes his hands. I've long nicknamed him Dr Stickynose. You think I'm joking, don't you?'

Lenie was shaking with silent laughter, Sally and her verifiable facts!

'But I'm a hundred per cent serious,' said Sally, indignantly. 'In my country, patients are being influenced to tell doctors to wash their hands. Pity we don't do it here!'

THE CANNON BALL

The winter started to creep in. For the first time in years Sally had the time to observe the changing of a season. She was alone and the rain sounded like music on the window panes. She was looking forward to Christmas: goodness knows where or with whom, just the thought of it cheered her up. 'Let's get the presents ready now,' she told herself, 'no last minute nonsense. If only this tiredness would go away. I haven't done anything and already I feel knackered. Go to bed early,' she told herself, 'stop trying to fight the tiredness, stop trying to prove yourself fit when you're not.' It was pouring outside. There was a feeling of anticipation in the air. Sally was nervous. She hated being alone. She knew she only had to ask Lenie or Ray to come and they, like others, would have willingly kept her company. Bed is always the best place to be when you're feeling out of sorts; it's your own personal fortress, and it makes you feel safe. That is if you're sure the windows are closed and the front and back doors are locked! Sal still hadn't got used to the idea that Cloggie was no longer around her. As sick as he was, he was always the one to lock up, lights out, the usual domestic chores that men always seem to adopt and maintain. There was always something that Sal forgot. As long as the gas is out, the rest is of minor importance, she told herself.

On that fatal night three weeks before Christmas, Sally crept into her bed, sheets high enough to eliminate the deafening noise of the rain, or was it sleet? She felt thirsty. The bedroom door was open, and the garden lights shared their orange glow with her. She could see the furniture on the landing. It all looked peaceful and safe. 'Close your eyes,' Sal told herself. 'Count sheep, black sheep, white sheep. Just keep on counting. If they murmur, fight with each other, tell them you'll turn them into a shepherd's pie and have them slaughtered. They've got to keep in line then you can continue to count them!'

In her fantasy she dressed each and every one of them in sheep's clothing. The final lamb was dressed with a black bow tie around its neck and matching black and white socks to keep the cold out. There is not a shred of evidence that sheep or lambs get themselves dressed up, but the myth that was created on that specific night certainly kept her company for many hours to come.

A cannon ball went off. An explosion indescribable took place in her head. It jolted her awake. The room started to spin. It was spinning like a top, faster and faster. Sal was ice frozen with fear; she could not move. Keep your eyes closed, lie still, it will all be over in one minute. You are dreaming. 'Oh my God!' she screamed. 'I am not dreaming, my head's spinning, the room is spinning. Stop!' she screamed. Every movement she tried to make confirmed the drama that was taking place. Just keep still, eyes closed, the 'top' will slow down, it must slow down. Count sheep, think who you can phone; you cannot phone. Stay still, for God's sake, woman, keep still, she shouted to herself.

Don't move. Eyes must remain closed, don't look, look? Look at what? She could hear the French clock banging the life out of itself. It was telling her it was five o'clock. It will soon be nine o'clock, four more hours to go, she told herself, Lenie always comes at nine, just keep your eyes closed, don't move. Try and sing to the sheep, put them all in a choir; at least you can hear your voice. How about Mary had a little lamb, its feet were white as snow, and everywhere that Mary went, the lamb was sure to go. She felt awful, she felt as if she was seasick. If only the boat would sink, it would all be over.

I'll phone Ray, get him out of his bed, he has got a key, he can phone a doctor. 'You will be okay, Sal,' she murmured, 'you are not going to die yet.' She turned to stretch out her arm. It was dark. She tried to feel for the phone, but the 'top' took over. The room started to spin like a fan on a hot summer's day, but this was a winter's night of horror, cold, indescribable horror!

'I want to pee!' she screamed. 'I can't even turn my head, let alone exercise the soles of my feet, but I must pee.' Her voice, the sound of her voice, kept her intact; her heartbeat was in her throat. She was gasping for breath. She heard the five thirty bang throughout the house. 'How I love that clock!' she cried. Her bladder was about to erupt, no, it did erupt; where it came from, heaven knows, perhaps one of the sheep in the choir had a key to her waterworks. Within five minutes she was lying from her neck to her toes in a fountain of stinking urine. Every ten minutes the water tap turned itself on again and again and again. She continued to talk loudly to herself. 'Now if I stretch my left arm out and try and get that telephone on to my belly I'm sure I know Ray's telephone number by heart. I'll just scream for help. He will understand, I'm sure he will. Settle down,' she told herself, 'ask the sheep not to leave, just think of stupid moments.'

Feel free to imagine the impossible: sex with an oil baron, strange footsteps echoing in the darkness, dancing in your birthday suit in front of a beautiful crackling fire occupying an elaborate curved mantelpiece.

The top began to lose its energy, it was losing speed. She didn't dare to open her eyes.

She had the telephone on her stomach. Its number blocks felt so incredibly small. 'Practise first,' she told herself. 'Kid yourself you're practising Handel's Water Music on Aunt Jessie's piano. You're doing okay. Think positively. Thousands would give out a small fortune for a luxury waterbed; you've got yourself an original one filled with your own personal body lotion, and by the sounds of it the tap is still running. She heard a noise that sounded like Ray's; she recognised the foreign accent. All she could say was, 'Get here as quick as your car can get you here. I don't know whether I am dead or alive.'

'Stay calm, Sal, I'll be with you in a jiffy.' Ray's voice sounded like achievement itself. He asked nothing, her voice told him sufficient.

Now if you live in a house in which wood is the dominating feature, the dweller is truly never alone! Wood will always continue to make itself heard. It shifts, which by the way is an extremely unpleasant ugly noise. A shrinking noise is much worse, or in the heights of summer when it expands giving anyone who wants to listen and who is blessed with an overdose of imagination a sense of mice crawling around, or rather scratching around, in their private apartments between the ceiling and the roof. If you want to, you can even imagine them cooking their eggs and bacon, but on this particular day our patient's imagination, as she later disclosed, didn't get any further than mice, cookies and bread-crumbs! That night Sally fell in love with all her house creatures great and small. She never knew there were so many cracks and shadows in the house. 'Must remember to make a note of all this when I'm on my feet,' she whispered, 'an excellent sales tool: Sally's ghost house.'

Ray's scratching wheels were no ghost; he took the bend as if his life depended on it. Sally closed her eyes and thanked in her imagination the only ruler of her life. 'We are going to make it, I don't know how,' she whispered, 'but we are on our way. I beg you, don't leave me!' She knew it was Ray's car, only he could drive around a corner with such speed but where was he? 'I know he's got a key,' she told herself. At that very moment an unfamiliar noise came from downstairs, the noise one associates with a carpenter's hammer and nails melody. It went on and on, louder and louder! 'The key, you stupid idiot. The key! When will you learn that you have lost your husband and that you should, by now, have taken over his domestic tasks. He would never have left the key in the door. He was methodical, he could be relied upon; he would have locked the door and placed the key where it belongs! His tasks are now my tasks, when will I automatically take over his role? Ray will use his brains,' whispered Sally to herself. 'He always does. He will think up something, even if it means climbing over the roof and breaking in a window.'

How well she knew him: his love for the theatre, his love for an exhibition, making sure that everyone is drawn into everything right down to their toes. I wonder what colour his hair will be today? 'No Sal,' she said, 'tonight! It is still dark! When he is blond, his mood is excellent; let's hope he's not brunette, that means he's out of sorts and needs a stimulator!'

Ray had anticipated practically everything but key destruction at six in the morning was really the limit. Those neighbours, two houses away, Sal called them world citizens, lovely people, right down her street. I'll wake them. Perhaps he might have a good hammer, if not we shall have to call a locksmith; I have got to get myself into that house somehow! Ray looked around him. He admitted later he had no idea where to start. How do you wake up people you don't know? Should he call the police?

He had even secretly hoped that a burglar was in the neighbourhood. At least he would have had the right tools.

There is to my knowledge, no film company in the world who could have cooked up and exercised the scenes that took place on that morning in late November. Try to imagine a Mexican with limited knowledge of Dutch trying to explain why two perfect strangers should get themselves out of bed! Two men in the pouring rain, with hammers of various sizes, wire of various thicknesses, with the intention to breaking the door down, or whatever action these two adorable fake burglars anticipated was necessary to force the door open. The only female in the group was marching backwards and forwards from one house to the other with steaming coffee and home made cake. Michel, who was definitely the most experienced in such situations, instructed his wife to look up a locksmith: put a message on his tape, offer him a double tariff and tell him to get to the scene as fast as his car can take him. We're not making much progress and she has been alone too long up there, Michel decided. The lights are still not on. I said right from the beginning she should have stayed in that hospital. I'll bet you my whole existence Sally is suffering from head injuries, ignored by those doctors. Have you seen that photo? I am an everyday guy, but even I can see that a bashed up head like she had, cannot go ignored. She still doesn't look sharp out of her eyes and I'm sure she doesn't hear me half the time.

The locksmith was on the scene, on the dot at eight fifteen. What Sally had been waiting for for three and a half long hours took place in exactly three minutes. Tick, tick, the key flew out and all three of them came charging up the stairs, lights switching on everywhere, to find Sally lying there in a pool of urine, dressed in a long blue nightie, completely saturated from her toes to her neck.

THE DOCTOR

Her world of imagination had kept her spirits up throughout those final hours of sheer fear and loneliness. She had managed not to cry, but now, pretence was no longer in the air. Tears flowed over her cheeks. 'I am sorry, folks,' said Sally, 'please help me. I can't help crying. I've been having a sing-song with the clouds and the residents above them, and thank God someone was listening.'

Ray couldn't resist teasing her. 'Sal,' he said, 'there is enough of your water in this luxury four poster bed, a few drops more will not make any difference.' By this time Michel had crept back downstairs to Sal's office with the intention of phoning a doctor. We don't know whether he shouted, cursed, or politely demanded, but we must remain honest. Dr Leopold Niggins took five, no four, minutes to arrive on the scene. Everyone wanted her to remain in her current predicament.

'The doctor must see you, Sal,' said all three, 'exactly the way things truly are. He cannot evaluate a sickness if the true symptoms are not looking at him,' sang the three musketeers, blond, brown, and black. 'We must give the poor man the opportunities to show his skills, so early in the morning.'

Now Professor Niggins had already been spied upon by our Sally. He was the young someone who walked around a surgery, usually for twelve months. This gentle member of the male sex had made, at the time, an immense impression on her. The type, as Sally would say, one would pray to be sick for, in the hope his angelic figure would visit your bed, soothe your brow, and secretly hold your hand. He truly was everything a woman could ever hope for when she was sick, feeling down, miserable and out of sorts.

His hand felt like a jelly when he attempted to shake yours. Dandruff was a permanent accessory to his jacket and the plump darling had that certain thing about him which made you think: I bet he lives with Mummy, and Mummy says every day, 'Daddy would have been so proud of you, do your best, darling, make everyone better, kissie, kiss, goodbye.' Sally couldn't believe her luck: the same great huggy teddy bear was standing in the doorway. Perhaps it was the smell that filled the air, the fear that he might have to make a quick decision; whatever, something certainly stopped him from approaching the little waterbed filled with Sally's own pearly drops, all of which contained an aroma unknown to most, but well known to our medical visitor.

The three night watchers had politely left the stage, giving him all the space and confidentiality he as a doctor required. Slowly but surely he squatted himself on the corner of the twin bed next to Sally's. He sat rubbing his knees. Perhaps he's got fleas, thought Sal, you never know these days what these doctors get up to. He started to clear his throat, asked her what was wrong, his eyes looking up to the ceiling while he waited for her answer. He probably thinks I've got bad breath, that's it. That is why he is being so evasive, Sally decided.

'I'm tired, Doctor, I'm exhausted. I've been lying here since five this morning waiting for someone to tell me what's wrong. I'll try to explain to you how I experienced this disaster and I'm hoping you can tell me what has gone wrong.'

Sally to this day never knew if the man had listened to one single word she had said. She was still lying on her back practically tasting her own urine, which by that time had filled every corner of the bed. Now, did he approach the bed? Did he feel her pulse? Did he check her blood pressure? What stupid things one can think of at such a time. The poor man was probably still digesting his breakfast, probably wondering whether he had cleaned his teeth or not. However, Dr Niggins was a man of words; he did not need to bring his medical equipment with him. His knowledge came from his knees. He was still rubbing his knees when the medical statement of the year was pronounced. A statement so original, so universal, it brings tears to one's eyes every time one hears it being pronounced. It is stress, he said, stress. It was almost poetical the way he greeted his own conclusion. If he had had the opportunity, he would have given himself a kiss for being so talented. This was sheer brilliance. He only had to rub his knees and his magical voice produced 'STRESS'.

'Thank you so much, Doctor,' said Sally through gritted teeth. 'I do hope my own GP will look in later. You've been most helpful.' She desperately wanted to say, 'Go back to where you came from,' but she knew, like so many others, that regardless as to whether they rub their knees, pick their noses, or never ever wash their hands, you need them, if only to get the necessary doors to open.

Sally, who after four hours was almost beginning to feel at home in her private swimming pool, knew she would have to find that right door. But at that certain moment she was too emotional and grateful that the front door of her own warm house had responded to her cry for help and security. Ray and Michel, the old darlings, came back upstairs. Both were anxious to know what his reverence had pronounced.

'I'll make it quick, guys,' said Sal, silently laughing. 'He found a marble in my left ear. The dizziness, the spinning of the room, the fact that I could not or did not dare to move for all those hours, comes from reading too many horror books in my youth. And if you, Michel, will make me a lovely cup of tea, and you, Blondie, my old chum, will fetch a wet flannel, I'll survive until Lenie gets here!'

'I'll stay,' said Ray. 'I am not leaving you here alone. Do you mind, Sal, if I open the window, just a little peep?'

Now our Michel, putting all jokes aside, was a handsome, secretive type of man, the type every normal inquisitive woman would look at twice. He had that certain 'something'. He was double sexy, whatever that means, and as far as Sally was concerned, he could do no wrong and vice versa. From the moment that Cloggs was no longer with her, he was always the neighbour who would cross the threshold to check if everything was in order. The tea and cookies that he served on that last stage of Sally's unplanned adventure would remain for ever in her feelings of gratitude.

'I'll call in later, Sally,' he said. 'I can hear Lenie downstairs; I'll go quickly before she throws me out!'

To those who do not know or have the privilege of having a Lenie around the place and therefore have no visual concept of the rules of the house, Lenie was someone who decided for you! Lovely grey hair, sparkling eyes. Sally's house was her house and anyone who approached the serenity of her domestic environment was totally ignored and banned from her acknowledgement. She didn't even ask what was going on here, why should she?

'I have been waiting for something to go wrong,' she uttered. 'What did he say?'

'He, I assume, is the young doctor, Lenie?' said Sally. 'Let us have a little respect please!'

The two of them helped her into the spare bed, the one that had given poor Niggins so much inspiration.

'Ray, go downstairs,' said Lenie, 'make fresh tea for us. I'm going to clean this baby: talcum powder, safety pins, the whole lot.'

Sally could spot the tears in her eyes. She squeezed her hand tenderly. 'Stop worrying, Lenie, how many years do we know each other? I'll dig deep enough to find the right people. Lenie, find me my sunglasses, the light is killing me,' Sally whispered. 'And from where I'm situated, I can see four paintings on the wall and not one.'

'Sally,' whispered Lenie, 'what shall I do with your bed?'

'Throw it all away, and I mean everything. This bed and all its belongings has protected me for sufficient hours. Let's make a fresh start. Find someone to help you throw it all down into the garden and have it taken away.'

No sooner said than done, Lenie had the famous twin bed and all its belongings confiscated within, to be precise, four hours. Where it went to Sally never knew and she never asked!

Cardiologists can be a bore. You can never imagine them doing the Highland Fling or the rumba; one always has the feeling they despise yummy, yummy cakes with loads of cream, and even more, despise the folks who eat them. There had been sufficient cardiologists in Cloggs' life, all serious, all of them caring. Sally was always aware that, due only to them, Cloggie had reached the late sixties. 'I know we are wasting this man's time, Cindy, we both know there is nothing wrong with my heart.' My assumption is Niggins felt he had to do something after they had more or less practically murdered the poor bod for doing absolutely nothing. But really, a cardiologist of all people; if I were twenty years younger, I am sure his magical knees would have sent me to a gynaecologist.'

One could sense that the young cardiologist, who was doing his utmost to be secure and professional, could not combine her answers or problems with those of the heart. He completed his routine checks and asked her if she had any questions.

'I am too tired, Doctor, to even talk to you. Your white coat is driving my eyes crazy. I would love nothing more at this moment than to get back into my bed. I want to find myself gone! I did not know how to find my way into this place and if I were alone, you would have to help me find my way out.' For Sally it was over and out. The tears rolled down her cheeks. 'This is me, Doctor, this for God's sake is me.'

She opened her bag and took out the cruel photo of her accident. She handed it to him, the tears still streaming down her cheeks. The silence in the room of coldness, unfamiliarity and speciality expressed the feelings and thoughts of the first medic she had finally found who understood that more than one blunder had occurred since that fatal day in October. After two minutes of deathly silence he informed Sally that he would send his report through to them. His obvious respect for colleagues did not get him any further than to address them with the title of 'them'.

'I shall also phone them today for you. It is not standard procedure.' He went on in English. 'I am the heart man and you certainly don't need me at this moment.' Sally in the midst of her tears and snotty nose forgot to mention, 'Don't phone Niggins.' She only realised what she had done wrong when she painfully discovered that nothing was occurring. 'Nothing' is a form of exaggeration and one must give credit where credit is due. One of Niggins' colleagues, with many years of experience and subscribing to her own pension, popped her head around the door and prescribed 'Internet'. 'Chat with people on the Internet, see what they have got; thousands of people in this country have a whiplash injury. You could undoubtedly find some compassion from them.'

Poor Sal; the symptoms continued like clockwork. Two days out of bed, four days in. Sally was becoming an invalid. To her friends it was so obvious: her energy was slipping away; she became dependant on all of those around her. The dizziness continued; the background scenery on the television moved as if it was on a train. She felt so ill, so sick, she wanted to end it all. 'I cannot go on like this,' she told Lenie. 'This is not what life is all about.' Her speech was slow; she could no longer find the words in Dutch. She spoke, when she spoke, in her native language. A trip in a car was out of the question. The traffic rushing past, or movements from any direction, made her feel completely insane, and finally the movement of someone's face when speaking to her drove her out of her mind.

Christmas passed. It was New Year's Eve. Our patient and her loyal secretary, Cindy, who had worked for Sally during the last twelve years, were sitting at the table, both trying to evaluate what had happened in the last three months.

'Write it all down, please Cindy, week by week, day by day. I've got to find another doctor. This bunch have got to go. Maikel – remember, Sonja's hubby – has asked around. They have no doubts whatsoever that a good neurologist has got to be found. We are looking at severe brain concussion. No one, either in the hospital or here in this antique village, has paid any attention to the obvious. Now you go home, enjoy your end of year party and this old lady who looks more like death warmed up will retire to her jewel of comfort, her bed.'

Cindy did not trust her; in fact, she confessed later, she did not trust her for one second alone. 'You go to bed, Sal. I'll watch a little television, then round about midnight I shall come upstairs with the champagne and glasses. Don't be scared, no one is going to leave you alone in this house. That's a promise,' Cindy declared. 'I shall be here most of the time.'

Sally knew from experience that Cindy would never let her down. She also knew that Dennis the Menace, a house friend of the family for many years, would be looking after her the following day. The list of carers for day and night was complete, Cindy informed her, and starting as of 2 January, we are going to attack this arrogant bunch of so-called doctors. How often have I not heard you say, 'We pay them, they don't pay us!'

GOING HOME

'Go on, up you go,' said Cindy, trying to be cheerful. 'I'll help you get undressed and if you need to walk to the bathroom later, just ring your lucky fortune bell.'

Sally fell immediately into a deep, deep sleep. Cindy was sitting on the floor next to the bed at midnight, champagne and glasses on the floor. There was an immense storm that made a noise loud enough to keep anyone awake. The fireworks had not yet started, the dogs not yet barking, but Sally was miles and miles away. It made Cindy wonder whether she should wake Sally up. Cindy had always had so much respect for her, had admired her for her achievements in their country, and no matter how long she looked at her, she could not accept how any person, male or female, could become such an absolute wreck in such a short time. Her instinct told her to forget the champagne. Let the poor woman sleep, she told herself. Sleep is the best medicine she can have. Knowing this woman as I do, she is probably fighting for her life, instructing her lawyer to sue the wholesaler, playing her Handel's Water Music on the piano that she always intended to buy, finding a way to chop the doctor's tail off for being so passive and uninterested.

Cindy could not at this stage resist having a little giggle. I wouldn't like to be in his or anyone's shoes when Sal gets on her feet. She took hold of Sally's hand, knowing she wouldn't waken, and whispered, 'Come out of this alive, Sally, we cannot miss you. You're a right so and so at times but we all love you.'

Where did the word 'love' come from? What made Cindy use such an emotional phrase? Was Sally's face so peaceful? Was there a smile on her face? How could Cindy sense that Sal had already left us for twelve long hours? The final stage of her lifelong adventure had closed in and swept her away. She was floating, she was speeding through a tunnel of love; she was travelling back to her village, her little kingdom, where she as a child had acted as the queen. She went to the roots of her childhood, which had showered her with safety and excitement. She could hear the engine of her darling Uncle Fred's car, and see the flowered dress that Aunty Joyce frequently wore. Aunt Jess, whom she adored, was playing her favourite hymn, 'Onward Christian Soldiers, marching on to war, with the cross of Jesus going on before.' Sally saw a little girl, unknown to her, standing next to the organ, singing to her heart's content, an expression on her face that one can only describe as serene innocence.

The trees, the flowers in the forest, so frequently visited by herself and Joyce, she could smell them all. It was as if she was holding them in her hands. Their fragrance was pure, exquisite, and unforgettable. The sun was shining over the tiny waves moving in the tadpole pond, Sally's forbidden territory, but frequently visited if only to count the frogs. She could smell the water; it always smelled so chalky.

The old school house was still the same. She was sure she could see St Patrick's flag floating in the wind. She could smell the heat of the old coal fireplace and the smelly feet of so many of the children. She looked for Trevor and Geoffrey. She couldn't find them. She couldn't smell them, she couldn't hear their voices. She floated on to her final destination. She wanted to be near Pearl and the Christmas tree and finally her desire to kiss and thank her darling Aunt Jess for teaching her the code of living, a code that Sally had never forgotten and that remained with her till her death. The smell of lavender, Pearl's perfume, was unbelievably strong.

The jingling of the Christmas tree bells was clear but try as she might, she couldn't see or find Aunt Jess a second time. She could smell her. She could smell her oven. She wanted so much to find her, but all was in vain. Her window sill was still clustered with books. She knew this was the room where Aunt Jess had died. The room where she had conversed for so many hours with her Mr Jesus, her room of make believe. A room full of emotions and childhood secrets.

The delicious smell of Arthur's tobacco was suddenly everywhere: the man who had spontaneously taken her into his care, so many, many years ago, in that old fashioned railway carriage; the teacher who had placed her on her imaginary throne. Sally could smell him around her. He was everywhere. She could not escape from his presence. She could hear a sound in her room, the window sill was occupied, she could not grasp who or what it was. She tried to move on, she wanted to see more. She still had not found Trevor and Geoffrey. Where were they? They were part of her family. She loved them. She wanted to be near them. She could not move on. Everything around her gave her the impression of a meeting point. Her trip was over. She could go no further. She could hear a voice, a child's voice. It was her favourite hymn being repeated, the rustling of trees, murmuring tones, magical voices, inspiring her to live and relive her days in her village.

Cindy, who had kept a close watch on Sally, could determine she was coming back to the world of the living. She saw one huge tear gliding slowly over Sal's cheek. She bent over, aiming to hear what her patient was murmuring, but all she could hear was, 'Goodbye.'

More we are not allowed to know; additional pieces remained Sally's secret. There was, however, one aspect that no living soul could deny: she came back to this planet with a determination to fight and restore her life. No one was going to stand in her way, and no idiot was going to play around with her life any more.

'Cindy, get your notebook, please, let us get the engine started. I know I am a perfect wreck; together we'll put a plan together, a plan that doesn't have to be dependent for one hundred per cent on the faculties of others. Now step number one, get Niggins here on the dot! Say anything. Tell him I'm dying. Tell him I have fallen out of bed, just get him here!

Prof. Dr Niggins arrived, sheepish, empty handed, but to Sally's delight he was still the occupant of the magical brown trousers. If he sits on my new twin bed, if he dares to rub his knees, I'll scream at him. I swear to God I will! I have got the steering wheel in my hands now, and he, the little darling, is going to do what I want him to do and not vice versa.

'Good afternoon, Doctor. No, no, not there, not on my twin bed, please. There is a chair patiently waiting for you. Sit yourself down. What I have to say won't take long! The cardiologist contacted you three, four weeks ago? I have not seen or heard from you, what have you done? Where are we going to?' Before poor Niggins could restore his image, Sally continued: 'You will make an appointment for me with the best neurologist available. No, I am not going to do it, so don't even think about it. You are going to make that phone call. Explain how urgent it is. Try and get me there by tomorrow. Three months delay is more than enough, especially at my time of life.'

You nutcase, she thought, the classic symptoms of a severe concussion were looking at you all the time. She didn't allow poor Niggins to say a word, she didn't give him the chance to rub his knees, and she certainly didn't give him the opportunity to look up at the ceiling.

'Just make the appointment,' said Sally. 'Cindy will call in and collect the necessary papers.' I'd jail him if I had the chance, she thought. Put him behind bars for at least a week. Then he would know what it feels like to be humiliated, helpless, scared out of one's wits, and above all ignored by those who have been trained to restore life. I'd even pay for his board and lodgings. On second thoughts, the tax man might even pay for it. 'Indoctrination' is still deductible! And this chap could do with a lesson or two!

MR CONCERN AND PARTNERS

'Cindy, a little lipstick, please, dear, a little powder over the nose, perfume behind my ears and a little green eye shadow just to make me look alive. We are off on a day's outing, coffee and cream cake, we are heading to a hospital. This bed has been my sanctuary for three quarters of every day; let us celebrate that help could be on its way. After all's said and done, we only had to wait eight days to get in. Let us look now on the bright side of things. Up till now, I have become a burden and not a concern. Who knows, we might, you never know, we just might meet a Mr Concern. Now, there should be loads of lovely exclusive perfumes for men, downstairs. Choose something classic, how about a lovely Lalique? Wrap it nicely in silver paper, not gold; gold is a bit too swanky for someone we haven't yet met!'

'Are you sure you've finished?' said Cindy. 'If our Mr Concern hears you're chattering, he will follow suit and refer you also to the Internet.'

Never will Sally forget that first taxi drive to the hospital. Every single bobble in the road made her feel sick and lifeless. She wanted desperately to return home. The morning energy was slowly diminishing. She was terrified, petrified as to what the outcome would be. There are times in our lives when we secretly hope that certain institutions will forget our names, in fact forget that we exist all together, but the sheer tone of almost welcome in the doctor's voice made both females want to hug each other. They wanted to stand up and cheer. His appearance was professional. He did not, thank God, look like a would-be basketball player. In one second this gentleman expressed knowledge and confidence. Cindy showed him the photo of Sally, a bruised and broken woman. She looked as if she had been run over by a truck. Slowly she began to unfold how she had lived in the past four months.

'How do you feel at this moment?' was his reaction.

'Your posters on the wall are moving, and that white coat you're wearing is driving me insane. My knowledge of Dutch is practically nil. I can only speak my native language, and my co-ordination has gone to the wind.'

His reaction was a combination of anger, disgust and sympathy. 'On behalf of my colleagues, I apologise.' It was as if he was saying, Right, let's close the past, forget everything and everyone, you are a winner, a survivor; we both know it, now let's get cracking! Within ten minutes this gorgeous man had rung every bell at his disposal. Scans, therapists, you mention it, Sally had won the day!

'I'm sorry, but it's all going to take a long, long time, I warn you. Come back and see me any time you want to.'

Luckily for Sally the doctor did not mention how long, and what he also forgot to mention was that her future therapist was and probably still is one of the most experienced and thoughtful persons in his field. A jewel! A man of decisions, a special someone who had respect for himself and his patients.

'Satisfied, Sal?' asked Cindy, who had very modestly left the thank you parcel behind on the doctor's desk.

'Satisfied? Satisfied? We've only just started. Now, when we get home I would like you to send a fax to an old acquaintance. He used to be our GP some ten years ago, an absolute nutcase, but a nutcase with a story to tell. He always had the guts to tell you what he thought you were doing wrong with your life, not that poor old Cloggie could ever understand him, but still, I must admit there was something refreshing about the man. I remember telling him one day to shave his disgusting beard off. It used to hang from his chin to his navel. One could visualise ants running about between the long thin hairs. I even asked him if he thought he was Jesus. Do you know, Cindy, I never found out whether it was the association with Jesus that made the beard disappear, but off it went and my guess is, he is probably today as bald as a badger! Ask him if he would for old times sake pop in and see me. If he comes we are in business; let us be honest, you don't know if you don't try!'

The following day was a day of rest and excitement, unbelievable excitement. A day one should remember with gratitude and everlasting joy, a day of truth and forgiveness. Totally unannounced, no warning in advance, Sally's local GP made a personal visit.

'Do you know, Cindy, I almost felt sorry for him. It sounds silly but he looked so sheepish, so "forgive me please" looking. He had some medicine with him and he actually said "Sorry".'

Now, instead of saying, 'It's a bit too late for all of this nonsense,' Sally surprised us all by telling her visitor that she would forgive him, on one condition only. He had to promise to lecture that idiot of an assistant of his, explain in details the wrongs and the rights, the unprofessional mistakes he had made, and what's more keep a permanent watch on him.

'Not only does the poor chap not dare to make a decision,' Sally declared, 'he should never have been a doctor in the first place. Do you realise I can only read a few sentences in the newspaper? My own writing I can't make sense of, someone has to hold my hand from here to the bathroom and all the rooms are lopsided. The only place where I feel safe is in this bed! My best friends are my sunglasses. Be honest with me, Doctor, do you understand my anger, the reason why I would like to shoot the whole bunch of you? I still cannot understand why this had to happen to me. I tell myself that only now can I feel and understand the desperate fear that always surrounded my husband. The feeling of having no control over one's self; being dependent on the knowledge of others and hoping to God they know what they're doing.'

A silence descended on the room. It was peaceful. 'I would give anything to speak to my husband, to tell him I now understand why he was as he was. I'd love nothing more, Doctor, than to punch you on your nose. You know what I mean, a good old fashioned punch, but when I look at you and evaluate the past, you were a good egg for my hubby. Can you remember how many nights, early hours of the morning, good weather, ice, snow, take your choice, you had to spring out of your bed and rush down here? It was not the injections he had that impressed me, but the fact that you always stayed sitting next to him, until you were fully satisfied that we did not need the ambulance. Do you know how many times I sat next to the driver, praying that the ambulance would reach the hospital on time? Go on, Doctor! Guess! Be a good sport and make a reasonable choice.'

'Well, I know,' said the doctor, 'that I've called them at least six times. Tell me, Sally, how often is it?'

'To be exact, thirteen, and he died while I was out doing some shopping, in his old, old chair, no fuss, no hospitals, no doctors, all alone and peaceful. We all spoilt him, Doctor, we all spoilt him; we all exaggerated! He was a good man and believe me, they are few and far between. You've built up a lot of credit in this house, thus, as a judge would say, "I'll let you off with a sharp warning." I know I am the only one who can pick up the pieces; restore my life and finish my adventure. Before you go, Doctor, how is your little boy getting on?' She knew he loved nothing better than to tell anyone who would listen about his son. He had lost his wife in a car accident, and his son was his whole world.

* * *

168

When you have not seen someone for fifteen years, it is either a shock, or one continues to talk and act as if it was only yesterday. Within six hours of receiving Sally's fax, our Mr Ex-Bluebeard, the ultimate example of a medical nutcase, someone who specialises in doing that and only that which is not allowed, let alone understood, rang the bell and entered the house as if his last visit was only yesterday. He deposited himself on the bed, took her face in his hands and whispered, 'What have they done to you? You're unrecognisable. Don't cry, please Sally, don't cry.' He put his arms around her; he wanted so much to comfort her! 'I'm not going away. I'll take over. I promise. You gave enough of your life to your husband, now it's your turn to live. I saw your photo some time back in the newspaper. I've still got it somewhere in my desk; couldn't think at the time why I cut it out. Come on, Sal, try and laugh. Together we can restore you back to that glamour photo. I'll be back tomorrow.'

He knew she couldn't take any more. Enough was enough. Clearing his throat loudly, he stepped into Lenie's kitchen and pronounced his first intention of control in Sally's house.

'Lenie.'

'Yes, Doctor.'

'Where is her medicine?'

'Here, Doctor, here.'

'Right, give me a plastic bag,' he replied, 'I am taking the whole lot with me. See you tomorrow,' and out he went. A complete nutcase, a divine manipulator: perfect, just perfect, for getting his patient back on her toes!

The door had hardly closed. Our doctor had not even reached his car before Lenie charged up the stairs, terrified about what she had allowed him to do.

'Sally, I could not help it, he took the medicine as if it was his own, he didn't even ask. Sal, he's taken over, he's coming back tomorrow; I'm frightened of him, Sal.'

Is he now, thought Sally. First he tells me he's coming back, then my faithful Lenie.

'I have a feeling, Lenie, we are in business.'

'In business,' said Lenie. 'Sally, you are sick, you're not in business.'

'I know, my dear, I know, but the majority of the human race forgets that the profession of medicine is a business, a well organised and beautifully camouflaged business and nothing else. It's so simple, he takes away all the medicine his colleague has sold me; he will have twice the amount of the identical medicine delivered by this evening from his own pharmacy. We'll be paying two bills, identical period, and no one will say a single word. All the bills go to the insurance company and bob's your uncle!

'Now, how about one of your lovely cups of coffee? No more bics. Today I am going to walk to that bathroom alone. I am going to wash myself; forget my back, it can take care of itself for now. I shall then dress myself slowly but surely. No help please. I know you mean well and I love you dearly for it. There is a little war going on inside me, especially in my head, and I have long accepted that I am the only one who can fight and win this war. When we have got all the aliens dispersed we'll have a wonderful celebration, I promise you; it will be something you will never forget.'

WUDY

Wudy, the hospital therapist, was an utter scream: a scream to look at, and a scream to understand. He had the charm of a film star and the capacity to return one's confidence. 'Let us start by taking off those glasses. There is no sun here!' said Wudy.

'Oh yes, there is,' snapped Sally, 'there is sun everywhere. Those lights are terrifying and those white walls are worse than Omo white.'

Now, we are not sure whether it was the Omo that broke the ice, but from that moment on the two of them got on like a house on fire. His programme was exhausting. He didn't miss a trick.

'I'm falling, Wudy, I'm falling.'

'No, you're not,' said Wudy, 'don't argue, just keep going!'

'Will I ever walk in one line, throw a ball up and catch it when it is coming down? Be able to remember someone's name without having to see it written down first? Be my friend, Wudy, and say the day will come when I shall be driving my own car again!'

'How about playing badminton,' replied Wudy, 'in six months time? You can, you know. If you practise every single day at home each exercise that we have taught you.'

That her Wudy meant five minutes of badminton in which half the shuttles would fall on the floor, did not enter Sally's mind. To Sally badminton meant her youth, her little white skirt, her gym shoes and Omo white socks. That she would, after only six months, be dancing and prancing like a ballet dancer was certainly something worth fighting for.

That she was twelve kilos overweight and in the age group of viewers and not doers didn't enter her dismantled mind for one single second. If her Wudy said badminton in six months then six months it was.

She believed every word the good man said. Every morning no later than six o'clock she would creep downstairs to the garage and practise. She would talk, sing and swear to herself. Coordination, Sal, coordination: click, click, with the feeties and nod the same time with the head. Lovely, lovely; now throw the balls up and catch them, don't drop them! Think of badminton with Wudy, a night flight to New York. The verbal nonsense created in those early hours of dawn, month in month out, would fill a TV show. At two o'clock a darling neighbour whom she had never spoken to before the accident would come and take her out for a short walk in the nearby park. They would count the trees together; yesterday five, today six.

Never would Sal forget that the biggest wish in her life, at that moment, was to open the door and say to him: 'I have already been, I wasn't frightened. I've made it, all twenty-five trees, there and back!' Seven days a week for three months they went tree walking. What they didn't chat about wasn't worth mentioning: dogs' poop, dogs' behaviour, owners' behaviour. Breeds, dogs, dogs and dogs! Sally called it her war against fear. She was terrified of dogs and always, without fail, the little darlings would come with their sweet wet noses, their arrogant artistic tails wagging in the wind, to Sally's inviting legs. The owners would introduce them, announce the dog's official name, tell you a thousand and one times that every dog in the universe bites, but not theirs. 'Look,' they would say. 'Look how much he likes you, he doesn't jump up at everyone, he's very particular whom he takes a liking to!'

'He's organised everything, Lenie.'

'Who's organised everything?'

'The doctor, silly,' replied Sally. 'Honestly, hand on my heart, he has everything in its place. He's coming three times a week to check on my progress and Lenie, why are you looking so doubtful? We're not opening our doors to the devil. Or are we? You must admit a little excitement, cross and daggers would be most welcome. Personally I think he looks too mild, too friendly to represent any dark and evil spirits.'

A horrible thought went through Lenie's mind as horrible thoughts always do when one is nervous. However, she looked back at Sally, smiling, and saw that Sally for the first time in months was beaming. She looked almost mischievous.

'I'll be ten years younger, Lenie, when I'm back in the world of the living. I've decided I'm going to explore the secret weapon of beauty and Charlie is going to help me. I know it doesn't do to dwell on dreams, but we all need something to look forward to in life. Now cheer up, Lenie, I promise I'll keep you informed on everything we get up to. If there are any restrictions, I'm sure you won't be too shy to tell me.'

Charlie Cohen didn't look Jewish. With the exception of his name, his features were too fine, his voice too smooth and quiet. His elixir of life was alcohol. It was common knowledge that he was a heavy drinker. The type that wore knickerbockers in his youth, went to church twice on a Sunday or to the synagogue twice on Saturday, and couldn't wait to fly out of the parental nest. His obsession was money: big houses, flashy cars, golf clubs and boats. The entire community was indoctrinated in the behaviour of our Mr Charlie Cohen. Our prince of medicine lived a life of luxury. The banks loved him. They gave and they gave and to please them he took and he took. A wonderful marriage between the two institutions, but like all marriages, divorce is always spying on us, always waiting for the right moment to spring, always waiting for a theme to expose our lives and those around us.

Sally appeared at the right moment. Charlie Cohen couldn't believe his luck. A widow, no family, no relatives and not just someone. In his eyes she was an extremely successful business woman. She might be a wreck now, Charlie told himself, but within six months he would have her back in her network: a little guidance here, a little manipulation there, he was oh so confidant all his dark clouds would pass over. He could remember she had offered to help him fifteen years ago – something to do with a new car, the actual details had vanished from his memory – but he could recollect her impulse to be generous. He found her intriguing, but could never fathom why she had stayed with that husband of hers. He was so sure of himself, so desperately in love with himself and his status in society: the simple idea that someone might pierce through his transparent plan was too ridiculous for words.

Thanks to Wudy life began to exist again. He had her on the bikes, the feet exerciser, the eye exerciser, climbing up and down the wall-bars, standing on the gym ball holding Wudy's hands as if her whole life depended on it. Her homework continued. Juggling with tennis balls in the garage. Reading one to three pages a day. Television and computers

172

were taboo, far too heavy. She tried it once but the backgrounds were moving with greater speed than the actors. She missed having Cloggs to evaluate her results with, and like most of us she didn't want to discuss all the private details with friends and staff. Thus, in the back of a taxi, which in those days meant eyes closed in order to avoid 'flying saucers', Sally's nickname for trees advancing and passing traffic, she gave birth to the SBO team, the 'Sally Bone Option' team. This meant she could talk to herself without feeling insane, use her imagination, and add and subtract all elements relevant to movements occurring around her. Her intuition, in the past, had never played havoc with her. 'It's your Bible, Sally,' Albert would chant. 'Always rely on it. It's there to be used, so use it!' She wanted desperately to play badminton with Wudy; to dismiss the intruders who were slowly gliding their backsides on to the chair behind her German steering wheel. She wanted to drive her car again, and not remain the passenger. Her plan, her ultimate goal, the final task that still had to be conquered, was her secret and her secret only, and no one, no doctor, no living creature, was going to take it away from her.

Without Brother Charlie, Sally's SBO team would have been liquidated. Charlie certainly gave her and her team constant food for thought. The seeds that poor dear Charlie sowed never reached their ultimate growth. Was it perhaps the lack of water that the SBO gave them or was Sally's SBO constantly one step ahead of him? The word 'constantly' would be giving a slightly incorrect vision of this period in her house. She would tell you with gales of laughter: 'He was such a bloody good actor – Jekyll and Hyde type – I love you, I love you not – that most women who are alone and hungry for romance and see affection only on the TV screen, would have fallen for it all, lock, stock and barrel!

How lovely it was: the rain no longer looked like rain, who could even think about rain, it was Monday and Charlie always came on Monday. Kissie kiss on the left cheek, kissie kiss on the right. Sally's heart, amongst the medicine for organs A, B and C, fluttered like a butterfly spooning with her mate. He, like all males on the prowl, wore her favourite eau de toilette, Guerlain Vertevier; to be more precise, it was Guerlain that first entered the hall, followed by Charlie.

'Sally, why are those photos of your husband still on show? Take them away. Get the past behind you. It's a year now since he died. You've got to think of new emotions, a fresh environment. Think of selling this house. I've got a few projects myself at home, a little castle in Spain,

Sally, or perhaps France? I'll bring some photos with me next time I come.'

'When will you come, Charlie?' Sally thought, I don't want to be here alone with him! I'm tired, my SBO team isn't working. He's going too fast for us. I still can't balance on Wudy's gym ball without holding his hand, and already I'm furnishing a castle in France or was it Spain and poor old Cloggie's photos have to go in storage.

The medical papers had already been switched from her old GP to Charlie's office. There was no turning back. She could be wrong, she told herself; why distrust the poor man, perhaps he does mean well. Give him a chance, woman; give him some space in your life. You knew from the start that he promotes himself as being the master of the mind, all that 'do you love your mother more than your father? If so, why so, if no, why no' stuff. However, all that mumbo jumbo is still no excuse for grumbling about his own wife. Divorce, yes or no, she, Sally, certainly didn't want his baggage in her house.

He started to take an interest in her clothes: where did she have them made? He assisted in the selling of Cloggs' car, but try as the poor chap might, Sally with her restricted energy still managed to slip away from any deal he was making with a brand she wouldn't dream of driving in. Sal had been a BMW nutter for years. There was no reason to change. She couldn't grasp his tactics. Was she looking at something new in the medical profession? He did not hesitate to bill for everything he did. The telephone calls, asking her if she had slept well, the unexpected house call, the chats about her business, his domestic problems, his background, the history of his family, it all went on the monthly invoice. Perhaps I'm old fashioned: could this be modern technique? Sally asked herself. It's after all years since I needed a doctor. This could be modern medicine, specially designed for the rich and the lonely; a new method originating from America? That's right, said Sally to herself, just like Charlie to get himself interested in a new relationship style for doctors!

In her book she wrote, 'Maybe he is genuine. He has a sense of humour, he makes himself at home, gets his beer out of the garage, his wine out of the cellar; he now comes at the end of the day and stays for at least two hours. He phones late at night; another six months and he'll know more about me than I know myself. He's clever: if he bills everything, he can always clear himself of any emotional involvement. But we know,' Sally wrote, 'the time will come when he gets greedy. His bills won't be enough.' Curiosity, excitement, and the knitting needles from Miss Marple were rushing through her veins. Just what I need to get the grey cells in optimum condition, she told herself. Must keep Cindy updated! Thank goodness Cloggs isn't around; he would have kittens.'

Lenie was anything but happy with the goings on in the house, regardless of the fact that she saw Sally improving by the day. It was no longer necessary for someone to stay the night, but why let him come in after she had left the house? She didn't like him, he was too smooth, trying to get her Sally to sell her house and buy something abroad; where did the chap get the nerve from? 'He is after one thing only,' she told her hubby that evening. 'Mark my words, one thing only! He's got a plan. I'm sure he has, he thinks he's got it all worked out and if it doesn't work with one injection, then he'll give it two or three. He's desperate, he'll do anything to make it work.'

'Will it?' her hubby asked her. 'I can't believe Sally hasn't seen through his behaviour; she's a smart businesswoman. Shouldn't we sit down and warn her? We've known her and her late husband for so many years. Do something, Lenie. The woman has worked so hard her whole life, we can't sit back and do nothing.'

'Hand me another cigar,' said Lenie. 'I'll think about it. Perhaps I should phone her lifelong friend Dot; she's the only one Sally ever confides in and the only one who has the nerve to put Sally in her place.' Her lips twitched in a weak smile. 'And if that doesn't work, I always have a last resort, one telephone call from him and our potential lover boy will be on the next train to wherever he wanted Sally to move to.

'He's desperate,' Lenie repeated, 'I'm sure he's desperate. I give him another six months, then he won't know what's hit him. She'll have his balls cut off and if no one will do it she'll do it herself. He underestimates her. He knows too much or rather he thinks he does. Sally is not one of his many victims, she's a woman who's is going to get back to where she came from and he, the ignorant twit, will be paid to get her there.'

'Are you telling me she knows what he's up to?' asked hubby dear. 'Are you sure she's not scared of him? Make sure, Lenie, he doesn't get hold of a key. The whole atmosphere certainly scares me: a smooth talker like him could get away with murder, there's no one who ever doubts a doctor's words. For twenty-four hours a day, he could make up any cock and bull story, and every bull and cock would believe him. Don't tell me he drinks, Lenie, and don't tell me he has his own pharmacy.'

'Not only does he drink – give me some sugar, please, your tea's a little strong – but I think he lost his driving licence some years back and of course he has his own pharmacy, where do you think he gets his money from? His lifestyle costs money and as we both know, hubby dear, money doesn't grow on trees.'

'Is he looking over his shoulder, Lenie?'

'Is he what?'

'Looking over his shoulder?'

'Is that dog language or army slang?' Lenie asked. 'Whatever, it's too late. I'm tired, my bed is calling me. I must just phone her, just check if all is well.'

'Say goodnight to her from me,' said hubby dear, 'she's a nice lady; I'd hate anything to happen to her.'

The days passed by. They were all enjoying the beauty of spring when Dennis the Menace, as they always called him, decided he would take his good friend Sal away for a weekend. It was time she got out, away from the atmosphere at home. He knew her favourite hotel. A nice room looking out on to the sea would do her the world of good. He too was concerned; our new medical hero was too much of a hero for his liking. He'd made two efforts to meet him, drop in unexpectedly system, but it never worked. Charlie always had to rush off. Dennis, like many of the charming men in the cosmetic world, was a homosexual. Sal always felt at ease with him. She knew he could be relied upon. His concern was genuine. Many a night he had slept in his sleeping bag in Cloggie's old room, a faithful nightwatchman in the early stadium of Sally's illness. The way he would cart his sleeping bag up the stairs was a scream for all who loved this amiable clown.

'Sal, I've booked two rooms with adjoining doors. We can have breakfast in yours and if you're up to it, I'll take you for a beach walk, a sleep in the afternoon and dinner nice and posh in the evening. If it's all too much, no problem, I'll take you back home.'

What Sally did not know and had never anticipated was Dennis's intense curiosity to check out our Mr Charlie. He had phoned him to inform him of his plans; did he, Charlie, feel that Sally was up to it? He desperately wanted to record his reaction: would he be talking to a professional guy or a softie wearing hand-knitted socks? This bizarre telephone call was the first piece of evidence that was being presented to them both. Actually, it was screaming at them, yet neither one of them could spot the first scenario let alone the last. Neither of them was smart enough to evaluate Charlie's refusal to accept Dennis' invitation to come and have dinner on the Saturday evening. Dennis could smell a twinge of jealousy; his laughter was forced. The steely glint in Charlie's eyes was saved by the phone. Dennis was his enemy. He knew everything about Sally's close friend. Sally always talked about him, joked about him. It was so obvious few secrets were kept from him. Charlie knew only too well that after one evening with a world citizen like Dennis, there would be no secrets left to unfold. Charlie had many many secrets and too many people to hide them from. Dennis was a threat and had to be kept out of his sight until he had been accepted as one of Sally's network of confidantes.

'Dennis, do you mind putting out the candle; it's too much for the eyes. The rest is great. I'm so grateful. Now let's have it, you haven't brought me here for nothing,' Sally inquired. 'What do you want to hear? I'm in the mood for a confidential chat, so cough up the questions. If I can I'll fill in the answers.'

'I've been asking around, Sal. Be honest with me, we're all worried about you. This man is isolating you.'

'Nonsense,' Sally replied, 'he's not isolating me, he just criticises everyone I know. Now let me see, thanks to him, I've got a new dentist, he's fabulous, simply out of this world . . .'

'. . . and I bet his bill was out of this world,' Dennis responded. 'Go on, I'm listening,' said our host.

'Well,' continued Sally, 'he wanted me to visit his local therapist, but I love Wudy, so why take two alike?'

'Did you go?'

'Yes, just once, couldn't stand the woman. I heard the two of them were seen often together in the past, it was local gossip. I'm sure he still gives her a kiss and a cuddle; so what, if it makes them both happy.'

'Go on, Sal, keep talking.'

'Well, a PR bureau suddenly came on the screen. The owner could do wonders for our company,' said Sally.

'Did you go visiting, Sal?'

'Yes; it was obvious the two of them knew each other well, but I didn't feel at ease there. There was something sinister. I was intruding. It was so evident. She was talking about everything, but not prices. Charming woman. I couldn't catch the link between them, medical brochures perhaps? I must admit, Dennis, the feeling of everything being sinister remained with me the entire day.'

'And?' Dennis replied.

'And what?' said Sally. 'You're making me tired; let me enjoy my lovely meal, there's a good boy. Oh yes, I remember now: Charlie thinks I should learn to play golf, wonderful sport for the concentration and, before I forget, Cindy says he is sexless. No sex whatsoever, no passion, no emotions, and now let's shut up and eat.'

Dennis didn't need to be told to shut up; he was speechless. Is this a doctor-patient relationship? he asked himself. Before the night is out, she'll be telling me he is going on a golf holiday with her. Compliments of the company.

Dennis couldn't sleep that night; he had too much on his mind. His dear friend was still so tired, and this Samaritan in the background wasn't exactly improving matters. She can't tackle him, that's what it is. She knows he is crooking her mentally; he is twisting her mind around. She'd like to kick him out, I'm sure she would, but doesn't have the strength to face reality. She's still a good looking woman, looks years younger than her age. He could be spraying any sort of bullshit in the air; the question is, can she analyse it?

The cocktail bar in Dennis's room was a welcome luxury on that particular night. Our friend's brain was, that night, a book; the whisky supported him whilst he flicked frantically through the pages. By the time he found himself between the sheets, just a few more hours before daylight, his final conclusion was reached. This was no light reading! Sal wasn't his first victim, there were more floating around, of that he was sure. Dennis closed his eyes and allowed his early morning fantasy to complete his perception.

There are some people who will do anything for money. My guess is he has at least four telephone numbers of victims in his mobile, all widows, divorcees, women who are vulnerable. He's a born manipulator, knows how to create expectations, knows how to disappoint and then please. Drinks, sniffs, steals from his own stockroom, lives a double life and obviously doesn't want to meet me! God help him when this victim wakes up; she'll crucify him in her own sophisticated style. He could hear Sally's voice, her eyes glittering, her hands forever drawing attention to her words. 'Dennis, always remember,' she would say, 'the most crucifying punishment you can give to anyone is kindness. Is the victim aware, yes or no? Will he or she strike back? The immense variation of questions which our Mr Genius has to play around with are, believe me, no emotional pleasure and the longer the waiting takes, the dimension of his wrongdoing increases day by day. His fear can be almost suffocating. He is no longer the manipulator, he is the victim. We kill him slowly but surely, with kindness, deep and beautiful kindness. We extend an emotional rope, and we watch him hang himself. Remember, love your friends, but love your enemies more!'

TREASURE ISLAND

There is always someone in one's family who tells you, 'You never know anyone until you live with them.' With Charlie, three days was enough! It was only when she was actually on the Island that she was capable of recollecting how she got there. She had been there twice, once with Dennis, once with Cindy. She called it her dream Island, a healthy place to retire in. There are kind gentle people and the scenery is out of this world. In a letter to Dot she wrote, 'You must come with me next time. We'll find a cosy house, bundle our memories together and sell them to the highest bidder! Dot, I'm positive I didn't ask this moron to accompany me. I recollect showing him a brochure of the hotel where I always stay; him saying, "I've never stayed in such luxury"; him marching back into my office announcing his intention to accept my offer to treat him to a ten day visit to the Island; his monthly bill arriving declaring the time required to make this enchanting house call. I remember he wanted his own room; and finally, the reason for accepting my offer was to create time to get to know each other and at the same time he would teach me to play golf. Dot, this chap could be a champion salesman. I constantly have to question my mental functions. Am I nuts or is he? I'm not sure if I'm living on this planet, or the one hereafter.'

It was still dark. The street lights were still on. The taxi driver and Charlie were waiting for her to open the front door, allowing them to collect the luggage and golf clubs and finally to speed through the empty roads, direction airport. Sally knew the driver; he had driven her so often to the hospital.

'Where are you going to?' he whispered. 'Are you taking him or is he taking you? Be careful, he stinks of alcohol. He must have been drinking all night. I warn you, he's so-called funny and that at three o'clock in the morning. What's he scared of? Flying? Perhaps he can't play golf. We might as well joke about it, but be careful and make sure you have a good time.'

This man's not scared of flying; he's scared of himself, Sal told herself. He's frightened of a situation, not a person. Poor Charlie was fast asleep in the plane's seat next to her. 'Thank God he doesn't snore,' she whispered to herself. 'I've seen some puffiness in my time but this joker wins the prize. This really is pathetic. I'm supposed to be the patient, he the doctor, if it gets any worse I'll be looking after him for the coming ten days. What's in that bag on his lap?' she asked herself. 'Go on, woman, feel it! Even in his sleep, he is holding onto it, as if it's full of drugs ... no, Sal, don't even think about it! Nice respectable citizens don't do that sort of thing. A far too expensive habit for dear Charlie; now just get it out of your mind, keep your hand in your lap and do not meddle in his private possessions.'

Could that bag be his wife's? It looks a bit too feminine for my liking. A man doesn't carry a bag like that. I don't like the colour, cheap material! Reminds me of a rag doll children suck when they go to sleep. Try as she did she couldn't take her eyes away from the linen bag, which by now reminded her of her grandmother's peg bag. 'I can't go on like this,' she told herself, 'I just can't! I've got to know what's in that horrible bag. Now when the stewardess walks down the aisle with coffee, instead of stretching out her arm to me, I'll do the stretching and on the way to receive the coffee, have a quick, quick, feel in the bag; a quick pinch, a little squeeze, use my hand as if it is a crab! Fabulous Sal, she told herself, the height of being a genius. Ten more minutes, she decided, and operation 'Crab' could go into action.

In the ten minutes to come, Charlie's precious mystery bag adopted many lives. It won't work, idiot, she said, it's lying on his willy! If he has a big willy, that doesn't give me much room to squeeze, have a little feel, circulate my small little claws here there and everywhere. Now, most men would be delighted with a wake-up squeeze of their willy, but with Charlie, her intuition told her he was very sparing with his penis. He only opened his flies on extremely special occasions. She couldn't agree entirely with Cindy on the sex subject, but she was getting there. She saw the trolley approaching their seats. Charlie was still fast asleep. Action, Sal, action! Don't get nervous, there's always tomorrow if it doesn't work. She was right on the verge of moving her arm, hand ready to squeeze, when a voice whispered in her ear, 'Sally, hold my bag please. I've go to try and find the loo, that is if I can make it.'

He had his own room, Sally hers. She had as always the same room. Lovely flowers from the gardens were telling her how welcome she was. Charlie's room, next to her, was total luxury: bar, all the trimmings, were at his disposal. The setting was inspiring for ten wonderful days of rest, sport and future dreams. There would be chats with locals; she would take her favourite waiter, his wife and daughter out for dinner. She could introduce Charlie to them and give him the opportunity to talk to people who are so unlike us: folks who make you feel guilty when you grumble about a roof leaking or a few holes in the street.

The beauty of this Island, at least for Sally, was intoxicating: the flowers, the colours were like an oil painting that never fades.

'Charlie is a pain in the arse, Dot,' she wrote. 'I'd like to smother him! He's a moron. You won't believe it. In the first three days he has raised more questions in my mind than in the last six months. My mind, by the way, to which I've long granted the title of the SBO team, gives me the chance to natter to myself without feeling a fool, which to be here with him, I certainly must be! The golf programme started on day one. Don't laugh, Dot, I go with him in a cute little buggy, both of us looking as if we were the world champions. His favourite colour was black, mine pink. Disneyland would give a fortune for such photos! His golf bag looked very shabby. I'm sure it wasn't his. However he had established himself as a golfer, very low handicap, so low I can't even remember it, and he was going to teach me how to play golf? I know now, Dot, you don't teach someone golf on a course, you start on the driving range. Now why he got me into that buggy the first day, I'll never know and something warns me not to know. If you could have seen my first swing, you would have been so proud of me. How was I, Dot, how was I for goodness sake, to know in which direction the silly little ball had to go. I couldn't see anyone walking in a certain direction. I couldn't see a flag anywhere and as for those coloured bits of wood, they meant nothing to me. On that certain day, on one of the loveliest golf courses in the world, I, Sally Bone, made history, truly Dot, I'm going in the *Guinness Book of Records*. I walked on to a little piece of earth which golfers call a tee, looked at the ball, which I had by now christened Benny, took my position, told Benny I was going to send him flying and bingo off he went. Never will I forget seeing that ball take off. It was a sight for sore eyes. There was, however, one snag. It was going in the wrong direction and it took poor Charlie's hat with him. He was on the verge of taking it off when Benny decided to assist him. Poor old Benny, he was disqualified for the rest of the holiday and so was your friend Sally. I decided there and then, Dot, to drive back to the golf shop, speak to the golf pro and hire him for the rest of the holiday, at least for each morning. It wasn't fair on Charlie, Dot, it meant he could now play with experienced golfers and to play eighteen holes exclusively with a pro would also be a perfect treat for him. You know me, Dot, I like everything well organised, thus as far as I was concerned nothing else could go wrong.

'How well do you remember, Mother, Dot? How she would have said, "Can't stand the man, Frank, can't stand him, and don't stick up for him." There isn't a day that she doesn't enter my mind: her vision, her approach to her surroundings. She would have watched this moron like a cat watches a mouse. Now I may be naïve, but regardless of the day's programme, Charlie boy goes to his room, every day, truly, Dot, I'm not telling porkies, every day at exactly four p.m. he closes the door and stays there until seven. He then knocks on my door, gives me a kiss, takes my hand and walks me into the bar. From then onwards he's a different person: he's cheerful, he talks to the waiters, he's a different personality altogether. Now, four o'clock here on the island is five o'clock where he lives. Should he not be out of the country? Does he have to report every day to an institution, the tax people maybe? Perhaps he owes money to the underworld? He's under pressure and he's frightened. He's nasty when he sees me talking to other guests.

'The taxi driver whom I have known for three years has been cut off. Charlie told the receptionist to phone for someone else. It all happens before you can realise it has happened. He's false and jealous. I saw him chatting up the young boy who cleans and stocks the golf equipment. I could see the boy waving his hands, saying no. I heard later, Dot, he had asked the kid to play golf with him. There is danger around me, I know it. He's talking about France. He's created absurd stories as to why I shouldn't purchase a house on this Island. He drinks in a day what others consume in a week. There are now, dear Dot, five more days to go. I'll be glad to get back home. I'm lonely! P.S. I still have not seen one centimetre of his room and the grey linen bag is completely out of sight! Why is this man taking such a professional risk to be here with me? I'm sure I'll find the answer. Dot, try and digest all of this. I'll phone when I return, I promise.'

And so it was for ten days, twenty-four hours a day, a complete scenario that any film company would have fought for. Ten days of Miss Marple, with high heels, long red painted nails, jewellery that usually lived eleven months in the safe and golf clubs to replace the knitting.

CREDIT

For the first few weeks back home all was quiet on the western front. Our Charlie was so sweet, so attentive. Flowers as a thank you for the holiday, domestic news red hot from the press. He was definitely getting a divorce. They had indeed had plenty of time to get to know each other on the Island. He was now looking for temporary living quarters and he was looking forward to more 'free time' together. Little did he know that his credit with Sally had long been diminished; she knew he was a first class manipulator. She told no one, not even Dot, but in her mind he was definitely a homosexual. This accounted for all the female victims he so-called danced and pranced with; it was all camouflage to escape from reality, the double life he led, or was forced to live in. She did not believe in the divorce nonsense. This man couldn't afford a divorce, she told herself, it would ruin him. She was certain he was up to his neck in debt. He needed that practice and pharmacy. He had no means to buy his partner out. He needed someone to buy him out, or was such a conclusion past tense?

Their last spending trip together was to a fabulous golf showroom, where every golf nutter could empty his pockets and bank account. Charlie boy knew just where he was taking her. If you're not an experienced player, then you think you require everything. She saw, or rather she smelled, one foot past the door, what was going to take place. The golf bags had his full attention. She couldn't believe her ears. This man must be insane, she thought. He is telling me that I said when we got back home that we, that means I, would buy him a new golf bag. Sally watched him purchase an expensive golf bag, as if it was the most normal thing in the world. He even had the cheek to request that the bag be placed next to the counter, along with the latest fashion garments he knew they still had to purchase.

Always be kind to your enemies. Always smile at those who think you are an idiot. How many times had she not preached these words to her staff? People always win, she would say, when you get angry. Stay cool and you will always be the winner.

'Go ahead, Charlie,' said Sally. 'Choose anything you want. Do you need a jumper, a nice pair of trousers? Ask the sales girl if the latest fashion has arrived.' Charlie saw dollars. He saw the American Express card being aired. Lovely, lovely, let the lady pay. He had no genuine love for women and what he was doing gave him no feeling of disrespect for himself. He had a right to it. Her late husband had been spoilt, why not him? Poor old Charlie, if only he had been a little brighter. He had no idea that his final act of utter greediness was a vibrating exercise for Sally's brain. One she had for months wanted to put into operation. One she knew would come to exist, if only she could retain her emotions, her patience and finally her belief in herself! No emotionally disturbed prat was going to pull her down to his level.

Charlie, lovely big shopping bags in his hands, left the showrooms grinning from ear to ear; he was madly satisfied with himself. He was so satisfied, he even forgot to say thank you!

'Sally, would you like to see my new house?' Charlie inquired. 'It is furnished. I am living there alone. I'll cook for you. I am a good cook as you well know; what shall we have, spaghetti, macaroni, shrimps?'

'You know me, Charlie, I am a glamorous dustbin. I'll eat anything. I'd love to see your house, I really would,' Sally continued. 'I'm sure you're going to be so happy in the future!' Sally started to observe every movement he made, every twitch of every muscle. His eyes were as always emotionless. He doesn't want to be alone, she told herself. He is frightened. He's got that 'look over the shoulder atmosphere' about him.

The rented house was the answer to all her questions. It was huge. This must cost a bomb every month; who the hell is paying for it? I'm sure he isn't, Sally told herself. 'Divorce period' my foot. He really must think we are a bunch of idiots to believe a fairy story like that. He showed her the entire adequately furnished rooms. I didn't miss a single inch, she told Dot later. His motorbike was in the garage. The pillows in his bed gave no evidence of some bimbo.

He was silent. It was time to drink. He made tea; he put glasses and a jug of water on the table. Charlie and water, what the hell was going on here? The mobile went. She heard him mumble. It went again; he disappeared into the garage. It went another time and every time our Charlie disappeared into the garage. Water on the table, Charlie an alcoholic; nervous as hell, telephone, telephone, heaven forbid I hear the conversation. Someone is telling him what to do; he is under pressure. He's as white as a sheet. He's got to obey a call. I am sure I am right. I know I am on the right track. Her heart was beating something crazy. Someone was putting our Charlie to work. Perhaps he had something to sell; whatever the game, it was smothered in fear, he had no control, someone was certainly telling him what to do! He was not in a position to say no. They gave the order, he had to run. The meal was, though tasty, devoured in complete silence. Charlie ate enough for a cat. Sally for three.

Not a drop of wine touched his lips. Lovely, thought Sal, simply divine. I am not sure I have discovered the plot. I think I have, but it is so lovely to see you sweat, you bastard. How many people have you not been rotten to in the past, when they needed your sympathy? The rich ones were always number one, the poor never really interested you. In the period of one hour, to be precise eight calls came through on his mobile.

'Let me take a taxi home, Charlie, these calls are obviously so important. It must be very cold talking in the garage. Let me disappear, it should help matters for you.'

'Sally, I am sorry, I must go. It is a patient, she's got cancer. I must help her.'

'Do you want to know, Charlie, what I truly think? It is either one of your victims, one of your old girlfriends who is screaming she'll commit suicide if you don't go to her, or the Mafia or whatever they call themselves these days, telling you to make a drop now and not when you feel like it.'

He didn't contradict either suggestion. 'It is not what you think, Sal. I beg you don't leave me.' On his way to whoever he was meeting, he dropped Sally off at her house.

She spent hours looking out of the window, trying to recollect all the details relevant or irrelevant in the last fourteen months. Time had gone so quickly. There were no more doubts in her mind as to the danger she had been in, especially in the time when she was so vulnerable. It was her true and faithful friends who had constantly warned her; Wudy who had kept her alert with all his tiring but positive exercises; and lastly, her determination to restore her old self.

Charlie was up to his neck in trouble, but to what extent could her name be listed in someone's notebook? His stories always contained so many holes; a few extra would not disturb his nights rest.

Sally called in a detective bureau. She wanted one hundred per cent proof that she was right. She wanted to finally test her faculties, see if her little grey cells were back to normal. She was prepared to accept the bureau's verdict. She could, let's be honest, be wrong. Their instructions to Sally were to stay friendly to him. Be careful; don't let him catch on for one moment that you suspect him in any way. Act as if everything is normal. There wasn't a stone these guys didn't turn over. They even visited his surgery, the cafés, his sports school. They introduced themselves as new inhabitants of the area who wanted to meet the local doctor. Poor Charlie was so arrogant, he even thought they liked him; in fact he announced he wouldn't even charge them for their visit.

Sally confided in Dot. She knew she was walking on thin ice. Had she gone too far? Was she capable of accepting the consequences, accepting a possible defeat? It took exactly four weeks for a team of experts to free Sally from her doubts. She read their notes again and again and again. She went out into her lovely garden; she could hardly breathe. She felt as if she was choking. 'What a drama,' she whispered, 'what a drama. No one starts off this way. I was obviously his last chance. Thank God we all knew he had a plan. I suppose I should be grateful to him. The poison in his veins, his childish manipulations; his obscene desire to cheat the rules of our establishment kept my targets going. I am free,' said Sally. 'I am free to expedite my one last goal in my life, my last wish, my long kept secret, but before I go I must pop down to Cloggie's grave, tell him I'll be away for quite some time. Put some beautiful red roses over his name and throw him a kiss goodbye.'

That evening Lenie received a phone call from Sal. 'I am off, my dear friend, for a few months. I am going to find my roots. I am going to see if there is anyone around who still remembers me. Take care of everything for me. Your money is in the kitchen. See you soon. I'll keep in touch. Don't worry, Lenie, I am back in the world of the living. Nothing is going to happen to me now!'

Sally knew she had to fulfil her final wish, her final dream. A power stronger than hers was guiding her back to the past. She couldn't leave this earth before returning to her little kingdom, to visit her little chapel where she had spent so many hours singing. She wanted to hear the music and pay her respects to those whom she would never forget. To those who had brought her back to life.

HOME

'Please park the car here, Ron.' Ron was the son of her parents' driver. 'I'll walk the rest.'

The little village church was still standing in all its beauty at the top of the hill, daffodils and bluebells were everywhere, just like in the olden days. Where could that grave be? thought Sally. It is, after all more than fifty-six years since Joyce died. Perhaps the weather, storms, gales have destroyed the stone. Sally decided to just walk amongst the graves, read what was still readable. She was certain she would discover the grave she was looking for. It took exactly three minutes for Sally to find Joyce's grave. Sally couldn't believe what she saw. It was as if someone had

186

washed the tombstone. It was marble, pinkish colour, gold lettering: 'In Loving Memory, Joyce Beatrix Cranwell. Aged 36 years, died 1948.' Don't be silly, Sally, she told herself, every grave is lonely, but why did this one remind her so much of loneliness? Was it because there were no Cranwell graves around Joyce's? No plants, no flowers. What do you expect, Sally, she asked herself, a kitchen with cakes and pastries? That is life, you idiot, not death. I must, I must, do something. I am sure her brother Bernard used to take care of her grave: spring flowers, roses. I remember they used to be his specialty. The dear kind man used to cycle every two weeks to the churchyard in order to keep everything tidy. Sally made up her mind there and then to pay a local gardener to take care of the grave; it was the least she could do.

Joyce was part of her village memories, and regardless of what anyone thought, her village had brought her back to life. There was no crying, no tears; it was just a situation which she felt needed her attention. She walked up to the Vicarage and rang the bell but as usual there was no one in. Nothing has changed, thought Sally. Vicars only ever worked two days a week, so how on earth can I expect him to be at home on a Wednesday? She decided to write to him, to explain the situation, put him to work, gardener included, and give the pair of them exactly two months to restore the appearance of the grave.

'Excuse me, good morning. Do you mind if I interrupt your work for one moment?' Sally asked an extremely charming, in her eyes, young man. 'Do you happen to know any of the village inhabitants? Are there any Cranwells left? Trevor, Geoffrey? Is the old school still here, the chapel?'

The young man, who was on his knees doing his best to tile a path, looked up, smiled a good old fashioned Macleans smile and said, 'Some are still alive; Trevor, his father Harold.'

'Harold? That's impossible,' Sally replied.

'No, he's still with us. He is ninety-four, lives with his son and his wife.'

'Geoffrey, where is Geoffrey?' screamed Sally.

'Somewhere near Cheltenham, I think,' the young man replied.

'Impossible, I have just come from there. This can't be happening to me. I am not even in the village and already it is all coming to life. Who are you, may I ask?'

'I am Foxley, married to Diana, Godfrey Kent's daughter.'

'Godfrey Kent!' screamed Sally. 'Is he still alive? Is he still the same?' After a moment's thought she said, 'Where can I find Trevor?'

She didn't wait for an answer. Sally thought, I shall ring the bell, introduce myself and we shall take it from there. She could not remember when she had felt so excited. She was in *her* village. It had been her little kingdom. Behind her was Joyce's grave, and next to the graveyard was the little forest where Joyce had taken her to pick bluebells and wild violets. She could hear Joyce's voice warning her never to go into the forest alone; and she could see the two of them putting the flowers into two vases, one for Joyce and one for Aunt Jess. Oh, my God, thought Sally, I cannot go through with this, I am going to make an utter fool of myself. I am returning home. This is my home and I have never stopped loving it.

She found Trevor's house. It was opposite the old pub, another forbidden dwelling in the old days. She rang the bell and hoped for the best.

'I don't know you!' was Sally's reaction when a friendly female opened the door. 'Please excuse my utter rudeness, but I am looking,' said Sally, 'for Trevor Cranwell. Does he by any chance live here?'

'I will call him for you. I am his wife, Jean. One moment, he is around somewhere.'

Sally closed her eyes. This cannot be happening. I am in dreamland. Please, someone, hit me on the head and wake me up.

Trevor's voice woke her up. 'Are you looking for me? How can I help you?' Trevor undoubtedly thought someone wanted a house built, or the kitchen renewed. She had worked it out. She had not seen him since she was twenty. So we are talking about an absence of forty-nine years.

'Hello, Trevor, I cannot believe it is you, any idea who I am?'

'Of course I know who you are. I would recognise your face anywhere, you're Sally. Sally Bone, you used to live with Nana in Banyards.'

Poor Sally went over the top to hear someone mention her Aunt Jessie. After all these years it was all too much. Thus, the rivers of Babylon entered Chrishall.

'Sorry, Trevor, I cannot help making a fool of myself.'

'Don't be silly, Sally. Come here. You always made an exhibition of everything. Let us give you a welcome home, a hug, a kiss, a fresh cup of tea and your favourite chocolate biscuits.'

She sat on the settee and chatted with Trevor and his wife Jean as if they had all been on a holiday, as if they had been on some ridiculous adventure and had finally found their way back home. The number of friends still alive was unbelievable.

'Remember Faerie Cottage?' said Trevor. 'Well, Irene Cranwell is still about. She must be ninety-three or ninety-four. She works with the local TV and radio on the history of the village and surroundings. Susan, her daughter, you went to school with her, remember, lives opposite. Dad, your Uncle Harold, is upstairs. Knowing him, he will be down any minute. I doubt whether he will remember you. He is ninety-four.'

'You're joking, Trevor,' said Sally, 'you don't mean Uncle Harold, Pearl's brother, your father?'

'I certainly do,' said Trevor. 'When we're not looking he still tries to drive his car around the village. Tell you what, Jean, why don't you get the car out and drive Sally around the village. Take her to Ellerslie, the bungalow, Banyards where Nana used to live, pass by Faerie Cottage. You always used to tiptoe past that cottage, Sal, remember? Jean, take her anywhere she wants to go to.'

They passed the old school, the pond, the chapel, the Red Cow pub which had its origins in Norman times, the thatched and attractive cottages. If only someone could tell me what I have done to deserve such joy and happiness, if only everyone could be so happy.

'Please stop the car, Jean, I want so desperately to peep through the windows of the bungalow.'

They parked the car alongside the drive, allowing Sally to quickly have her peep through the little dining room window. No one was at home at Ellerslie and in all these years nothing except the furniture had changed.

'Sally dear, go and see if you can find Robin ... Are you coming to pick plums with me tomorrow? ... You left your favourite book here yesterday, you know which one I mean, *The Cuckoo Clock*.' Sally was sure she could hear Joyce's voice, could see her walking around the room, her very slim body dressed in the pleated skirt of those days, and the lovely embroidered white blouse which was always worn on Sundays. She swore she could see the same toasting fork lying in the fireplace, used a million times for toasting crumpets on a winter's day.

Porkie pie hat man, the letter and many more thrilling adventures from her youth came rushing into her memory. She peeped through the sitting room window: nothing, but then nothing had changed.

The construction of the tiny bungalow was still the same. If this bungalow was for sale I would buy it, then I could live with my memories until I die. We English always say, 'You always end up the way you start,' so why shouldn't I buy this bungalow? Fortunately for Sally, Jean broke up the daydreaming, as knowing Sal, she was quite capable of dialling the number of an estate agent and instructing the man to give her an option on the lovely little bungalow should it ever come onto the market.

From the bungalow Sally walked on to what she used to call the big house, Banyards. Nothing had changed; it was as if time had stood still. She wanted to run up the drive, but try as she might, her legs wouldn't move. She felt like someone in outer space. She was playing her favourite *Midsummer Night's Dream* with John in their wigwam. His ears were still as big as any donkey's. Aunt Jess in her fold-over apron was walking towards them, a plate in her hand. She was bringing them a piece of their favourite treacle tart. She could sense Pearl looking out of her own bedroom window; she looked up, there was no one. How many years had she sat on that window sill gazing up to the stars, dreaming of the future, asking Mr Jesus to give Santa a push in the right direction; hours of chatting with her darling Aunt Jessie.

At that specific moment control over her mind and speech was gone. Her thoughts were geared to one incident only, the accident, her inability to function and the energy from this wonderful period in her life which had brought her back to the spot where she was now standing. Unrehearsed, as if it was the most normal act in the world, Sally whispered her gratitude for her life. Without all you wonderful people I would have slipped away. Your hymns and music gave me the energy and determination to live; the freedom to experience the excitement of returning to my precious village. To feel and smell the presence of the most beautiful people I have ever had the privilege to know. My life has been a success. Without you all, it would have had no meaning. The exquisite daffodils, the bluebells, the romantic wild flowers are still blooming in our beautiful village. Let no one destroy its beauty or the memory of the people who once lived in it. This is the end of my adventure. I've found my way back home!

Sally Bone kept in contact with her old and new friends. She visited her village regularly. A reunion took place and they all found themselves on the local TV. Sally paid for the maintenance of Joyce's grave. It was her secret! She felt it was the least she could do.

Sally found her Geoffrey; she went to his second marriage.

At this stage in her life, Sally had promised herself, no more 'I spy' games. No more secrets from the grave. No more detectives and bank accounts. Life was going to be pleasant. Toast in the morning, the odd telephone call at midday; golf in the afternoon; gossip hour from four o'clock to five. A small sherry at six o'clock and the rest of the evening preferably with men. If unavailable, then as a last resort, women! Dot being the only exception.

Now, why, oh why, did Geoffrey's nose destroy her well planned intentions? Geoffrey's feet never resembled a Yank's; even as a baby, he never looked American. The shape of his head was European. As a young boy, Sally used to love playing with him. To look at, he was a typical Cranwell. His nose was identical to that of his Granddad's: straight and long. He had the Cranwell charm. He spoke easily, could put his mind to anything.

He was, like all the young children who had lived with or near Sally's royal family, spoilt! He only had to put his finger up, result? His wish was their command. The darling folks undoubtedly wanted to pamper him. He had, after all, lost Joyce, his mother, the mother who had agreed to give him her married name, to take him into her loving care and treat him as if he was her and Eric's first born.

Sally never liked Eric. He gave her the creeps. He had the habit of always putting his arm over her shoulder, plus the bonus of a little pat here and there. One could never deny he was a super charmer. His abundance of attention and charm to the women was in total contradiction to the support and comfort which he gave his son. From day one, after Joyce's death, he withdrew his entire responsibility.

Sal was ten years older than Geoffrey, and during her school vacation trips to her kingdom, she would observe and register in her mind the rejection the village Casanova had for his adopted son. Eric remarried and had, at long last, a child of his own. He divorced, got himself married again, and off we go!

There was no fibre of attention for the new generation. Geoffrey had been well educated. He could have restyled the company: modern ideas, latest techniques. Sal couldn't understand why the father had pushed him aside. In later years, when destiny had chosen to reunite the two chums, Sally still maintained her doubts about the past. She sensed a deep longing deriving from long chats with her dear friend to know and understand from where his true roots originated. Who was the Yank? Why had he, Geoffrey, always had emotional problems, domestic situations which he couldn't handle?

Always being the loser, whilst in true faith, he wanted so much to please.

He shocked Sally by describing, after so many years, the colour of Joyce's dress, the dress she'd worn on the Monday morning, the day she left for the hospital; the last day of her life. He'd served in the Royal Marines. He had seen every country one could dream of. But the colour of his mother's dress, the goodbye wave when the car drove away: these scenes were always with him.

Later in life he survived by offering his services to various building companies. He had a chip on his shoulder. He felt cheated: no one had felt responsible for his inheritance. He was sure Aunt Pearl had wanted him to have something.

In his absence, houses had been built. The ground allotted to him by his grandfather had also been used for a commercial purpose. Why was the ground not purchased from him, a reserve in the company's books? It was just too obvious to Sal that her make-believe brother had been a threat to someone; but who? Why? Adopting a child is a deed of charity. Was someone against this adoption? Geoffrey had never found true happiness. Perhaps, he had now succeeded, his new wife was charming. She knew her new husband was always searching for a light from the past. It was almost an obsession of his to talk about his past; who was who and what was the bare truth, once all the village gossip had been destroyed by time.

Sally decided to get herself fully acquainted with the gossip and authentic history of Eric and Joyce, both inhabitants of esteem in her little kingdom many years ago. She was convinced that only she could solve the mystery. Thus, a revisit to her village friends was the final solution.

She knew, previous to her preparations, exactly who she had to speak to. Children are always the most reliable bearers of gossip. They hear their parents exchanging juicy, sexy fables. The next day, the children have something to discuss in the playground with each other. If it's gossip relevant to one of their pals, then one can rely on the intensity of the details. No one would doubt the core of the stories.

With this ingredient in mind, Sally expressed her wish to find someone who went to the village school at that specific time.

Was anyone still alive who had known Joyce? Had Joyce confided in someone before she left for the hospital? Eric was dead. Pearl was dead. Would Trevor know any family gossip? She doubted it! She would leave him as a last resort.

Sally Bone, you're disgusting, she told herself. The way you are manipulating these delightful people, you are a disgrace to the community. The start is good! I'll have this little village mystery solved in no time.

Now Iris, who lives right next to the church, has made some sensible comments! There were indeed five babies adopted, all in the same year. Yes, Geoffrey was one of them.

'How do you know?' Sal asked.

'I just do,' Iris replied, 'I can remember my Mum talking about it, and as old as I am, I can still remember the christening. Very posh it was for those days. Mind you, the Cranwell family were very much respected back then.' It was a complete puzzle why Iris felt she had to whisper, 'They still are!' Sally wanted to whisper back, 'There's no one around us, Duckie.'

Daily village whispers are at all times food for thought; think again, Sal, think! Iris knew more than she was willing to express. If only I could find someone who was a member of the church; someone who was active in the church; someone who arranged the flowers at the time or year of the famous christening. It's all very morbid, Sally told herself, but it's keeping my grey cells active. If I find Geoffrey's true roots I'll treat myself to a world trip, a new fur coat, the latest Ferrari, just a little something to remember myself by.

Geoffrey had confided in Sally by telling her that he had heard his mother crying in her bed so often, weeks, perhaps months, before she had set off on her final trip to the hospital.

Sal asked herself a thousand times, Why would Aunt Joyce cry herself to sleep? Did she know, did she feel, she would never return? Was she desperate for the future of her darling little son? Who would look after him? The grandparents were no longer young.

You're just surmising, Sal, she told herself. Remember again and again, it's never what you think it is. And with these famous Sally B. words, the little old lady who had once crowned herself the queen of the village found herself talking to Betty, undoubtedly the oldest inhabitant in the village, and still the most intelligent! Lo and behold, the church member who in the past had always arranged the flowers so often with Joyce.

Sally, felt unpleasant. She knew she had found the only person who could be trusted on this subject and at this particular time.

'I've come a long way to find you, Betty,' said Sally her lips twitching in a weak smile. 'Forgive me if I shed a tear or two whilst I talk, Joyce was someone who always remains in my memory. I loved her when I was a child so much. I beg you tell me anything you know about her, especially her last days on earth. I've found her son; I want so much to help him. In his mind he has always been searching for explanations. I'm positive there's a secret in his mother's grave. Tell me anything. Just anything that could clear the way! People shouldn't have to live with doubts and uncertainty, when others so near can restore their peace of mind.'

Betty, frail and composed, decided she would have a chat, if only for old times' sake. Sally must, however, promise to take her secret to her grave! Sally's immediate thoughts were, First the secret, then I'll decide if it goes to my grave or not!

Betty leant back in her little leather chair, folded her hands neatly in her lap, and with a nod that described she was ready to begin, she revealed the truth which only she could know. Why the certainty? Joyce Cranwell had poured her heart out to Betty the day before she left the village, two days before she died.

The information was short. Joyce had left the church on the Sunday morning. Betty wanted to say goodbye to her, to wish her a speedy recovery and tell her they would all be praying for her.

Joyce, whose eyes were filled with tears, asked Betty if she had heard the latest news. Before her friend Betty could reply, Joyce almost screamed, 'I can't forgive him for what he has done. He placed his own son in my lap four years ago. Eric, my husband, is Geoffrey's father. I have no will to live. I have no energy in my body to bring me back.'

Joyce left her village a heart-broken woman. She returned a week later in her coffin.

In the plane back home, Sally was completely preoccupied with her unspoken promise to Betty, and a man who had every right to hear who his true father was. She was also sure that the jigsaw was now complete and perhaps Geoffrey could put the past away, close the book and enjoy his life, in an atmosphere that Sally knew he deserved.

She confided in her lawyer, in various other male friends. Should she, could she, tell him? Was it her task? All gave an identical answer. Every man should know who his father is or was.

Thus an extremely emotional Sally B. told her chum forever, all the ins and outs of their little village. Never will she forget the look on his face when he said, 'Sally, I'm real! Do you think Granddad knew?'

'Knew,' Sally replied. 'He would have shouted so loud, our lovely little village would have left the ground, and by this time we might have reached the other end of the world.'

Sally wiped her tears. No more tasks, she told herself, no more meddling in other people's affairs, enjoy what is left of your life. Exercise your golfing. Try and eat more sensibly, and mind your own business back home. She was just about to put the kettle on when the telephone came to life.

It was one of her female friends telling her that her lover, Graham, had left his wife and was moving in with her. Sally was desperate to say, 'Has he shown you his latest bank statement, and whose name is the house in? You're going to have his children every weekend.'

'Are you there, Sal?' her friend said eagerly. 'It isn't like you to be so quiet.'

'No,' Sal replied. 'Thanks to you, my dear, I'm off: truly, madly, wonderfully off. Somewhere no one can find me.

'I'm off to enjoy the memories of my life and the happiness which my close and very dear friends have given me.'